END

"The creative approach o_____ ...____ ... in God's Word, yet in such an expansive and imaginative way as David Orlowski has done is in the tradition of Bunyan's *Pilgrim's Progress* and Milton's *Paradise Lost*. It is more than an interesting read; it is a Bible-based, inspiring message of hope rooted in the living truth of Christ."

-Pastor Jack Hayford, Chancellor, King's University

"I could not put this book down! I seldom think about death. I cry when a friend dies. Dr. Orlowski has pulled me out of denial into reality. I now see Heaven three-dimensionally. It has provoked thought and discovery."

- Barry Goldwater Jr., U.S. Congressman

"This book blew me away! Heaven is powerfully presented. Like C.S. Lewis' writing, this story deeply touches of its own accord, but add the tremendously compelling theology, and it's amazing! I was transported to a place of sight, sound and imagination that was powerful and transforming."

- Dr. Michael Richardson

"It's brilliant! I had no idea what I was about to read. It brought clarity to scriptures I had read as a child but never understood. I finally have answers to those things that seemed fragmented before. I now really get it! I can't wait for the next book."

- Dr. Brenda Taege, DDS, LLC

"This book is tremendously gifted with imagination. It has aroused and expanded our conceptions of Heaven. It just made us love God more."

- Pastor Paul and Judy Andrews, Faith Family Church

"After reading the first chapter, I was hooked. I read the book twice in two days. It really helped me love more as a wife and mother."

- Khristy Thompson

"This book is the Avatar version of Heaven! It's a fully vivid, technicolor rendering of what Heaven is really like!"

- A. Avila Smith

OUR FIRST 22 DAYS IN
HEAVEN

The Apocalypse Trilogy

Dr. David W. Orlowski, D-Min, LPC

TWO TREES
PUBLISHING

OUR FIRST 22 DAYS IN HEAVEN
The Apocalypse Trilogy

By Dr. David W. Orlowski, D-Min, LPC

Book orders at: www.TwoTreesPublishing.com
or call: 480.619.8486

International Standard Book Number: 978-0-615-39779-5

Two Trees Publishing, LLC
P.O. Box 15411, Scottsdale, AZ 85267-5411

Printed in the United States of America.
Edited by Drew Berding and Kim Orlowski.
Cover design by Max Niseem Soussan.
Cover and book layout by Natasha Bartinelli.

CONTENTS

For my beloved wife Kim, whom I have loved
from the moment our eyes first met

For June, my mother, who waited for these chapters
prior to passing into the light

For Drew, without whose help the discoveries may
not have happened

OUT OF TRAGEDY

"All things work together for good to those who love God."

Romans 8:28

"Mom, can I drive?" ventured the young Michael Gates, as he, his mother, and his sister approached the forest green SUV in their driveway.

"No, Michael," his mother, Deborah, answered tersely. "I'm too tired for that." She threw back her dark hair and put on her sunglasses.

"Mom, I've got my license," he appealed earnestly. "And it's Saturday."

His mother paused in front of the driver's side door. She looked at him with an appraising glance as she mulled it over and decided to give in. "Alright, but no speeding."

Michael was elated as he grabbed the keys, opened the

car door, and jumped into the driver's seat. "No problem!"

His mother turned her attention towards his sister. "Rachel, in the back. Seatbelt!" she commanded, simmering to herself.

Rachel just shook her head at the unfairness of it all, climbed in the back, plopped down, and slammed the door harder than was necessary. As Rachel delayed clicking her seatbelt, her mother craned her head back and eyed her icily, her lips compressed into a thin line. Click.

Rachel muttered under her breath, "Excuse me for not being like Michael, your *Golden Boy.*"

For a pair of heartbeats, Deborah stared Rachel down, challenging the flicker of defiance she saw, until she realized the engine had roared to life. She turned back to Michael and cautioned, "Okay, take it easy."

Michael situated himself behind the wheel with his typical apprehension. Tucking his golden blonde hair behind his ears, he peered into the rearview mirror with his lucid brown eyes.

*   *   *

"Babe," said Damien Westin emphatically. "If you're afraid of a little speed, I can help you face your fear *real* fast." He pushed the accelerator and felt the power surge in what he called his "high-riding beast." His truck struts lifted the base of the cab to tire height, allowing him to tower over the traffic. It was a red monster pick-up, his dream machine.

"You're going, what, twenty over?" charged his latest girlfriend as she leaned in closer to read the speedometer. "No, almost thirty. Slow down Damien! Please, before you get us both killed," she pleaded.

"Chill," he said with a hint of condescension audible

in his voice. He reached out, as he mockingly asked, "Like this song?" and turned up the volume.

She turned away. For a moment, she stared out the window feeling dismayed. *I can't believe I'm here again. He seemed so good on paper.* "You're not all there, are you?" she blurted. "Oh, you're a charmer, but that's just a ruse. You make a ton of money at your father's bigwig architecture firm, but even that doesn't seem to mean anything to you. Tell me I'm wrong. What freaks me, is you're so calloused. Nothing matters – not me, not anything," she concluded levelly.

Damien acknowledged her with a hint of a smile. "Good girl, standing up for yourself, speaking your mind, all of it makes you sexier. Now we're making progress."

"Yeah, you're a creeper." Her incredulity threatened to spill out further before she resigned herself and softened her tone. "What happened to you when you were younger? What's wrong?"

Damien felt his face tighten. "You want to ratchet it up? Sometimes it's best to let sleeping dogs lie," he countered darkly, shooting her a poisonous glare. He pressed the accelerator further toward the floor. Out of the corner of his eye, he saw her grip the door-handle tighter, her knuckles whitening.

"Damien...," she implored over the music.

"Sweetness, you would really do well to look death in the face and smirk. It works for me." He let out a wolfish chuckle that worked itself into a wry smile.

* * *

Within minutes of their departure, Michael was heading south down Mountain Boulevard under the midday sun, staying right at the speed limit. He even stopped at a yellow light he could have made. Mom was nagging Rachel again. He decided to interrupt and try to change the subject.

"Hey, look how cool the mountainside is; the rain's like, really made the flowers pop."

"Keep your eyes on the road," his mother snapped. Still, he noticed that she did look at the hill to their right that slowly climbed toward the mountain. He knew she loved flowers, and thought maybe they would distract her from critiquing Rachel. Michael glanced in the rearview mirror, and Rachel's glowering eyes said it all.

Further ahead on the right, Michael noted, was the beginning of one of those new mile-square subdivisions. It was a strange thing, seeing the expansive mountain hillside, and then suddenly houses, lots of expensive houses that all looked the same.

*   *   *

Vic Dunham stood on the sidewalk, proud as a dad could be. His auburn haired daughter, Katie, had just turned three-and-a-half, but she was picking up riding her new bike as though she had no learning curve. He had run alongside her two or three times while holding the back of her t-shirt, but she had brushed him off. *It had always been that way*, he thought, *from her speaking in three-word sentences by 10 months, to reading and writing by age 3 - My little Mensa IQ girl; and now this.* His eyes glittered and his lips curled up at the corners as he raised his chin ever so slightly, pondering the "whiz-kid" media attention, and whether they would want video of this as well. Clearly, her indelible memory also translated to her astute physical dexterity, he posited, himself an engineer.

Vic noted with some uncertainty that Katie was not

at all afraid to keep up her speed. She hasn't fallen yet, he considered cautiously. Still, he could not resist finding an audience for her. First, triple-checking to make sure the street was clear of cars, he jetted across the lawn to their front door.

"Honey, come out here," he called. "You've got to see Katie."

Vic was halfway back across the grass, preening just a bit, when he realized Katie was not turning back in her usual circle.

"Katie!" he shouted. "Katie, come back!" It was no big deal, but still it made him nervous. "Katie, you listen to Daddy right now!" *Damn her independence*, he thought, *she's too smart for her own good*, and began jogging after her.

Katie was almost two houses farther than she had gone before, four from their home. Suddenly he became alarmed. After two more houses, the slope of the road would take her downhill. Instinctively, he looked beyond her down the block. Then he saw it – Mountain Boulevard. It had always seemed out of reach, but now it felt much too close. He shifted his eyes down the street to the left and saw an ice cream truck.

"My God," he muttered in panic. "Katie stop!" he shouted.

Vic broke into a full run. *That's it*, he thought, *she's heading to the ice cream truck.*

His wife, Olivia, was now on the front lawn, her face distraught, as she recognized what was transpiring.

Katie crossed the threshold where the street sloped downward. She gasped with delight as the bike picked up more speed. In the span of a few seconds however, the bike began traveling uncomfortably fast. For the first time she thought something could be wrong and automatically splayed out her legs, as she had not used her brakes before.

Olivia ran out to the middle of the street and could not accept what she saw happening. With sudden alarm, she started half-jogging in the one direction she was afraid to go. "Katie! Katie, stop! I said stop!" she screamed, despair already compromising the strength of her voice. She realized that Katie's bike was going almost as fast as Vic could run. She pulled up in pure anguish, drawing her hands to her face, her soul thrown into agony. This was all happening too fast. From her innermost being poured out the plea, "Somebody help us! Somebody help us!"

Sprinting now, Vic had closed the distance by half. His lungs and legs burned. He commanded himself to run faster.

Katie's head turned a little. In a panic she screamed, "Daddy! Daddy!"

At that instant, the ice cream man looked up from the cluster of children around him. His musical chime and the kids' commotion had drowned out what was transpiring. His eyes moved from Katie to Vic, who was still too far away, and then back to Katie. As he comprehended the situation, he lost precious seconds. Realizing he could not catch her by going in front of his truck, he turned back, crashing into a boy, which sent his ice cream flying. Everything slowed as his acuity sharpened, the ice cream seemingly suspended in the air, the music groaning on note by note, the boy's face showing bewilderment, his hand stretching out to push the boy aside as he pressed past him.

*   *   *

Michael continued heading south on the four-lane road in the right-hand lane as their vehicle reached the beginning of the new subdivision.

*   *   *

Damien was approaching from the opposite direction, heading north, arrogantly speeding up Mountain in the passing lane.

*   *   *

The ice cream man bolted into the street and reached out to grab Katie but just missed her. Then with every effort he forced his body to turn left in full pursuit, his eyes affixed to her pink shirt.

Vic's body began giving way, but his mind screamed to keep going. His legs rose and fell like dead weights. Still, he pressed forward. All he could see was Katie heading straight into the fast moving traffic.

Almost immediately, Michael's eyes caught sight of the little girl on a bike coming from the side street on his right. In a split second, he deftly pulled his SUV into the passing lane, his mother suddenly reaching for the wheel. There was no meaningful time for braking. This little girl was going to cross their path. When he thought to move to the right behind her, a man in a white uniform was in the way. His only choice now was to cross the center white lines, and swerve into the oncoming traffic.

Damien's eyes registered the SUV pulling into his lane straight ahead, and then the little girl on the bike entering from his left. He thought to throw the steering wheel to the right but realized he was boxed in by a moving van. His hand thumped off the music as his girlfriend screamed, her arms waving hysterically at what she saw bearing down on them.

Both Michael and Damien slammed on their brakes. Both saw the little girl. There was no preventing that she was going to be sandwiched right between them. Michael looked across at Damien and could see his face communicating disgust as he lifted his hands off the steering wheel, derisively asking "What the hell?!"

In that split second, Michael's senses sharpened as he registered the screeching of the tires and the smoke from the treads. He heard his mother scream, her hands bracing on the dash. He saw the utter panic in the woman's eyes that was directly ahead of him in the passenger seat of the truck, her arms reaching out frantically. He felt his grip tighten as he braced himself for the inevitable.

Michael saw the ice cream man re-enter his peripheral vision. He was throwing all caution to the wind. His legs pumping, his lungs puffing hard, he stretched his arm out as the gap closed inch by inch. Michael had no idea if the man could stop his forward momentum even if he did reach the girl. The reverberating sound of the tires screeched with ferocious alarm. In the last possible instant, the man's hand grabbed the little girl's shirt and yanked her up into the air, his shoes skidding on the pavement to keep from ending up between the two vehicles. Katie's feet went flying over her head as he whisked her off the bike. Michael's eyes followed the bicycle until the instant it was smashed between the vehicles. Then everything went black.

*   *   *

The ice cream man recoiled from the earsplitting tumult of steel and shattering glass. Falling back, he drew Katie to his chest unharmed. Because Damien's truck was raised off the ground, Michael's SUV went under Damien's front bumper striking the pick-up truck's large wheels. In that instant, the abrupt halt of the truck's forward momentum caused its tail-end to lift upward and flip headlong until all the truck's mass came crashing down inverted on top of the SUV. Both vehicles were crushed.

Vic arrived within seconds, gasping for breath. He reached down and took hold of Katie in desperation. Olivia was doing a shuffle trot in her flip-flops, her eyes seeing nothing but her daughter. As they reached each other, they grabbed hold, burying their heads in each others' bodies, and crying out in relief.

The ice cream man wiped blood from his face as he stood up and shakily backed away from the accident. He had a gash over his left eye that would require attention. Turning, he beheld the family reunited. After several moments, he forced himself to look back at the vehicles. The large red pick-up truck was lying upside down on top of the SUV. All were probably dead. Although still dazed, he reached into his pocket, pulled out his cell phone, and with trembling hands, dialed three numbers.

2

ASLEEP IN WAITING

*"Who makes His angels winds, and
His ministers a flame of fire."*
Hebrews 1:7

Michael sat upright in his vehicle, confused as to what was happening. Strangely, despite the chaos that had just transpired, he felt at perfect peace. It was as though stillness and serenity filled the air. Looking to his right and slightly above, he was face to face with Damien. Both he and Damien were trying to comprehend their circumstances. They could see their bloodied bodies, crushed and mangled, but there was calm everywhere. It felt surreal. As they looked about, unsure of what to say, they noticed the others.

"Mom, Rach. You're okay!" Michael exclaimed.

Damien said coarsely, "Babydoll, if you hadn't called for the object lesson, this would never have happened."

"What?" she asked rather carefree, "What did you...?" Suddenly she recognized that he was shifting the blame onto her, but she had no interest in entertaining it. For several moments, she drank in the tranquility and then offered, "Damien, that's shameful. I mean it . Obviously, we're dead, and even now you can't lighten up. I'm sad for you. If we're not already broken up, I am breaking up with you now. I hope you can fix yourself."

"That's funny," he said cynically, utterly unmoved. "You're breaking up with me? Sayonara," but she had already moved outside the vehicle and was gone.

Michael lowered his head and moved closer to his mother. "Mom, I'm sorry. I was just trying not to hit the little girl," he sighed.

"There's nothing you could've done."

"Nothing he could've done?" Damien replied hauntingly. "Hello? Take a good look, darlin'. Oh, is that you bleeding?" he added with deadpanned disdain. He left before anyone could respond.

Michael, Rachel and their mom, Deborah, slid out of the vehicle and stood there trying to get a handle on what had just occurred. As the firemen and paramedics arrived and hustled about, one of them passed right through Deborah, startling her. As the police were now redirecting traffic, Michael made his hand pass through a small tree. He touched his face and grabbed hold of his hair to check if he still felt like himself. He did. Looking down, he saw that he was dressed in an off-white ridged linen shirt with shorts that were of the same material. He smiled to himself, *Wow, this is nice*. Checking under his shirt, he found an undergarment that was silky and entirely comfortable[1]. He noticed sandals on his feet that were unique, yet functional.

"Kid, my name is Turk. It's standard attire, everybody gets it."

Michael raised his eyes, surprised to hear someone talking to him.

Turk then offered, "I have to admit, that was quite sacrificial of you. You saved her life."

Michael looked up at him cockeyed, "You can see me?"

"Isn't that obvious?" Turk turned, and Michael followed his gaze and found they were looking at Katie's family that was sitting on the curb, huddled together. Michael's heart went out to them.

Michael questioned the oddity of his own peaceful demeanor, "Why am I okay with this, I mean you, and well, everything?"

"Because of grace. There is a peace that surpasses understanding with it." Turk seemed bothered at having to further explain, but continued, "Most people don't expect to be more alive the moment they die, but such is the case."

Turk's powerful features were perfectly accented by his shoulder-length dark hair. There seemed to be a glint of light coming from his eyes. His burnished bronze skin glistened in the afternoon sun revealing a strongly contoured physique. Michael's eyes were taken with what he surmised to be white-translucent wings folded tightly behind him, but nobly rising above his shoulders and flowing down his sides like the robe of a general. He was struck by the strength of his appearance, and the play of his muscles clearly evident underneath his rust-colored tunic and breeches. He could easily imagine him being in command.

"Wow. I mean, wow. You look like you're one bad-ass angel. Oh, I'm sorry, I probably shouldn't say that, now that I'm... but wow!"

"I am a warrior angel," said Turk matter-of-factly, almost with pleasure. After hesitating, he replied, "Kid, I've never been given a civilian assignment before, so let's take it easy with all the yammering. Let's just try to keep it as simple as possible."

Michael interjected, "Unbelievable. I don't think I could've known what to expect, but I know it wasn't this. I'm just trying to wrap my head around it. I mean, I'm in that SUV! They're trying to get our bodies out. And yet, here I am talking to a Rambo angel. Is this for real? I mean, I can tell it is, but, wow!"

"Yes, it's all real. There is life after death," Turk replied. "Like Scripture says, 'Your dead will live; their corpses will rise. You who lie in the dust, awake and shout for joy, for the earth will give birth to the departed spirits.'"[2]

"You're kidding. I've never heard that before. That's cool. And you, what are you, my Guardian Angel? You? I could have used you with this one nut-case back in my freshman year."

"That's true. That guy was all talk. You let him punch you in the mouth for free. You just walked away. That annoyed me."

"I was joking. Wait, were you actually there?"

"From before you were born, I was given charge over you.[3] I've been with you all your life, especially when you needed me to intervene. Admittedly, I fast-forwarded a lot of parts to get to the actionable events."

"What do you mean, fast-forwarded? You skipped big sections? What's that mean?"

"What, you've never used a remote? I sped up time when you were sleeping and such. Don't discount my efforts. I was there for all the important moments. Handbook 101, 'Are they not all ministering spirits, sent out to render service for the sake of those who will inherit salvation.'[4] I rendered. Got it?" replied Turk, slightly defensive.

"Um, sure." Michael thought it time to change the subject, "Wow. I'd like a body like yours, all bronzy and everything!"

"Soon enough."

As the firefighters pulled out another one of their mangled remains, Michael's thoughts turned. "If you're my great protector, why didn't you, well, guard me, or us, from all this?"

"That didn't take long," mused Turk. "You've always been into questions, lots of questions, but don't think I'm your tour guide. Control yourself. Still, I liked what you said that one time, 'We shouldn't be afraid of...'"

"'...where the truth will lead,'" Michael finished. "We shouldn't be afraid of where it will take us."

Turk continued, "Look kid, the long and the short of it is your mother let you drive, Mountain Boulevard allowed Damien to speed, and little Katie was drawn to the ice cream truck."

"I don't understand."

"If your mother had driven, she would have gone through the yellow light that you stopped for, and that would have changed the time line. But that's not what you're asking, is it?"

"No. Why didn't you just stop it?"

"Now you're asking a question that will reveal itself with time. Wait until you see it from Heaven's vantage point. That's all," he replied rather tersely.

Michael laughed in unbelief, "What? Will my *knowing* mess up the space-time continuum?"

"Funny. Maybe."

"Wow. I didn't...okay, we'll drop that. Where did my mom and Rach go?"

"Your mother went with her angel Arrack, and Rachel

went with Tam. I'm sure they're having a much better time with the civilian angels. Worry not. Let's go." Turk led Michael to what appeared to be a shimmering portal of light.[5] They stepped into it, pausing momentarily, and then passed through.

*   *   *

To his surprise, Michael found himself several days later at a rather large funeral that overflowed the chapel. Toward the front were three coffins draped with flowers. Michael saw his father surrounded by extended family members that were trying to console him. Invisible, Deborah and Rachel were standing nearby taking in the moment with their escorts.

Michael turned to Turk and asked, "Is this actually our funeral?"

"Yes, we've moved forward in time."

Over the next hour, Michael noted the dismay that many wrestled with over the tragic circumstances of their deaths. Still, many could not shake the sense that something important had taken place.

Following the service, Michael, his mom, and his sister reconnected briefly before moving about to appreciate the sentiments of their family and friends.

Afterwards everyone relocated to their house for a reception. Turk led Michael into the backyard. Michael's sensitivity to his father's loss moved him to ask, "Is my dad going to be okay?"

"He'll be fine," said Turk not intending to elaborate.

"But..."

"Your dad spoke well, composed himself. It's a tough assignment," he answered.

"Assignment?" asked Michael incredulously.

"Everything's an assignment, kid; nothing personal. I like your dad."

"Yeah, he's a great dad." Michael's eyes narrowed slightly and his eyebrows furrowed, as he studied his mom. "I'm not sure how my mom is handling all this. She seems a bit distant," he put forth, trailing off with uncertainty.

Turk let Michael's concern hang for a moment before agreeing reluctantly, "You're right, she's not doing well. She can sense that something has been taken away from her, but she can't pin-point it yet. It has to do with her role of being a mother. The problem is that in Heaven, she's not free to control you or your sister in an attempt to feel superior. She's lost all that. In the days ahead, she's going to be faced with the grim realities of her strategy to use the both of you to get love for herself."

"I get it. I've seen that with my Mom," replied Michael with a spark of clarity. "There have been a lot of times I've had to step in to protect Rach... but Mom'll let it go. I'm sure she will. So what happens now? I mean with us," he asked, sitting on the end of the picnic table.

"Next, it's into the light."

"Sounds great, but what does that mean?"

"I'm not into answering such questions. Ready?" asked Turk curtly.

"No. I'm not ready, Mr. Can't-Deal-With-Your-New-Assignment-Warrior-Kick-Butt-Angel. What does 'into the light' mean?" retorted Michael in semi-jest.

"It means you pass through that portal and end up at your resting place. It's back to the mortuary, where you've been laid," stated Turk with finality.

Not satisfied, Michael stared him down with a prying resoluteness. He held fast his gaze and raised eyebrows until he saw that Turk was willing to capitulate. Turk's lips compressed as he eyed him dubiously, and then with bemused acknowledgment, obliged, "Remember when we passed through the portal to get here? Recall how time advanced? In the span of one second, four days had passed. Yes?"

"Yes."

"Well, a thousand years of your time is as a day in our terms,[6] which is to say that when you enter into the light, time on earth is going to pass more quickly."

"Einstein's Theory of Relativity," replied Michael.

"That's right. There's a major misconception, however, that each of you goes straight to Heaven at the moment of your death. Most consider it only logical. Actually, in the not too distant future, everyone who has died from the time of the Resurrection onward will be brought into Heaven at the same instant. All of you will arrive together in the Outer Court as one large group."[7]

"Is that true? I've never heard that."

"You heard it. It just didn't register."

"No, I mean it, I've never heard that."

"I was there in church with you when you did. In fact, I helped arrange for you to go to that church. Recall the Apostle Paul's words; he spoke repeatedly of 'those who fell asleep in Christ.'[8] For example, Paul said, 'But now Christ has been raised from the dead, the first fruits of those who are asleep.'[9] Do you remember when Jesus referred to Lazarus as being asleep, not actually being dead, though his life had passed out of him?[10] You probably don't recall, but King Saul called the Prophet Samuel out of his sleep.[11] Even in the Book of Daniel it says, 'Many of those who sleep in the dust of the ground will awake.'[12] The point is that all those who die are better understood as being asleep, but soon they will be raised at His coming."

"I'm kind of getting what you're saying, I think," responded Michael, his eyes registering minutely.

"Everyone who dies goes into the light, something the Scripture compares to sleep. Scripture says, 'Behold, I tell you a mystery, we shall not all sleep...'[13] That means those who pass do, well, sleep... And how about the Scripture we just heard from the pastor at the funeral, 'For if we believe that Jesus died and rose again, even so God will bring with Him those who have fallen asleep in Jesus. For this we say to you by the word of the Lord, that we who are alive, and remain until the coming of the Lord, shall not precede those who have fallen asleep.'[14] Make note of the words, 'fallen asleep.' Paul classifies everyone into two groups, those who are asleep and those who are yet alive. In the end, he says, 'whether we are awake or asleep, we will live together with Him.'[15] For this reason it says, 'Awake sleeper, and arise from the dead, and Christ will shine on you.'[16]

"Over and over, the passages indicate that those who die, fall asleep, and are then raised up together at His coming.[17] Why do you think many headstones read, 'Rest in peace'? What's happened is that some people haven't believed the Scriptures because they appear not to make sense. People come up with various theories to discount them, from disembodied souls waiting for their heavenly bodies, to what have you."

"Exactly! Why would God leave people asleep for, what, since the time the Bible was written or whatever? That's about two thousand years," replied Michael, his face showing some incredulity.

"See. That is what I was just talking about," retorted Turk defensively. "This is why I didn't want to get into this. I'm sure the civilian angels do a much better job at explaining than me. My warrior comrades are probably roaring with laughter." Turk looked back at the house and saw a slender angel eyeing him, at which point, the angel immediately turned away mortified.

Turk then offered emphatically, "I'm saying time is relative. For the apostles, it would feel like, what, two days? For you, it might be ten or twenty minutes. Suffice it to say, the time you spend in the light will be negligible. Then, the trumpet will sound, and you, and all those in the light, will hear a voice calling, 'Come up here.'[18] Scripture calls this great ingathering the Harvest.[19] When it happens, we'll meet up again, okay?" added Turk, trying to compose himself. Suddenly, a shimmering portal of light appeared before them. "There's your doorway," he prodded.

"Wait! Two more questions, come on?"

Turk paused, trying to subdue any hint of irritation, "Make them quick."

"I thought people who've died have been looking down from Heaven?"

"There has been a great cloud of witnesses, but that ties back to the Old Testament saints, not those of the New Testament.[20] I am not saying that your loved ones cannot look in on you whenever they want, you know, big events, weddings and such, as you can right now. They can and do. All they have to do is alert themselves to wake up for something, and they return to this time frame. Some keep tabs and visit more often than others, but most want their living loved ones to keep moving forward in life as God leads. In some unfortunate instances, people who have passed refuse to go into the light altogether. They exist haunted, being unresolved as to the circumstances of their death. But that's less common. Last question."

"Why is it important that everybody goes to Heaven at the same time?"

"All are caught up together[21] because everyone will be invited to share the same experiences during their first twenty-two days."

"Why twenty-two days?"

"That's three. Ready?"

Michael smiled, paused, and then nodded his head slowly with deliberateness. "Yup," and began to walk toward the portal.

"Okay, I'll see you shortly."

JACOB'S LADDER

"Behold, the angels of God
were ascending and descending"
Genesis 28:12

Michael found himself resting in the light in perfect peace, as though floating down a lazy river. Suddenly he was startled by the sound of a great trumpet, and a voice that called him out of the light, "Come up here!"[22] In an instant, he was floating upwards through dirt and soil like a balloon from his grave's resting place. All about him, others were rising from their sites. His eyes glanced around, and he witnessed a great number ascending from the mausoleum, past the confines of the cemetery[23], and into the sky. "Wow!" he shouted, as it all became real to him. Throughout the sky, he saw people moving toward the majestic clouds.[24]

Michael turned his gaze heavenward, and found he was approaching a radiantly beautiful man who was sitting on a cloud that served as a throne. His eyes appeared as a flame of fire. His face was colored like Turk's, with a burnished bronze appearance. His hair fell below His shoulders, and was dazzling like white wool, like shimmering snow. He was clothed in a white luminescent material interwoven with gold strands that draped across his chest. His hands and feet, like His face, were also glistening as bronze, as if they had been caused to glow in a furnace.[25] Michael saw a golden crown on His head, and what appeared to be a sharp sickle in His hand.[26] Michael could hear the echo of words already spoken, "Put in Your sickle and reap, because the hour to reap has come, because the harvest of the earth is ripe."[27]

Then, in an unexpected moment, Michael's eyes met those of the Son of Man. In that instant, as in a vision, he found himself watching Jesus during His ministry days.

Jesus turned to his disciples, "Our friend Lazarus has fallen asleep, but I go, so that I may awaken him out of sleep."

The disciples then said to Him, "Lord, if he has fallen asleep, he will recover."

Jesus paused a moment, not wanting to say out loud that they were on their way to raise Lazarus from the dead. He had hoped that speaking of Lazarus' spiritual state of sleep[28] would be enough. *He then spoke to them plainly, "Lazarus is dead. I am glad for your sakes that I was not there, so that you may believe, but let us go to him."*[29]

It was at this point in Michael's vision that Jesus turned His focus to him, "Welcome Michael. As was true with Lazarus, I am also the resurrection and the life for you, your mother, and your sister.[30] Thank you for laying your life down for little Katie. 'Greater love has no man than this, that a man lay down his life.'[31] Your deed will be remembered."

In an instant, Michael found himself back amongst the growing throng. He could not contain his emotions as love washed over him, as though the years of living famished were over. Tears spilled over as every longing he had ever felt seemed answered.

As the moment lingered, Turk appeared with his wings unfurled, and his face steadfast. "I told you it would seem like just minutes even though it's actually been years since you fell asleep." As he noted Michael's sublime reaction, he closed the distance, discerning the Lord's presence. "You made eye contact with Him."

"What? Umm, yes," stumbled Michael. "His eyes, from the side they look like fire[32], but when you look into them, I mean…" Michael found it hard to return to the present.

Turk could feel the eddying presence of the Spirit, and raised his face to bask in it. "He is the embodiment of love, so when eye contact is made, we see what He sees," he replied reverently, remembering something distant.

"Just leave me wherever He is," mused Michael.

After a moment, Turk commented, "Kid, time to go," indicating with the pointing of his eyes that the multitude was thinning out.

"Oh, right," Michael responded in recognition of the diminishing throng passing into the great shimmering portal of light. As he and Turk proceeded forward, feeling almost sucked into it, Michael felt his body suddenly elongate as they came to trans-light speed. He called out to Turk, "Wow! We're going warp speed!"

Turk smiled to himself. Moments passed as Michael got his bearings. His eyes widened like saucers as he looked beyond the translucent, yet multi-colored tunnel and saw star clusters and more distant galaxies speeding by. "This is amazing! Is this a worm-hole?"

"Yes. Some call it Jacob's Ladder.[33] We are heading to the recesses of the north[34], toward the North Star. There we will come to Eden's Gardens, which is the Outer Court of Heaven. We'll be there shortly."

"No way! Heaven's been in the direction of the North Star?" inquired Michael.

"That's true. People in the northern hemisphere were looking toward Heaven every time they found the celestial pole, whereas the people in the southern hemisphere were given the Southern Cross."

"Wow! Man, we're flying! This is wild! You're right, being in the light only felt like a few minutes. It was like no time had gone by. Oh! So what's today's date?" queried Michael.

Turk hesitated momentarily, but acquiesced, "Late September, 2023. Today begins Rosh Hashanah[35], the Feast of Trumpets."

"Why late September, 2023? Why now?"

"The timeline for the end of the age was hidden in plain sight. Scripture says the Sabbath 'is a sign from God, for in six days He made the Heaven and Earth, but on the seventh day He rested.'[36] It also says, 'Do not let this one fact escape your notice, beloved, that with the Lord a day is as a thousand years, and a thousand years is as a day.'[37] What this means is just like there are six days for working in a week, and then comes the Sabbath, likewise, the Almighty ordained 6,000 years for humanity to work its pride. However, for the seventh day, or the seventh thousand-year period of time, there will be rest and peace. Another name for this is the Millennium.[38] Understand?"

"Sort of. But why did He choose September, 2023?" Michael pressed tenaciously.

Turk took a deliberate breath, regretting his initial willingness to respond. "With the exception of the upcoming seven-year Tribulation, today marks the end of the 6,000 years granted to humanity. Without a reliable calendar from Adam to Christ, scholars guestimated the time frame as being 4,000 years or four 'days'. Also, from Christ until now, there have been some 2,000 years or two more 'days'. However, it would have taken faith to discern that the first 4,000 years, or the first four days, actually ended at the resurrection, rather than the birth of Christ.

"A new dispensation started with the resurrection.[39] The resurrection represented the end of the Old Covenant, and the beginning of the New Covenant. From that day, the last two thousand years have been the fifth and sixth day. We're now almost approaching the seventh day, or the thousand year reign."

"So what you're telling me is that there have been 2,000 years, minus seven for the Tribulation, that ran from the resurrection 'til now?" asked Michael.

"That's correct. The completion of mankind's six days of work are about to be concluded during the Tribulation period. Paul called them the 'last days,' not flippantly, but because there were two remaining days before the dawning of the seventh day, or the Millennial Sabbath."

"That's makes sense. Seven days in a week, six to work, and then the Sabbath to rest. Simple. Why didn't people see this before?"

"God intended more to be understood near the end."[40]

4

DAYS ONE TO NINE:
EDEN'S GARDENS

"The land is like the Garden of Eden before them"

Joel 2:3

Michael and Turk emerged from Jacob's Ladder, and entered Heaven's atmosphere. Michael extended his hands before his face as he felt wind for the first time, which left him with the sensation of flying. "Whoa!" was all he managed in a voice that was a bit wistful.

Beneath raised eyebrows, Michael's eyes flashed back and forth as he tried to take in the great multitude that was descending before him. He was immediately struck by the agility and ease with which their angelic escorts moved about through the air. He was surprised to see that many of the angels had varied skin hues, akin to a rainbow.[41] Each shade, though subdued from its primary color, was elegant and pleasing to the eye.

Even as Michael and Turk were still some distance above, they beheld a glorious paradise that stretched out before a large sea, overlooked by a towering mountain range. Throughout the panorama, there arose enormous trees that climbed like noble giants hundreds of feet into the air, and some thousands.

The whole of it elicited a squeal of delight, and his mouth remained open in awe. As they drew closer, he could see numerous rivers and streams, some frothy with white water, others meandering, coursing their way from the mountainous terrain toward a great sea.

Turk spoke up, "Behold, Eden's Gardens[42] descending toward the Crystal Sea. There are over ten thousand waterfalls of various sizes. The cascading waters originate from the southern mountains."

In front of Michael was a richly gardened landscape filled with celestial beauty. His eyes danced about over the pristine and enchanting topography. While he was still a mile high, he realized that this panoramic milieu went on for as far as he could see to his right and to his left. In all of it, he beheld a geological wonderland of unique rock formations strewn with rugged outcroppings. In one instance, Michael was awestruck by a regal waterfall that dropped grandly from a cliff opening to a secluded pool below. As he peered down, he saw a giant log bridge that forded the tributary halfway up the tall basalt bluff. The grandeur of the scenic view was magnificent and breathtaking. Everywhere he looked, he found it to be a veritable banquet for the eyes. He could not help but smile at the jubilance of the descending people with their "oohing" and "ahhing", and sounds of merriment.

Something happened at this point that he could not
have anticipated. As he beheld these inescapable splendors,
his heart was deeply moved with an overture of gratefulness. He had heard of Heaven's beauty, but never could he
have imagined how intimately he would be touched by it.
Without warning, tears began welling which he attempted
to blink away, to no avail. He shrugged his shoulders at
Turk, unable to speak.

Turk reached out and awkwardly half hugged him
in midair as the others continued to descend. As Michael
quieted within, he spoke in an almost inaudible whisper
against the excited din, "I want to meet the One who created this." At that very moment from across the northern
mountain, Mount Sinai, thunder pealed forth as if answering his heart's cry. Turk then realized that more than two
dozen angels had paused in their descent to peer back at
Michael.

As Michael stared up at Mount Sinai, he was struck by
its majestic grandeur that stretched far into the sky beyond
his vision.[43] He held his gaze upward for a long moment,
awestruck by Sinai's stateliness. He saw what appeared to
be a single passage, or corridor, that separated the mountain into two parts, running all the way to its base which
opened up on the opposite side of the sea. Fire spilled violently into the channel, concealing any visibility into the
passage. Michael questioned whether the torrent of flames
was spilling down from above, or actually ascending upwards from below. After eyeing the flames' churnings with
alarm, he suspected that the fire was in fact rising from the
base.

"Turk, that looks like 'wrath of God' stuff. What's happening?"

"That is the corridor that connects Eden's Gardens to

the Inner Court of Heaven. You are seeing the Pillar of Fire that guards the passage into Heaven. The fire is actually rising up, as you surmised, from the Stones of Fire at the base."[44]

Michael's attention was drawn to the great throng that had begun alighting to the ground. He had never seen so many people. And yet, in relation with the magnificent surroundings, their number seemed to fit perfectly. When he was still some distance away, he could make out the nuances of the landscape that jutted up and down in a beautiful mélange of configurations and colors. Trees and flowers were everywhere, and richly colored grasses and floral ground covers seemed to hold it all together. He saw entire meadows made up of varied flowers, or just one kind of flower, as he exclaimed, "Is that Daisy Field?"

"Good call."

Michael noticed people congregating about the trees, and as he and Turk drew closer, he could see them animated in their excitement as they were eating the various fruits.[45] Many people had two or three different kinds in their hands, laughing and making gestures of astonishment. Michael smiled in anticipation.

Turk tugged on Michael's arm slightly, indicating that they were flying further in the direction of the sea beyond the larger gathering. Michael, looking north, took note of a great stone wall with a number of arched gateways that stretched along the sea shore for as far as his eyes could see in both directions. It stood 1,000 feet tall and 100 feet thick, with a well manicured walkway on top to allow people to view the surrounding landscape from its elevated position. Michael thought the marble must be illuminated from within because of the way it glistened in the light.

The wall supported large arches that rose above each gateway. These gateways were evenly spaced to allow easy access from Eden's Gardens to the Crystal Sea. From each arch hung gloriously colored banners within the gateways, that even as he wondered, he understood depicted the twelve tribes of Israel.

Michael's heart leapt when he realized the entire wall was beautifully chiseled to memorialize the great stories of love. So well crafted, so filled with emotion, were the historical accounts that he felt as though he was beholding the narratives as they were happening. His eyes widened when he thought the characters to be moving, only to discern that as his vantage point was shifting, it was causing him to see the scene as it played out. It suddenly occurred to him the entire wall was ingeniously sculpted to chronicle the events as a person moved along it. He noted the wall etchings to be deeply cut into the granite, which if viewed from up close, could not be made out, but from a distance, perfectly told their story.

Pausing mid-air, Turk found Michael captivated by a scene on the wall where a lad dressed in sheepskin was approaching a ten-foot tall warrior, clad in full military gear.[46] Michael's eyes grew wide, "Look! Look at that kid. That's David, isn't it? Wow, that other dude's huge." Michael began moving to his right to take in more of the story, his eyes transfixed.

Turk offered, "This is the Wall of Love where every great moment of surrender has been depicted. If you look far enough down the wall, you will see yourself driving the SUV, swerving to the left, and Katie being lifted up and pulled from certain death."

Michael's smile broadened, "Really? No way!"

*   *   *

Turk and Michael floated smoothly down, reaching a

grassy knoll adjacent to a perfectly clear stream. Michael's jaw dropped when he beheld the varied animals traversing the long limbed trees which were all about. Lushly nestled beneath their branches bustled exotic species of flora that regaled his senses as a sumptuous feast. His eyes gleefully drank in the profusion of exotic parakeets, cockatoos, and peacocks, as though he were in a wondrous bird sanctuary. His attention was immediately redirected to a huge pterodactyl's swooping trajectory as it came diving through the tree-line passing right before his face. "Unbelievable! Did you see its clawed hands and long beak? It even had teeth; how cool! Are there dinosaurs here too?"

"Yes, northwest, down on the Lower Plateau. I'll take you there. It's Jurassic Park on steroids. In fact, every kind of plant, tree, fish, and beast that's ever been created can be found here somewhere, all coexisting harmoniously."

Turk changed the subject, "Kid, you hungry?" Turk moved toward the majestically overhanging tree before them. Michael did not answer, being caught up with the realization that light was emanating from all the surrounding landscape. It was as though every plant were iridescent, shimmering from within. He swiped his foot quickly through the grass to see what would happen and crystallized light, like dew, splattered forth. "Wow. Check this out! It's amazing!" he said, and did it again.

Turk picked several pieces of the purple-hued fruit that resembled plums. He tossed one to Michael who grabbed it from the air. "There are only a few of these trees in the garden," remarked Turk, as he bit into his own piece of fruit. Michael lifted it to his mouth and with his first bite, felt a shiver of pleasure run through him causing him to fall back on the grass. For several seconds he felt he was in la-la land, after which he just looked up with boyish giddiness. "These are my favorite," said Turk, as he picked several more and sat down. "Relax, we're not in any hurry."

After a bit, Michael asked conversationally, while lying on his back, his knees in the air, "Do we need to eat here?"

"Yes, your body will need food for now. Soon, you'll have your glorified body, and it won't need food or sleep. Don't get me wrong, you'll be eating plenty for enjoyment, but less for sustenance. You'll love the food in the New Jerusalem. The chemistry here is different from what you know. The fruit on this tree, for example, will not fall to the ground. Nothing degrades, nothing is wearing down. Nothing is slowly dying. Remember the story of the loaves and fishes?"

"Sort of. Not really."

"Five loaves and two fish were multiplied to feed five thousand men, along with the women and children.[47] The point is, two fish became thousands of fish. Up here, we multiply the fish without harming the original. It has to do with multi-dimensional physics."

"Cool!"

"Yeah, cool."

Together the two of them enjoyed their surroundings as they each finished several pieces of the delicious fruit. The tree canopy above them swayed in the breeze as Michael tried to rework his overall understanding of his new environment.

This gave rise to another question, "Why did God hide Himself? Why not just let us know who He truly was, or is, from the beginning?"

"Interesting. He did hide himself, but that was so you could grow in faith and love.[48] He let you discover Him gradually, not only through the things He made, but also in your longing for Him. Each person's time on the earth is comparable to a baby in the womb, or a caterpillar in a cocoon. Over time, you were allowed to grow and mature into an ever-increasing expression of love. How far anyone allowed themselves to trust Him was a gift to them."

"What do you mean? I'm kind of following, but..."

"From the time you were born to the time you died, His hope was that you would come to recognize the negative ramifications of living after pride. Everyone searched after their own idea of what they thought would give them love, as if they were starving for it. Let me put it this way. Pride, as you discovered, led only to fear and various forms of work, which included all your striving efforts to gain love through lesser things, namely, in your case, your attempts to please and appease your mother in order to win her love. It was hoped, that with enough failure, you'd come to humble yourself, and really learn to love her rather than fear her."

Michael nodded admittedly, "Yeah, most of the time I just tried to avoid getting into trouble."

"Do you remember how, in those few instances, when you humbled yourself and stopped striving for her approval, how you were able to actually say what needed to be said? Love strengthened you." Michael smiled and nodded, and Turk could see he understood. "To varying degrees, most people learned the secret found in humility. As they aged, their faith increased all the more to believe in a love that had to be unconditional, because they had failed every condition to have deserved it otherwise."[49]

"That makes sense." Michael turned over onto his stomach, and facing Turk, raised his hand with his index finger extended to touch the bronze skin on Turk's arm. "May I?"

"Sure," he replied, bemused.

"Check it out. The texture's different from mine. Yours is firmer, and yet soft. The bronze coloring changes the deeper I look into it. It's not like the bronze is painted on. It shimmers as it reflects the light on different levels, like a diamond. Can you feel that?"

"Perfectly."

"I mean, can you feel it if I barely touch you?"

"Yes."

"How, if you have no skin cells? I mean, it's smooth like glass."

"I have them, they're just not like yours. 'All flesh is not the same flesh,' Scripture says, 'for the glory of the earthly is one, but the glory of the heavenly is another.'[50] My body is perfectly in tune with the environment, more so than yours. Can you smell that fragrance?"

"What? No, not really." A moment later, Michael was caught off guard as the wind brought with it a vibrant and familiar scent. "Wow, wicked! That smells great!"

Turk replied, "Wicked? That scent is from roses a half a mile away."

Michael could not contain himself. "It's like I just put my nose right up to one. It's awesome!"

"That's as much from your increased ability to smell as it is from the flowers' ability to give off their scent. Everything here is as it was meant to be."

Michael then turned back over on the grass, and looking up, remarked, "Hey, those…?"

"Wombats."

"Those *wombats*, man they've got big ears, they seem to be looking back at me! I mean, like, looking, like they're communicating with me!" Michael noted their testy reaction to his 'big ears' comment.

Turk responded, "Actually, they are looking at us. They're also hearing everything you're saying."

"Oh, umm, sorry," Michael projected sheepishly.

"All of Heaven's creatures, from the largest to the

smallest, even to a cellular level, are self-aware. In as much as you are now many times smarter than you were on the earth, so also their natural intelligence is amazingly heightened. In fact, it would be accurate to say that many of the animals are far more astute than humanity was while it was on the earth. Many speak. In fact, most birds sing, and I mean, in numerous languages. Still, with your current mental acuity, you are magnitudes more intelligent and, will be that much more so, as you are revealed as one of the sons of God.[51] While you were on the earth, you had limitations, but now that you're here, those barriers do not exist. Haven't you realized an increased ability to handle difficult concepts? Feel smarter? Not so much like a teenager?"

"Smarter? I feel like I'm not forgetting anything. I'm really able to connect the dots with what you're saying. I've never felt so in touch with things."

"That is because you are using the fullness of your brain's capacity. It is necessary so each person can comprehend all they are going to experience."

After a moment, Michael arose and moved toward the stream. Turk remarked, "What's up?"

"It's time for some fun," Michael replied enthusiastically. "Let's do something."

Turk stood up in agreement, "Alright, follow me." He then took the lead and began sloshing down the shaded streambed, kicking up water as he went. As Michael followed behind, he could not resist saying "Wow!" again as he looked more closely at Turk's white translucent wings.

Turk, taking notice, unfurled them which amazed Michael all the more. He drew them up slowly and brought them down violently, slamming them into the water, thoroughly splashing Michael. "Funny, real funny!" said Michael rather derisively. "You know, you hit me with a fish. Poor fish. Did the big mean angel throw you at nice Michael?" He then noted that the schools of fish were moving to the side as Turk vigorously trudged on. Michael thought, *He certainly isn't a picture of grace. Why'd I have to get the brute angel? Look out fish, here comes Turk.*

"I heard that."

"What, you can read my mind?"

"Everyone can communicate without words. Listen, tune into my thoughts," said Turk as he turned about, and then slowly blinked his eyes and waited for him to focus. Suddenly Michael heard, "...hear me now? Can you hear me now?" Michael smiled and nodded his head, somewhat inanely. Turk continued in silence. "Nothing need be hidden here, because there is nothing that anyone needs to be ashamed of thinking. Still, not all is transparent. All your failures and shortfalls are covered in grace unless you begin defending yourself. Nonetheless, when all thoughts proceed from love, which will be the case once we cross into the Inner Court, as my somewhat dorkish friend, making fun of your somewhat brutish angel will be fair game."

"Funny. Friend, huh? You said friend," he ventured, being awash in good feelings.

"We'll see."

As they came to a deeper pocket of water, Turk remarked, "I first need you to get used to breathing under water."

"What, what do you mean? We can..."

"The water here has more than enough air in it. Your body can utilize its oxygen quite efficiently. Suffice it to say, it takes just a moment to get used to breathing the liquid. You..."

Before Turk could finish, Michael shouted "Yeah," and dove into the pool before them.

Turk muttered, "I could like this kid," and followed after him. After a minute of staring the fish in the eyes,

Turk nudged him and they returned to an upright position in the stream. It took a moment to allow the water to drain from their lungs, but there was no coughing or discomfort. "Now you're sufficiently ready," Turk replied briskly.

"Ready for what?"

"See that sinkhole up ahead?" Thirty feet down the spring was a visible whirlpool.

"That's a water tube that travels underground, back and forth, beneath the landscape for several miles, before it shoots you out the other end like a water slide. You'll love it. See that drop off over there?" Turk pointed to a place up ahead toward the Wall of Love where the foreground suddenly disappeared. "That's where this stream converges with two larger ones, and together they drop off into a pool at the base of a sizable waterfall. This water will shoot us out from the tube at full speed through the waterfall. Got it?"

"After you, compadré."

Turk took off, aggressively lifting up his legs and arms to get maximum speed before he jumped and plunged himself headfirst, wings pulled tight, into the swirling vortex. Michael was right behind him shouting out in anticipation as he launched himself.

For a split second, Michael tested the smoothness of the tube's surface, and then being astonished, yelled his excitement into the water. With unexpected fury, the water tube dipped and then rose. As they followed the contours at extreme speeds, Michael was suddenly upside down, thrown right, and just as quickly thrown left. The tube dropped downward and he felt his stomach fall, but seconds later, he was shot back upward as though from a geyser. It was pure elation as he could not imagine having more fun. After minutes of chasing Turk, Michael found he had caught up with him, and when attempting to pass him by riding high in the tube, Turk grabbed him and they began wrestling. Within a moment, both were shot out of the tube into midair. The force of the jet stream launched them through the descending waterfall, and out over the water. They tumbled and fell, and both came crashing down into the pool below.

When Michael came up from the water laughing and howling near some people, a guy he almost fell into retorted, "Hey brainless, what's your problem?"

With the adrenaline still coursing through his veins, Michael turned in the water with surprise, trying to get a handle on what was happening. "Don't I know you?" inquired Michael, arching his eyebrows in recognition. By just asking the question, the answer came to him, "You're the guy in the truck. We smashed into each other. I'm so sorry. What's your name? Damien Westin is it? Damien, my name is Michael Gates."

Damien's eyes bore into him. "Who cares, *capiche*?" he countered with crass indifference. "You stole half my life from me. I'm here early because of you. I was finally settling in to this place, and now here you are – pity." Damien paused, affecting an air of boredom. After wagging his head disdainfully, he questioned Michael rudely, "Well, are you going to leave or are we?"

Michael bristled slightly and called after him with some agitation, "Hey, I didn't want to hit her!" He suddenly felt self-conscious, and sensed the need to fix his wildly tousled hair. In that split second, he realized something had changed, and threw a look at Turk who just lowered his face.

"Why not?" spit Damien. He turned about and rebuffed, "If you had hit her, she'd be here and I wouldn't be. Doesn't that about sum it up?" Damien paused looking deeper into Michael's eyes, and then as if inserting a dagger, said sardonically, "Yeah, that sums it up. How about it Golden Boy? Say 'hi' to Squirrel for me." He barked out a laugh, at which point Turk intervened and closed the distance to Damien with unnatural speed.

"Can I talk with your boy for sixty seconds?" grunted Turk in a militarily precise voice, to Damien's escort.

"I'm not sure I should authorize..." Instantly, a splash erupted from the water and both were gone.

Turk and Damien were suddenly beyond the reach of Eden's Gardens in a place called Outer Darkness. Turk held Damien by the back of his garment and forcefully turned him around to demonstrate the complete absence of light. "Welcome to Hades. You're almost earning the right to be here permanently. Those who rejected the Father's love, at the time of His Son's resurrection, have made this their home."

Damien was immediately struck by the bone-chilling bleakness of the dank surroundings. The weight of a thick pall pressed against him as an oppressive shroud. His nostrils were repulsed by a sulfurous stench, as a noxious ashy midst stung his eyes, and brought on guttural hacking. Shrieks cut through the blackness putting him on edge. There quickly arose what sounded like a distant rancor of a thousand voices babbling without regard to whether there was a listener. Yellow eyes began appearing throughout the blackened backdrop. A cryptic, snake-like voice asked, "Why are you here Commander of the Host of Heaven? You don't belong. Leave him and go."

"Back off rebels," ordered Turk, momentarily flashing his brilliant presence. At once, Damien beheld the horrid look of dread filling the eyes of a large gathering of withered and gnarled people floating in mid-air, who instantly burst into blood-curdling howls of torment at Turk's manifest presence. They trampled each other to get away, and the wailing subsided, whereupon they reverted to their primal Hell-speak cacophony.

"Those would be your bunkmates, but this your bed," retorted Turk as he quelled his luminescence. In the thick and foreboding darkness, Damien felt all vestiges of love abandon him as an eerie shadow flooded over his soul. All meaning and significance drained out of him. Time seemed to curve around on itself. His soul began spiraling into a nightmarish limbo. Dread closed over him, leaving him frozen in terror. He felt as though he could not quite catch his breath. As the long seconds of isolation droned on, Damien questioned whether everything he had experienced in Eden might have been some elaborately concocted dream. Just when he felt a profound sense of weeping about to take hold, Turk turned him about. Damien saw the light emanating from Turk's face and body, which immediately restored his focus.

"I don't want you getting all weepy or anything," said Turk. "This is the place where people elect to go who want to prove they *can* be loved apart from the Father. Now, I didn't notice you coming up with any love," he intoned dryly. "What, no witty comebacks? If I were you, I would adjust my attitude. Are we clear?"

"Yes," said Damien reservedly.

Instantly, they returned to the water with Michael, Damien looking like he had seen a ghost. Damien's escort did not look pleased as he turned Damien around to take him away. Turk unapologetically held his gaze as he watched them leave.

5

TWENTY-TWO
DAYS INTRODUCED

"The Lord's appointed times…"
Leviticus 23

"Where'd you go?" asked Michael.

"Don't worry about it," answered Turk crisply, with a strangely taut expression.

"How come he was able to call me Golden Boy? How did he know about Squirrel? I don't get it. I thought this was a place of love? I thought people forgive and forget. What just happened?" asked Michael incredulously.

Turk motioned for Michael to swim over to a large slab of marble. There, they rested their forearms on the stone as their bodies dangled in the water. Turk leaned into Michael and spoke softly, "Never mind about the Golden Boy comment, there is abundant grace here for you."

"What do you mean?"

"You don't need to fear his judgment," said Turk with a voice tightly controlled, despite his rushing adrenaline. After a moment of taking himself out of battle mode, his eyes softened and he said with muted emotion, "I need you to trust me. Can you do that?"

"Yeah, I just thought who we were was all left behind now."

"It was until you started defending yourself. As soon as you chose to protect your pride, you opened yourself up to his critique. Humility is like clothing, it covers your nakedness.[52] But if you, or anyone, become judgmental or boastful, you expose yourself for examination. When you defended yourself, he saw everything in an instant. What just happened was not an accident. This was obviously prepared by the Spirit to give him the opportunity to forgive and release you, trusting his fate to the Father.

"In the days to come… let me just say it, we haven't reached the time yet when everyone will be faced with forgiving and forgetting. We've only come to the courtyard, or Outer Court of Heaven. What you're describing takes place in the Inner Court. Everything you see is just the 'front yard'. We're not in the 'house' yet."

Michael remained silent, thoughts spilling over him. Suddenly, this paradise seemed flawed.

Turk continued in hushed tones with the soothing roar of the waterfall deadening all other sounds. "Twenty-two days from now, every person of this great multitude is going to be invited into Heaven. But not all will want to surrender their pride, and instead, will claim their right to hold onto resentments, unforgiveness and bitterness. If

Damien chooses not to forgive you, he will be choosing to forego Heaven. He, like all humanity, is being given twenty-two days to work it out in his heart."

"But I thought we were in Heaven. Where's Heaven, if not here?"

"Do you see Mount Sinai[53] across the Crystal Sea?"[54] asked Turk as he turned his head.

Michael looked in that direction. He could see the mountain reach so far into the sky that he couldn't see the top. It stood before them with a stately and imposing majesty. He responded, "Yeah, it's awesome."

"Beyond Sinai, beyond the reach of pride, is the Inner Court of Heaven or Paradise, where the New Jerusalem in all her glory is bordered on its southern side by Sinai's mountain and its northern side by Mount Zion.[55] At night you can see the light coming over Sinai's peaks. In order to live there, the part of you that is mortal must first put on immortality, and that which is perishable must put on the imperishable.[56] Flesh and blood simply could not survive there.[57] It would be like asking you, when you were back on the earth, to breathe through the water as you just did. Not possible. In the place we are going, love is so intense and glorious, that it would not only fry any pride that comes near it, but your flesh and blood as well."

"Okay, so this place is the Outer Court – these gardens?" Michael asked for clarity.

"Yes. Do you remember the Old Testament descriptions of the Tabernacle?" Michael's eyes were unsure, and he shook his head. "Alright, let me try to explain. The Outer Court led to an Inner Court, which in turn led to the Holy of Holies. There were three separate areas: the Outer Court where sacrificial offerings[58] were made, the Inner Court where the golden lampstand, incense offering and showbread were, and the Holy of Holies where the Ark of the

Covenant resided.[59] Those were copies or blueprints for what actually exists here in Heaven.[60]

"We are now in the Outer Court where you will again see Jesus, the Lamb of God.[61] Beyond the Crystal Sea, through Sinai's Passage, is the Inner Court of Heaven where there are glories beyond your imagination. That's where the golden lampstand, which speaks of God's presence, illumines the New Jerusalem[62], whereas the incense offering gives expression to our profound gratitude, and the showbread represents His wondrous provision. You'll understand what I'm saying when we cross over.

"North of the New Jerusalem is Heaven's centerpiece, Mount Zion. This is where the Holy of Holies resides, the very habitation of the Father. I don't know that you would remember, but Paul the Apostle was once taken in the Spirit to this third part of Heaven, where he heard 'inexpressible words,' which he was not permitted to speak."[63] Turk continued, "So, we are now in the first part of Heaven, the Outer Court. We are going to the second part shortly, or the New Jerusalem, and from there, we will be invited to the third part on Mount Zion which is the Holy of Holies. Make sense?"

"Yeah. I think I'm getting it: Outer Court, Inner Court, Holy of Holies. We're in the Outer Court that is Eden's Gardens. We are going to the Inner Court which is the New Jerusalem, and then to the Holy of Holies on Mount Zion. First Heaven, second Heaven, third Heaven."

"Very good, soldier," he offered with subdued acknowledgement.

"What do you mean people can't get into Heaven if they hold onto their pride?" probed Michael.

"Pride needs to be understood in terms of love. Throughout your life, rather than resting and abiding in the gift of God's unconditional love, your pride left you searching and striving for lesser forms of love---conditional love. In other words, your heart said, 'I can be *proud* of being loved and accepted if I can, for example, earn something, hide something or judge something.' Back on earth, all iniquity flowed from this falsehood. The boastful pride of life is the root of all evil, because it left every person selling out for a loveless result."[64]

Michael then replied, "And now you say we have twenty-two days to work this all out. Why twenty-two days?"

Despite his aversion to answering questions, Turk was pleased with Michael's curiosity. "The twenty-two days correlate with the three fall feasts of Israel which are exactly twenty-two days in length, as described in Leviticus 23 and Numbers 29 in Scripture. However, rather than being feasts of food, here they are actually feasts of love. The first feast will celebrate the Father's love as expressed through creation. The second feast will witness the Son's love given for redemption. The third feast will consummate the Spirit's love through the unifying of the humble.

"God required the children of Israel to observe seven feasts on an annual basis. All of these were prophetic celebrations, foreshadowing things to come. Three of them were in the spring, which included Passover, the Feast of Unleavened Bread and the Feast of First Fruits. These three spring feasts were fulfilled in Christ's crucifixion and resurrection. The fourth feast was Pentecost, which took place in the summer. This was fulfilled when the Spirit of God was given to humanity."

Turk then pulled himself out of the water, shook his wings, and sat on the edge of the rock slab. "We have just begun enjoying the three fall feasts. When the trumpet woke you up this morning, and Jesus declared, 'Come up here!'[65] that signified the beginning of the Feast of Trumpets, or what's better known as Rosh Hashanah, which means *Head of the Year*. Today is not only the start of a new year, but the first day of a new era in the life of mankind. In just a bit, we'll see an astonishing display of the Father's creation.

"Ten days from now, we will celebrate the second fall feast called the Day of Atonement, or Yom Kippur as it is commonly known. At that time, you will witness with your own eyes the full story of the Son of Man, and the kind of love He demonstrated in order for humanity to willingly surrender its pride.

"Then from day fifteen to twenty-one, all will celebrate the third fall feast, known as the Feast of Tabernacles. Through His love, everyone will be invited to reflect on the ramifications of their wilderness wanderings, and to forgive and heal the rifts created by pride.

"Finally, on day twenty-two, the congregation will be gathered back together, and each person will decide whether they want to enter into the kingdom where humility, faith and love reign, or else choose to depart to Outer Darkness where their pride, fear and judgment will rule. Thus, the last of the seven feasts will be fulfilled. That's what's before us. We have some time before we assemble for the festivities. You getting hungry?"

"Wait a second, you just said a lot. But I think I'm starting to get it," replied Michael.

"That's enough for now," said Turk. "You'll see it all unfold. It's time to eat. Do you smell that?"

Michael lifted his face, and suddenly caught the warm, homey aroma of baked bread. "Wow! Definitely hungry," Michael said excitedly.

Turk replied dryly, "No really 'wow,' or is it 'wow, wow!?'"

"Real funny."

6

THE CRYSTAL SEA

"Who art enthroned above the cherubim"
Isaiah 37:16

As Michael and Turk sat dining on a scrumptious meal before the Wall of Love, with lots of smiles to go around, Michael's mom arrived. She seemed troubled so Michael asked her, "How's it going Mom? Isn't this place great!?"

"It's okay," she offered unenthusiastically, looking down.

"Mom, what is it?"

"Where have you been? I've wanted to see you," she challenged.

"I've been with Turk. We've been talking and checking things out. What have you been up to?"

Begrudgingly she tamed her frustration, and after hesitating, answered, "I went and found all of us on the Wall of Love. The whole scene is played out. What you did is amazing a lot of people."

"Really? Wild," said Michael with some enthusiasm but still noting his mom's reserve. "So Mom, aren't you glad your kids got here intact and are alright? Amazing, huh? Isn't it great that we don't have to fear anything anymore? Everything's okay!"

"Did you know your sister left me after the funeral? I wanted her to stay, but she said she'd just see me later. How is that for honoring your parent?"

Michael looked at Turk, then at Arrack, his mom's angel, whose lips were pursed. "Well, Mom, um, does honoring your parent mean that children must stay by their side, even in Heaven?"

"Honor is honor, isn't it? Do you want to leave me, too?" she queried.

Michael's mind began to spin. Turk squeezed his arm to focus him. As Deborah looked back down, Turk slightly shook his head back and forth. He then blinked once slowly, and Michael suddenly remembered to tune in as Turk projected his thoughts, "Don't force anything at this point. She will have plenty of opportunities to begin seeing things differently. Just tell her how much you love her, and that we'll stick around for a while."

"Mom, I think you're amazing," he said with a gentle voice. "You did so much for us, waking up early, going to bed late, everything. I know Rach thinks the world of you. Both of us are blessed to have you as our mom. In this place, even though we'll be out and about, our love will never be away from you. Mom, please," as he took her hands, and waited for her to raise her eyes. "We love you. No matter how many friends we come to consider family, we will only have one mom. That's you. Okay?"

"I just wish Rachel…"

At that very moment, Rachel came up, and leaning down, gave them both an enthusiastic hug. "Hello family!" she said a bit singsong. "I've missed you both. I have so much to share. But, where's the food, I'm starved? Hey Mom, isn't all of this magical?! I hear you went to see Michael and us at the scene of the crime." Rachel caught Michael's eye and winked.

"Rachel?" was all her mom could allow out, sensing everyone's eyes upon her.

"Mom, looking back, don't you think that Michael did us right?" Without waiting for an answer, she accepted a plate of hearty and messy barbequed ribs, noodle salad and steaming rolls from her angel, Tam. "Ribs, excellent! You read my mind!" remarked Rachel with her eyes brimming.

"But ribs aren't kosher," protested Deborah. "I've taught the kids…" but sensing she was exposing herself in some way, she backed off as she said, "Their father, he wasn't…"

"All foods are clean," said Arrack with gentleness. He then politely validated her concern, and revisited Peter's vision of the sheet being lowered from Heaven.[66]

*　　*　　*

As evening arrived, there was a transition from the brilliant luminescence of the day, to a more subdued and elegant illumination from the low-hanging clouds. Michael compared the lambent light to being in his living room versus being outside. "There is a whole different beauty to the landscape. It's incredible!" he exclaimed to those about him.

Suddenly, they heard a great trumpet call from across the Crystal Sea, beckoning all to turn toward the foreboding Mount Sinai.[67] By looking through one of the Wall of Love's marble archways, they could see all the way to Sinai's base. Their focus was drawn toward its fiery passageway. Michael could see at its entrance seven angels standing erect with their rams' horns announcing the beginnings of a great procession of transfigured Old Testament saints. They were coming back out from Heaven's Inner Court through Sinai's Stones of Fire onto the Crystal Sea. As their number increased, he saw their radiance shimmering on the water as it glistened and danced about. Above the saints, myriads of angels were also coming out of the fire, filling the sky above them like a great canopy.

Michael could not resist responding to the call, and having already stood up, he moved toward the water. He caught himself, returned several steps and said, "Mom, come on, we have to go forward," tugging her by the arm. She complied reluctantly, and together the group of them crossed under the marble arch, from which a draping silk banner descended depicting a stately lion.[68] Michael could not help but look up as he moved forward, because the lion above him seemed to be alive and staring back. Michael simply mouthed, "Awesome!"

Then for the first time, he saw the whole panorama of the Crystal Sea reflecting the majestic glory of Mount Sinai. He could not contain himself. "Wow," he said and looked at Turk with his face glowing in unapologetic wonder.

In a moment, they arrived at the water's edge. Michael gazed at Turk with an inquiring smile, wondering how to proceed.

Turk replied, "Remember Peter? The water will support you if you trust it."

"Honey, I don't think..." was all his mom could get

out, before Michael let go of her and stepped forward with confidence.

"Wow! Check this out, we can walk on water! How about that?!" Michael returned and took his still hesitant mom by the hand and said with enthusiasm, "Come on, Mom."

But Deborah was reluctant, and when she reached out with her foot, it sank easily into the water. "Ohhh, I don't think…"

"Mom, have a little faith, will it to be firm. Come on. See? Everybody's doing it." She then realized that all the people were proceeding through the other gateways and onto the sea. Not wanting to be left behind, she gingerly stepped out on the water and to her surprise it supported her.

"This is the only place where everyone can meet together this side of the Inner Court,"[69] tendered Turk.

As the great host coming towards them began closing in, Michael inquired, "Who are all these people?"

"These are the Old Testament saints. Each of them was born and died between the time of Adam and the resurrection of Christ. Each said 'yes' in faith to God's love when He offered to liberate them from their captivity to pride, and lead them into Heaven.[70] Today, they offer their testimony and praise for all that God has done for them."

Michael stopped and turned to Turk, "When they first arrived, after the resurrection, did they also celebrate the three festivals of love for twenty-two days?"

"That is insightful. Flesh and blood has not revealed that to you. They sure did. Now you've got me amazed. All of the Old Testament Scriptures became clear to them during their first twenty-two days here. Ask me later, and I will share what happened when the Old Testament saints first arrived. Still, I'm sure you will hear some of the Elders' testimonies in the days ahead."

For a moment, Michael turned his attention to the sea below where he was standing, seeing through with perfect clarity the coral reef with schools of beautifully colored fish. Astounded by the sheer vividness and multi-hued coral teeming with life, he was flabbergasted at how much detail he was taking in. As the creatures noticed him, they naturally began gathering about, near his feet, as if to befriend him. He shook his head and looked about, wondering if anyone else was beholding it. He laughed in delight at the spectacle. His attention was quickly redirected when another trumpet signaled that something else was about to happen.

Michael looked up just as the glorified Old Testament saints were separating to the right and left, opening up a large aisle between them. His eyes narrowed as he sought to discern what was coming out of the fire of Sinai's Passage. It was something that towered over the people. Still, he could not make it out because a cloud was spontaneously forming before it, concealing it. Lightning flashed from the expanding cloud, as sounds and peals of thunder shook the very water under his feet.[72]

Within minutes, the ominous cloud filled the sky leaving every heart apprehensive. Michael's mother, who was now clutching his arm with dread, made a panicked utterance. But Michael, rather than being frightened, only wished to move closer but was prevented by the crowd that had pressed ahead of them. As each person tried to get a better look, their necks craning as best they could, the water responded by lifting the entire assembly upward, creating an amphitheater so the people in the rear could see without hindrance. Michael's jaw dropped as he looked from side to side recognizing how the water was adapting to the needs of the people. Everything was, as

Turk had said, *self-aware.*

Within moments, Michael's attention was riveted back toward the foreboding cloud that finished its approach with menacing rumblings. The cloud had rolled out all the way to the middle of the sea. As electricity flickered and hung in the air, every eye was transfixed as the cloud began to dissipate beginning from the bottom, revealing four great wheels that arose high into the air. Michael's curiosity could not wait, and he nudged Turk and asked, "What is that?"

Turk blinked slowly and Michael remembered to listen in silence. "Do you recall seeing the Ark of the Covenant in movies or pictures?" Michael nodded. "Well, this is the real thing, the very Throne of the Most High which you will see unveiled momentarily. Notice the lofty and awesome wheels. Standing atop them are four angels known as the four living creatures." Even as Turk said it, they came into view. "These are the archetypal cherubim who were created second only to His Begotten Son. They surround the Throne in a square. They are several times larger than any other angel you will see.[73] All four of them have four faces each, including the face of a man, a lion, a calf and an eagle.[74] Sometimes the living creatures change the appearance of their calf face to their cherub face."[75]

"So what are those huge wheels their standing on?" queried Michael.

"The wheels are part of the cherubim. It's kind of like a person on a unicycle, only for them, the wheels have been created into their very being, with their spirits being contained in them.[76] This allows them to follow the Spirit in whatever direction He is going. Also, because they have four faces each, they never have to turn around, but only need to turn the wheel in that direction."

Michael then saw what appeared to be eyes on the

wheels. "What are those things on them?"

"You're right. The wheels do have eyes everywhere on them. This allows the living creatures to not only see with perfect acuity the multi-faceted glory of God, but to move about without hindrance.[77] More than that, each eye independently sees and reasons, granting the living creatures a mental astuteness arising from many hundreds of viewpoints. This is why their praise is unblemished, because they see with perfect clarity.

"Notice each cherubim has six pairs of wings, four that cover their body front and back, and two that join together above their heads, and just below the part of the cloud that is not dissipating. Do you see that? When they flap their powerful wings to rise from the ground, it's like the sound of tumult. When it happens in the Inner Court, it can be heard all the way over here.[78] Can you see between them? That is the altar of incense that burns with fiery coals that glow white-hot.[79] This is where the lightening, sounds and peals of thunder are coming from, and the fire that is flashing back and forth."[80]

Michael asked, "Why is the part of the cloud above the cherubim not evaporating?"

"That's because the Cloud of Covering is protecting you from the Father's glorious presence that would otherwise be too much for your flesh to endure. Behind it is a brilliant expanse of pure light and love that is like the awesome gleam of crystal.[81] Even with the cloud, His presence will be mightily felt. For the moment, the Archangel Gabriel is also helping to cover the expanse by wrapping his wings around it to ease the people into what is coming."[82]

Turk expounded, "Do you see the seven pillars of fire that are hanging in the air about the Throne? Those are the seven Spirits of God that constantly burn before Him.[83] The seven pillars perfectly represent not only the Father's presence, but His wisdom, understanding, counsel, power, knowledge and holiness."[84]

For a moment, Michael took everything in as he turned around and viewed the Wall of Love and Eden's Gardens from his elevated position within the amphitheater. He could never have imagined what he was experiencing. As he lifted his gaze, he saw a great company of angels hovering some distance overhead singing a melodious refrain in a language he did not understand.[85] When he simply inquired, the words came to him and he felt their soulful balm wash over him like liquid grace. He wanted to stay in that moment but was compelled to look back across the great multitude that spanned as far as he could see. He found his capacity to take it all in to be wholly inadequate. The thought occurred to him that he needed more eyes, and then he laughed at how he first thought it strange that the four living creatures had so many.

Turk grabbed his attention, "Now watch the Ark of the Covenant. Above the Cloud of Covering[86] is the Throne where the Father has dressed Himself as a man, otherwise known as the Ancient of Days.[87] His presence in this form is as much as you can handle for now."

Michael beheld a brilliant Throne come into view with the Father sitting upon it. He studied His vesture and noted it to be like radiant white snow, and His hair to be like pure wool.[88] He could see that from His waist up, His body glowed like molten metal, brilliant in beauty, but from His waist down His legs had the radiance of fire.[89] Michael was awestruck as he felt the Father's presence wash over him. Suddenly words were spoken to him, intimate words, tender words, penetrating him to the core. "Welcome Michael, my son. Truly, you were conceived in love from the foundations of the world.[90] Much has been prepared for you.[91] I know the plans I have for you, plans for welfare and not calamity, to give you a future and a hope.[92] Soon, you shall be brought into the fullness of My perfect love. I have and will forever love you. Does this answer your heart?"

"Yes," was all Michael could utter, which he repeated again and again with all gratitude, while visibly trembling. Even as he was engrossed in the moment, Turk warned, "Get ready, Gabriel is about to pull back from the expanse."

Suddenly, there burst upon the congregation a great wave of love that washed over every person. Michael immediately beheld a rainbow of vividly colored brilliance emanating from the Cloud of Covering which spilled joy onto the multitudes. Michael, however, could see that many were compelled to reposition themselves within the assembly, some to pull back because of the intensity of the Throne's glory, others to draw in closer wanting to experience more of it.[93]

Michael's mom held tight to his arm, but he looked at her and said, "Mom, I love you, but I have to go closer. You'll be fine."

Deborah was already feeling vulnerable, like she was still too close. "Please back up a bit with me."

"Mom," he pleaded, but he could see her panic. "Okay, let's back up," he said relenting. After withdrawing a good distance, which actually led them to ascend higher up the water amphitheater, she indicated her acceptance.

"You alright?" asked Michael, as she reluctantly nodded her head. "Good. Mom, I really need to go. Arrack's here with you." By the time she let go, with a little help from his tug, he could see that the place where he had come from had closed up. It seemed that every position was filled in. Feeling at a loss, he looked at Turk, who indicated by pointing toward his feet, that they should drop down into the water.

"This way," signaled Turk, directing him to follow.

The water above closed over them without disruption. Michael immediately transitioned his breathing, when he found himself face to face with a very large seahorse, perhaps ten feet tall. Because he had been listening to Turk in silence for a while, his ears were still tuned in when he heard, in a squeaky, high-pitched voice, "It looks like you two need a ride?" Michael's face registered his shock, but the seahorse continued at a rather rapid pace, "Would you both like a lift up front?"

Michael, with childlike wonder, answered with thought, "Yes. I mean, please, we do, we would love one, if you can find us a spot a bit closer."

"That I can do. My name is Chester. I am at your service." At that, he dipped under Michael and Turk, allowing them to grab hold, at which point he took off with some speed. He shifted left and then right looking for a space above. All the while, fish of varied sorts swam merrily alongside of them, delighting in the spectacle.

Michael held on, laughing to himself at this sudden twist of events. He thought to Turk, "You really are full of surprises." Turk just smiled to himself.

THE THRONE OF GOD

"He dwells in unapproachable light"

I Timothy 6:16

Chester slowed as they approached the throne. "Here you go!" he squealed, as they slid off his back.

Michael beheld the Throne's vibrant rainbow of colors, not only shimmering above the waterline, but displaying itself all about him in the sea. Like a wondrously synchronized light extravaganza, the colors attracted the fish which pursued them as though on a feeding frenzy. As Michael asked what he was witnessing, he suddenly understood that the light was a physical manifestation of the Father's glorious love. No sooner did it register, than he was struck by a brilliant yellow ribbon of light which felt like a lightning bolt of joy that left him reeling. "Amazing!" he muttered into the water. "Unbelievable!"

Michael could not help but stretch out his arms to touch the ribbons. After several colors left him wobbling, he comprehended that every color introduced him to a different expression of love.

"Turk, you failed to mention the light," he said, mildly chiding him without sound.

"While at first, the lightning appears to be menacing and alarming, it is actually the Father's love discharging among the saints. These build-ups of love release themselves with transforming power. The closer a person is, the more humble they need to be, otherwise they will feel the love as a burning sensation on their pride. That is why many were 'moved up the table' so to speak, and others needed to pull themselves back from being too close."[94]

Turk turned to face Michael, his eyes sober, his inner voice glacially calm. "Before we go up, I need to let you know that the Writings of Truth[95] indicate you will again be called upon to love without regard to yourself. As such, you have been anointed to come before Him without fear. Prepare yourself, because the water shields His presence somewhat, but when we surface, you're going to feel its strength."

Michael's eyebrows crinkled fractionally as he searched Turk's eyes. As Turk was motioning upward, Michael mused, *so much for the clouds and harps.*

As they ascended, Michael could already feel the weight of the Father's glory.[96] His whole being resonated as a musical instrument as love reverberated through his every emotion and thought. As he came out of the water on his hands and knees, he released the liquid from his lungs, hardly aware of it. Any thought of looking around however, was beyond him as he was completely caught up in the Spirit.[97]

In another moment, he was struck with a bolt of lightning that ignited his worship, where his heart began confessing what his mind was only beginning to comprehend. Along with the four living creatures he found himself declaring, "Holy, holy, holy, is the Lord God Almighty, who was and who is, and who is to come."[98] From his innermost being, these words gave voice to an expanding revelation of the Father's eternal attributes. With a flood of insight washing over him, he could not contain his worship. Rather than being constrained, Michael felt himself to be totally uninhibited. As he took in an ever-emerging disclosure of the Father's heart, he could not help but fall prostrate, all strength leaving him.

Michael found himself repeating, "Only You, only You are worthy."[99]

At the moment when he was searching for the right words, he heard the twenty-four elders declare in unison, "Worthy are You, our Lord and our God, to receive glory and honor and power; for You did create all things, and because of Your will, they existed and were created."[100] As though he were perfectly united with them, he found himself confessing it, along with all the assembly, several times more.

Turk touched Michael's shoulder and his strength returned to him.[101] As Michael slowly lifted his face from the water, something strangely familiar caught him off guard. His heart sensed something about the water. He found his hand reaching down, and his fingers dipping into it, at which point he brought them up to his mouth. Immediately, his eyes brightened as he gasped at the revelation that the salty tasting water was actually made up of tears, but not just anyone's, his own.

Turk leaned over and offered evenly, "He saves all our tears…[102] The Crystal Sea is in part made up of humanity's tears. All your pain and sorrow are remembered by the

Father in this uniquely chosen place."

Full consciousness flooded over Michael as he reached back to his childhood. Never could he have imagined how intimately the Father had held him in His embrace. In the past, everything had felt so random, so happenstance, but now such a notion seemed profane against the intimacy of this revelation as it spilled over him.

Michael lifted his face, filled with awe, and for the first time recognized he was directly before the Throne. It loomed large above him and was overpowering. His eyes were dazzled as the jagged lightning bolts morphed into long, flowing ribbons of color. For whatever reason, perhaps because he was cleansed within, he found himself energized by the ribbons rather than overwhelmed by them. All about him flowed a rainbow of emerald greens, sapphire blues, beryl yellows, and royal jaspers, each of which came in an assortment of hues as did the sardis reds reflecting a variety of shades such as ruby, crimson, scarlet, and cherry. The kaleidoscope of colors, shapes and patterns created a veritable light show that held his gaze.

Michael's position allowed him to see the four living creatures in all their beauty. What sounded like a description of something a bit bizarre now appeared to be the perfect blend of beauty and functionality. These cherubim were gloriously designed to fully experience the Father's unconditional love. Michael considered the 'origins' question answered. The four living creatures were the first archetypes as Turk had said. They had the face of the first man, the first lion, the first calf and the first eagle.

*   *   *

All light faded about the Throne, darkening Eden to its outer reaches. The anticipation was electric, when suddenly, a loud declaration came forth, "Let there be light!"[103] Instantly, light exploded from the Throne as a glorious display, stretching over the heads of the people as though the cosmos were forming all about them. Before their eyes, galaxies drew together, brightly colored nebula painted the darkness, and supernova's exploded with brilliance.

Michael was taken aback as the Earth rushed up from a great distance, settling before the assembly. Within seconds, he found himself passing through the clouded atmosphere and descending to the waters below. As he beheld the beginnings of creation, he saw how the Spirit moved over the face of the waters[104] and how the Son was beside the Father as a master workman.[105] He saw the step-by-step involvement of the three Persons of the Godhead as the heavens and earth were created. Still, Michael could not shake the question as to Jesus' role.

As Michael turned to ask, Turk blinked slowly for him to listen. "Before Jesus was born of Mary and took on His name, He was long ago begotten of the Father[106] as the Spirit of Wisdom. As such, He was fully involved in all of the Father's creative work.[107] Jesus, as the Spirit of Wisdom, was beside the Father as a wise master builder, always rejoicing before Him and taking His delight in the creation of man.[108] It was His wisdom that helped craft the exquisiteness of the human body with all its inherent and genetic beauty. Thus, the Father willed creation into existence, the Son spoke wisdom[109] over its functionality, and the Spirit moved 'over the face of the waters'[110] to bring forth the world in which humanity would live. So it is, we begin the first feast celebrating God's creation."

Michael's smile broadened as he looked on with great wonder. Suddenly, an anthem arose like the sound of many waters.[111]

All creatures of our God and King, lift up your voice and with us sing, O praise Him, Alleluia! Thou burning sun with golden beam, thou silver moon with softer gleam, O praise Him, O praise Him, Alleluia, Alleluia, Alleluia.[112]

Unexpectedly, the translucent sea below lit up with great glory, as sea creatures of every kind made themselves fully known to all the saints. With magnificent acclaim, each creature's nature and activities, mating rituals and survival instincts were revealed with fascination and marvel. From all over the assembly, wondrous exclamations and applause spontaneously broke out.

Michael discovered that as he merely gave thought to a creature, a download of information flooded over him. He tested it by thinking of an elephant, and immediately learned of its amazing capacity to hear subsonic calls from great distances. He realized its ears were vital for temperature regulation, acting like a radiator for cooling heated blood. He noted its trunk's ability to smell was greater than that of a dog. Moreover, the trunk's 150,000 separate muscle units were adept at sensing vibrations from a distant storm or herd.

An instant later, Michael gasped when he turned his face to behold a woodpecker unexpectedly hovering before him. Instantaneously, he perceived its skull's biomechanical cushioning to endure hammering blows to tree wood, its ability to reach out its tongue through its eye socket and stretch it for inches into a tree, and its tongue's barbs and glue-like coating to extract insect larva. Michael's eyes widened in amazement, and just as quickly the woodpecker moved on.

Michael was astounded each time the image of another creature came to mind. He was flabbergasted at the camouflaging attributes of some creatures, the olfactory abilities of others, and the defensive capabilities of still others. He reveled in the ingenious design of the praying mantises, the neurotoxins of the poison dart frog, and the sonar hearing of the fruit bat. He could not imagine more enjoyable goings-on. He was astonished by the explosive chambers of the bombardier beetle that mixes its combustible agents and then shoots them out through twin rear-nozzles like a machine gun, to ward off predators. Again and again, creature after creature, left him amazed at the creative genius and utility instilled by the Father.

Then, as though synchronized with the anthem being sung, dolphins, blue marlins, and schools of fish, both small and great, broke the surface of the Crystal Sea and, throughout the assembly, leapt high into the air. Joy broke out on every face, as the throng sang all the louder.

Thou rushing wind that art so strong, Ye clouds that sail in Heaven along, O praise Him, Alleluia. Thou rising moon in praise rejoice, ye lights of evening find a voice. O praise Him, O praise Him, Alleluia, Alleluia, Alleluia.

Michael bent down to watch the multicolored schools below moving in unison like a synchronized water ballet, creating a rainbow configuration that astonished him. *Oh the beauty, oh the glory,* he thought. Deep purples, shimmering blues and greens, brilliant yellows, rich oranges and reds, all of it combined in a spiraling symphony. When Michael could not imagine there being more, he realized that Turk and all the angels were ascending toward the sky, their wings unfurled, singing at full voice. He was awestruck at their beauty. As he was wondering why they were ascending, he understood they were making way for living things of every kind to answer the call to worship.

*Let all things their Creator bless, and worship Him in humble-
ness, O praise Him, Alleluia. Praise, praise the Father, praise the
Son, and praise the Spirit three in One. O praise Him, O praise
Him, Alleluia, Alleluia, Alleluia.*

Again, Michael's understanding was taking leaps forward with every creature he beheld. Michael's eyes wan-
dered first to a lion, then a tiger, and then a bear, at which
point, he laughed and said, "Oh my!" Wonder and marvel
filled his spirit as the creative glory of the Father was on
complete display.

As Michael's eyes drifted upward, he beheld flocks of
birds hovering before the Throne. He was astounded by the
stature of the eagles with their visual acuity, the uniqueness
of the pelicans with their fishing prowess, and the elegance
of the hummingbirds with their aerodynamic wing circu-
lation, all in their groups. He could not fully take in their
witness, because his heart was saturated. He found himself
singing with every ounce of his being while wiping away
tears with both hands, and yet refusing to close his eyes, not
wanting to miss this exhibition.

Michael laughed out loud when a giraffe stopped next
to him, towering some eighteen feet into the air. In a moment's inquiry, he learned of its two and a half foot long
heart that is needed to pump its blood all the way up to
its head. More than that, he marveled at the ability of the
giraffe's neck valves and arteries to close and open when it
bends its head down to drink and then lifts itself back up.
Both, he saw, protected it from either hemorrhaging from
too much blood flow or passing out from too little.

For a hundred revelations of the giraffe's exquisite design, he lifted his face to look beyond the creature to the
Creator. For a long moment, his eyes remained locked on
the Father as his heart followed the evidence to its logical

conclusion: the beauty, design and utility of each creature testify of their Maker. Michael spoke without words, "These creatures tell Your story. They reveal Your nature. Your willingness to hide Yourself from our eyes, and to let our hearts find You, shows us how much humility there is in love. Even with all Your glory, You let the heavens declare the work of Your hands. Day to day they pour forth speech, night after night their knowledge is proclaimed.[113] Yet even now, You hope only for Your love to take hold by faith alone. I love You. I have always longed only for You. You are my all in all."[114]

After a time, Michael's attention was redirected when he heard a fluttering sound behind him. When he stood and turned, a cloud of butterflies began whisking past him, brushing against his skin, fully enveloping his senses. Time seemed to stand still.

Again and again over the hours and days that followed, numerous and creative moments unveiled themselves. Sea turtles suddenly breached the water, birds landed in people's hands, large animals became a source for children to ride upon. From all over Eden's Gardens, creatures heeded the call and paraded themselves among the captivated throng. When the dinosaurs of the Lower Plateau arrived on the eighth day to make their way to the Throne, the assembly hushed in uncertainty. Throughout the expansive sea, thousands of creatures, made up of hundreds of species, began passing through the gathering. Many towered to intimidating heights, sending chills through the congregation. Then, as if prompted, children everywhere began riding their tails, while others held onto their legs. Sensing no danger, the assembly burst into a roaring ovation.

Similarly, on the morning of the ninth day, when all seemed to be settling down, Michael was stunned to find a huge Leviathan dragon rising up from the depths of the sea right next to him.[115] As he looked about, he saw numerous Leviathans rising up amongst the people. The dragon before him was over sixty feet high, and one hundred and twenty feet long, with an orderly and agile frame coated in impenetrable armor. Michael understood that even air could not come between its scales. Its eyes were illuminated as though on fire, and when at one point it sneezed, the mucus ignited in flames. Smoke exited from its nostrils as though from something burning. When it lifted itself up on its hind feet, Michael backed up timidly. He noted that its underside was like sharp potsherds. Then, in perfect unison, all the Leviathans stood tall before the Throne, and shrieked forth a booming acknowledgement to their Maker. Like a magnificent light show, they breathed forth fire that reached high into the air, at which the people lifted up their voice in holy acclaim to the Lord. The Scripture came to Michael, "Nothing on earth is like him, one made without fear. He looks on everything that is high; he is king over all the sons of pride."[116]

Michael's heart could not help but be struck at his own insignificance. Leviathan's awesome and powerful features offered another crescendoing declaration of the Father's creative exploits. Michael just marveled.

Throughout the festival, no one was rushed, no one wanted to leave. Time seemed frozen, as all relished the experience of finally meeting their Creator and His creations. All stopped to eat at various times, enjoying the hospitality of both the angels and Old Testament saints. Others, Michael noted, spent more time with particular animals, being taken aback that certain ones could talk. Other people elected to drop down into the water, as he had, and were now fully experiencing the sea life.

Michael heard a Scripture echo within, "Eye has not seen and ear has not heard, nor has it entered the heart of man, all that God has prepared for those who love Him."[117] As he bore witness to the reality of it, he surveyed the Throne bursting with love, the four living creatures repeating their confession, the twenty-four elders laughing and interacting, the transfigured Old Testament saints serving hospitably by passing out food and drinks, the throng of people about him celebrating with faces beaming; all of it with the fish below, the animals about, the birds above, and the angels filling the sky as a canopy that reflected the Father's glory. Michael felt undone, and fell back as a holy laughter took hold for some time. He simply could not contain himself. It was all too glorious.

DAY TEN:
THE DAY OF ATONEMENT

"You shall humble your souls"

Leviticus 23:27

This feast of love continued unabated. Even the prideful cohort that had pulled toward the back of the amphitheater could not resist the interplay with the Father's creation. Michael's mom was delighted by the fascinating and enthralling creatures. In every way, all laughed and sang and celebrated with astonishment. But hour by hour, something more was transpiring. Michael recognized holy and intimate moments when individuals about him came to trust the Father's love unreservedly. Their eyes and ears had seen and heard enough. However, something at the outskirts of Michael's heart, something he had not realized was there, caused him to resist such unabashed abandon.

On the evening of the ninth day[118], the atmosphere and mood amongst the people started to change. There arose an awareness that passed from heart to heart, that something must be done about the pride of man. As each relished in the Father's creative love, they could not help but desire a complete restoration of relationship with Him. Like a thought that is transferred with only a glance, conviction spread from person to person. Like a wave of agreement breaking over the assembly, generations of fathers and mothers began bearing witness to the ravaging effects of their own pride, even to their children's children.

As each person realized the devastating repercussions of how they had negatively impacted so many others' lives, there arose a unified plea that something needed to be done once and for all. Stronger still did their voices become, that prayers and pleadings beseeched the Father for His intervention. Heart after heart realized that pride had left them enslaved to fear. Pride had promised love, but given only death.

Michael beheld this sudden turn in the assembly. Then, to his unease, it happened to him. He saw how his compromises had negatively affected his parents, his sister, and his friends. He saw how pride had wormed its way out of his heart, corrupting him with fear. His eyes widened appreciably as he comprehended the monstrosity of the prideful assertion that love could be gained through pleasure, work or relationship. Universal agreement spread that even religion had failed its calling by appealing to fear rather than love, and rules rather than grace.

As the Father identified with the prayerful pleas of the people, the cloud of His presence took on a foreboding apprehension. Since Michael was right beneath the Throne, he was suddenly subjected to groanings that were too deep to utter, as the Spirit Himself was interceding to help every person with their weakening faith.[119] The Spirit declared to every heart, "Encourage the exhausted, and strengthen the feeble. Say to those with anxious heart, 'Take courage, fear not. Behold your God will come with vengeance. The recompense of God will come. He will save you.'"[120]

As the assembly was transitioning towards the tenth day, love led humanity inexorably to one conclusion: the reign of pride must end. Suddenly, a transformation began occurring from within the Throne, where the coals of fire ignited with lightning and cracklings of thunder. The Crystal Sea took on a fiery hue.[121] Turk was again by Michael's side, and when he looked up to inquire of him, Turk answered in silence, "The Father does not want to force the hand of any of the prideful in this great assembly, nor any yet remaining on the earth."

"Why is this happening?"

"This great mass of humanity has recognized the depravity of pride and they are imploring the Father to put an end to it. That this would happen was foretold since the time of Moses, where God called for a Day of Atonement.[122] This is the second feast of which we spoke. As the Scripture says, this holy convocation begins a time when every person is called to humble their souls. No work of pride is allowed, no boasting, no defending, no justifying. It is a time for complete humility. Even as it says, 'If there is any person who will not humble himself on this same day, he shall be cut off from his people.'"[123]

For the first time, the Father stood up as the Ancient of Days[124], His radiance as the sun, His eyes bursting with the fire of love. When He lifted His hands, a wave of grace rushed over the assembly, leaving no one standing. Every heart felt His aversion to introducing tribulation as a necessary means for humbling the prideful who were still earthbound.[125] Because many on the earth had not been ready to humbly trust the Father's love above every lesser love, they had been left behind at the Harvest, that their faith might be refined.[126]

As visions filled each person's mind, they witnessed what their relatives and friends would be caused to go through in hopes of bringing them to humbly acknowledge their pride's depravity. The onlookers realized that only through suffering would their loved ones accept unconditional love as a gift, and release all their striving efforts. They felt their hunger and thirst, sensed their grief, saw the armies and destruction, and beheld the catastrophic plagues. But they also saw the turning of hearts, billions in number, and the wisdom wrought with pain.

One by one, the assembly stood to their feet, accepting the wisdom of giving the prideful, yet on the earth, what they were asking for: the right to dictate their own end. They would be allowed their demands to have the leader of their choosing, the right to have God removed from their decision making, and the right to do whatever they wanted. Like a growing crescendo, the great assembly's prayers were rising as incense[127] from every side of the Throne. Person after person, section after section stood, until with universal agreement, the seven pillars of fire burned with great intensity. When the people recognized this, they shouted all the more earnestly. Suddenly, lightning and the deafening roar of thunder rumbled through the assembly, silencing every voice, until stillness hung in the air.

Michael gripped Turk's arm. "What's going on?" he asked as he could barely will himself to look up.

"Hold on, that's Gabriel crossing the platform." Michael looked and saw a brilliantly illuminated angel approach the

Throne. Reaching out, he took from the Father's right hand a scroll which Michael instantly understood to contain the foretold judgments.[128]

Turk spoke in silence, "Gabriel has been handed the Book of Judgment. It is a scroll containing seven specific judgments, each sealed with a separate seal. There is one on the outside, and six more seals on the inside. Each has to be broken to unroll the next portion of the scroll and reveal its judgment. The first six judgments are God granting mankind the self-rule it is asking for. The seventh judgment, however, will express the Father's perfect compassion to draw them back to humility. Hold on."

Gabriel flew out over the front of the assembly, and questioned with a loud voice, "Who is worthy to open the book and to break its seals?!"[129]

Turk grabbed Michael's arm, looked him keenly in the eyes, and said, "Okay. Here comes the Spirit. Just remember, the grace of God is freely given. Do not fear. The Scripture says, 'It is by grace that you are saved, through faith, and that not of yourself, it is a gift of God, not of works, lest anyone should boast.'"[130]

Suddenly, the seven pillars of fire which were the seven spirits of God[131] began moving out from the Throne toward the congregation. Michael immediately began feeling the examination of unconditional love. Although gentle and without condemnation, he became acutely aware that circumstance after circumstance from his own life was being searched out, where every motive, decision and action, was coming under scrutiny.[132] The Spirit was asking whether he considered himself worthy to open the scroll.

As the Spirit moved further into the assembly, there remained something that looked like tongues of fire on every person.[133]

Even as Michael felt the probe of love draw closer to

his pain, he muttered, "No, no, I'm not ready." In an instant, he found himself observing an argument that had played out in his kitchen with his mom and sister.

"Why can't you be more like Michael?" charged Deborah. "Look at the kinds of grades he brings home. Rachel, I swear, if you don't get off that cell phone and start studying, we're not going to pay one more dime for your community college."

"Fine. Whatever," said Rachel acidly, "I study all the time. You know, I get good grades. B's and C's in college aren't easy, and I'm not ashamed of them. So do whatever you want."

"Don't get sassy with me," replied Deborah flatly.

"Mom," beseeched Michael, "her grades are good. She's passed every class which will get her into the U." Michael sought to immediately change the subject, and asked, "Mom, how long after finals do you think it will take to get my report card money?"

"A day or two, why? I'll have your father stop at the bank. How much are we up to?"

"Forty dollars an 'A,' five 'A's.' That's two hundred," replied Michael.

"You're costing us a pretty penny, but you're worth it," Deborah ruminated, almost to herself.

Michael did not want to be reliving this. For the first time, he could see the impact it was having on Rachel. She was distraught as she left the kitchen, and he followed her up to her room, passing from the first floor to the second through the floorboard. When she slammed her door, she fell onto her bed and just wept over never being good enough. He could see her angel, Tam, even back then, comforting her. When Tam made eye contact with him, he felt love cut right through. Michael just sat back wishing he could undo everything, all the lies, but found himself paralyzed.

When Rachel finally got up and wiped her eyes, Michael watched as she pulled her backpack up off the floor and began situating herself to study. When she realized she couldn't find a pencil, she went into Michael's room and took one out of his backpack.

Rachel sat back down at her desk, and lifted Michael's pencil to start working. When she looked at the pencil, she was shocked to discover how he had done so well on his math and science tests. Written along the length of one side of the pencil were answers, answers to a test, answers to a final. Abruptly, she stood up and moved toward the door, then stopped, reconsidered, turned in a circle, and sat down on the edge of her bed. Her mind spun as she added it all up: Michael never studies. He isn't overly smart, except perhaps in English and writing. Still, I can beat him in Trivial Pursuit, Scrabble, whatever.

Her thoughts then went to Michael's best friend Squirrel, who got his nickname from being squirrelly. She remembered his dad was the custodian for the school. "That's it!" she thought, as she nodded her head with understanding. "Squirrel must have access to a master key. I'll bet he's breaking into the teacher's offices and getting the test scores. Oh my God! He's selling them! That's why Michael asked about his report card money---he needs it to pay Squirrel." Rachel looked down at the pencil, laughed, and went and sat back down at her desk.

As Michael watched this scene replayed, everything suddenly made sense. Rachel had changed toward him from that very moment. He could not believe what he had just witnessed. She had never said a word. When he had gotten to his chemistry final the next day, and looked into his backpack, dread and dismay had come over him. He searched and searched, knowing the pencil had to be there. But it wasn't. When he started the test, he was at a loss as to what most of the questions were asking, let alone having any clue about the answers.

Then a strange thing happened. After about ten minutes, the vice-principal walked into the classroom, spoke quietly to Mr. Miller, who then stood up and spoke very sternly, making specific eye contact with Michael saying, "Listen to me students. I need you to immediately, and I mean immediately, lift up your pencils and pens into the air."

Michael complied, as did the others. It became uncomfortably clear that several students were singled out, Michael being one of them. But when they looked at Michael's pencil, there was nothing on it. Realizing they could do nothing about it, they moved on to the next student. Michael just breathed a sigh of relief, and thanked his lucky stars. By the third hour, forty-seven students had been taken out of their classes and suspended for cheating. It turned out that Squirrel had sold a test to a student whose parent found the pencil, and with Squirrel's dad's job on the line, Squirrel told them everything.

Michael remembered it being the talk of the town for some time. His mom was shocked, and wondered how Squirrel had gone so wrong. In all of it, Michael somehow never got exposed. His mother asked, but he just lied about it. He ended up almost flunking the final, but blamed it on the teacher. His mom believed him, esteeming him for how he always got such great grades.

Watching it played out, Michael now knew where his pencil had gone. He also knew why Rachel's attitude had changed. He hated himself for living the lie. He despised his nickname, "Golden Boy," that Squirrel dubbed him early on while he was holding his golden pencils. It stuck, and Squirrel ended up spreading the nickname as their inside secret. He never really reconnected with Squirrel after the big bust. The school board insisted that Squirrel be expelled, and that was that. Squirrel was just too much in the center of it to be caught near him.

Michael suddenly wanted the truth to be told. He wanted to be done with all the hiding and lying. As he opened himself up to let the Spirit show him just how far pride had taken him, he saw situation after situation where lies, deceit and half-truths played themselves out. He could not have imagined how many thousands upon thousands of instances there were. Still, the Spirit brought no condemnation, no shame, only truth.

Michael realized how pride was at the center of every concession, every indulgence. All his longings were to find love, but rather than accepting it as the free gift that it was, his pride had him searching relentlessly for counterfeits. Each time, he saw his pride work its cruel magic, deceiving him into concealing and covering. With compromise after compromise, he had justified his actions, only to turn around and judge others for the very things he himself had done.[134] He was dismayed when he realized just how pervasive his self-deception and self-justification had been.

Returning to the present, Michael could not contain himself. He was on his knees bent over with his hands upon the water, his hair falling forward. He had reached the unavoidable conclusion that he was unworthy of breaking the seals on the scroll and putting an end to pride. Tears of conviction and remorse fell straight to the water as the weeping and convulsing took hold. All around the congregation, there arose an uproar of grief as every person saw the far-reaching ramifications of their iniquity.

Still, there were some who rebelled against it. They swore and cursed, venting their judgments against the Father. "You can't blame me! I only did what was done to me! I'm the one who was abused! I will not be made to forgive! You're asking too much! I don't care what the truth is; I'm not the bad guy!" By the time the saints willed these naysayers to be gone, their angels were escorting them out. They would be given what their pride demanded, the freedom to be unforgiving and judgmental. Their self-worship left them self-absorbed, and now they were being led away to a place devoid of the Father's love – Outer Darkness.

Michael heard these grumblings, but could not bring himself to critique even them. He felt cut off at the knees, unable to offer any judgment. All he had ever wanted was love, but his twisted inclination had left him groping about in the dark.[135] As the love of the Spirit embraced him all the more, and the tongue of fire burned brightly upon him, he found himself wanting for nothing but to abide in love.[136] From his innermost being arose the words, "I'm sorry. I'm sorry for everything." His pride had broken, and he realized that he could never be considered worthy of opening the Book of Judgment and ending its rule. When Michael recognized through the Spirit's prompting, that 'no one in Heaven, or on the earth, or under the earth, was able to open the book, or to break its seals…that all had sinned and fallen short of the glory of God,'[137] he began to weep.[138] Everything within him wanted the reign of pride to stop, not just for himself, but for his mom, his sister – everyone.

In that moment, Turk touched his shoulder and said, "Stop weeping; behold, the Lion from the tribe of Judah, the Root of David, has overcome so as to open the book and break its seven seals."[139]

9

DAY TEN:
THE LAMB OF GOD

"Behold the Lamb of God"
John 1:36

Suddenly, after so much lamenting, so much mourning, there fell a great hush over the assembly. After collecting himself, Michael's eyes narrowed and his forehead wrinkled as he looked inquisitively past the twenty-four elders. He thought he saw movement around the base of the Throne. He looked up at Turk, who obviously saw something too. When he looked back, there came out from the Throne someone who was unrecognizable in appearance. Michael stared for several seconds before he realized it was

Jesus, appearing as a slain lamb that had been bloodied and beaten.[140] Michael reacted without a thought to those around him, and uttered, "Oh, my God."

Jesus ascended to the Mercy Seat, His head bowed and His demeanor humble. As He raised His face, through His flaming eyes, the scores of people beheld His life story, as though they had been present from the time of His birth. They saw His wit. They laughed at His sense of humor. They roared several times at the absurdity of some situations that Jesus had found Himself in with His family. It was all so ordinary at times, so similar to their lives. But still, He was anything but ordinary. They saw that His every word and deed arose from love. They beheld His uncompromising trust in the Father, always being patient to allow situations to play themselves out. They were struck to the heart when, after He had fasted for forty days, He faced soul-wrenching temptations. They were amazed as His ministry began, that He spoke with such authority about the very kingdom they were about to enter. When, again and again, He availed Himself to the sick and infirmed, healing all who were brought to Him, the people spontaneously clapped and cheered.

Toward the end of His ministry, Jesus demonstrated the Father's lavish love by raising Lazarus from the dead, after he had been in the grave for four days. Later, He was walking with a multitude in tow, when two blind men called out, "Lord, have mercy on us, Son of David!"[141] As the multitude sternly told them to be quiet, they cried out all the more. Many still did not recognize the Son of Man as the Son of God, and were adverse to such a proclamation. Jesus knowing this, stopped and asked the blind men, "What do you want Me to do for you?" They answered, "Lord, we want our eyes to be opened."[142] Being moved with compassion, He touched their eyes, and immediately

they regained their sight and followed Him. Jesus continued heading for Jerusalem along with His disciples, Lazarus, and the healed blind men.

As He mounted a donkey that was brought to Him,
the words of Zechariah the prophet were heard, "Say to
the daughter of Zion, 'Behold your King is coming to you,
gentle and mounted on a donkey, even a colt, the foal of a
beast of burden.'"[143] They saw how people spontaneously
laid their garments before Him, along with palm branches,
and shouted "Hosanna to the Son of David, blessed is He
who comes in the name of the Lord! Hosanna in the highest!"[144]

At that moment, all Heaven shouted and declared the
same, as though it was happening right then. The outcry
was deafening.

When Jesus entered Jerusalem's gates and proceeded
to the temple, the great assembly saw that the two men who
had been blind were bringing other blind and lame people
into the temple, against religious practice. Nevertheless,
Jesus healed them. The hearts of Heaven recognized for
the first time how all-surpassing His love truly was.

But just as suddenly, everything turned as the religious leaders rejected Jesus. As the Son of Man declared
with great authority the truths of Heaven, speaking against
injustice and confronting pride, there arose a voice of rebellion that spread from one religious leader to the next. Soon
they were plotting how to kill Him. The throng of Heaven
watched in dismay when, in the span of several days, His
own disciple Judas received monies to betray Him.[145]

Michael beheld Jesus and the disciples in the intimacy
of the upper room, breaking bread and passing the cup. At
that moment, Michael felt himself being nudged and handed some bread and wine, so that he too could participate.

During a pause in the vision, Jesus spoke for the first

time to the host of heaven, "I once said, 'I will not drink of this fruit of the vine from now on, until that day when I drink it new with you in My Father's kingdom.'[146] This is that moment of which I spoke. I now welcome you, under the New Covenant, into Our unconditional love." All of heaven ate and drank together in Holy Communion.

The Old Testament saints declared with so unified a voice that the water reverberated, "He was despised and forsaken of men, a man of sorrows, acquainted with grief, and like one from whom men hide their face. He was despised, and we did not esteem Him. Surely our griefs He Himself bore, and our sorrows He carried; yet we ourselves esteemed Him stricken, smitten of God and afflicted..."[147]

As the vision continued, all beheld Jesus' willingness to allow humanity to do whatever was in their heart, whether for good or evil. As Michael beheld Him being tried, scourged, crowned with thorns and clothed in a purple robe, he heard Pilate say, "Behold the man."[148] As Jesus was then marched up the Via Dolorosa, Michael could not help but fall to his knees. Tears spilled over as his stomach began convulsing.

All of Heaven shuddered as they witnessed Jesus crucified on the cross. As He died, they heard the centurion declare, "Truly, this was the Son of God."[149] In that moment, every knee in Heaven bowed[150], and every tongue confessed, "You are the Lord."[151]

No one stirred; no one moved. Michael was on his face for some time until he heard a single voice begin singing, which led to an anthem of praise,

My Jesus, my Savior
Lord there is none like You
All of my days, I want to praise
The wonders of Your mighty love

My comfort, my shelter, tower of refuge and strength
Let every breath, all that I am, never cease to worship You.

Shout to the Lord
All the earth let us sing
Power and majesty, praise to the King
Mountains bow down and the seas will roar
At the sound of Your name
I sing for joy at the work of Your hands
Forever I'll love You, forever I'll stand
Nothing compares to the promise I have in You.[152]

10

DAY TEN:
THE CROWNING

"An everlasting dominion"

Daniel 7:14

In the moments that followed, Gabriel stood before the congregation and spoke with great authority, "Do you want Jesus, the Son of God, to be Lord and King over you? If you do, say 'I do' now."

With a resounding voice, the assembly declared "I do!"

"All those opposed?" But there was only silence.

"Will you submit to His rule and reign in all things?"

"Yes!"

"Will you trust His love above every lesser love?"

"Yes!"

"Then let the Son of God present Himself before the Father."

Suddenly, there was great acclaim and a prolonged ovation. Jesus approached the Father who sat upon His great Throne, above the Cloud of Covering, which concealed the expanse of His awesome presence. After receiving much praise, the Father stood and motioned for the assembly to give way, but they grew even more pronounced in their applause. Finally, the congregation quieted.

For the first time, the Father spoke. Such was His voice that its sound was like many waters.[153] Its power was felt to each one's innermost being, where His love penetrated to their very core. "Peace to you. Strength to you. Do not fear."[154] But so overwhelming was His love, the people could only say, "Glory!" over and over again.[155]

With a soothing vulnerability in His tone, the Father invited, "Lift up your heads, O gates, and be lifted up, O ancient doors, that the King of glory may come in."[156] One by one, they lifted their faces to behold the Son kneeling before the Father. "Behold, My Servant, whom I have chosen; My Beloved in whom I am well pleased. I have put My Spirit upon Him. He will proclaim justice to the nations. He will not quarrel or cry out, nor will anyone hear His voice in the streets. A bruised reed He will not break, and a dimly burning wick He will not extinguish. He will faithfully bring forth justice. He will not be disheartened or crushed until He has established justice on the earth, and the coastlands have received His instruction."[157]

And then, turning to Jesus, the Father allowed His gaze to linger upon Him. He shared, "Because You have loved Me, therefore I have delivered You. I have set you securely on high, because You have known My name.[158] Therefore, to You is given dominion, glory and a kingdom, that all peoples, nations and men of every language might serve You. Your dominion will be an everlasting dominion which will not pass away; and one which will not be destroyed."[159]

Michael's eyes were drawn to the seven pillars of fire, which began rising from where they had been hovering above the water. As the pillars arose, their brilliance intensified with great love spilling over the assembly. After a moment, they encircled the Throne, drawing themselves together to fully envelop the Son.[160] It was dazzling and astounding, with shimmering light radiating forth with unrestrained glory.

But more than that, Michael found himself intimately caught up, being unable to contain his affections. Throughout the assembly, tears spilled forth, and arms were stretched out to take hold of loved ones. Such was the beauty and glory of this coronation. With every heart enraptured, all were witness to the most vulnerable and transparent expression of love ever shared. As love washed over the people, without reservation every heart was caught up in elation and ecstasy. Michael could not help but respond again and again, "I love You. I love You. I love You."

In the midst of this outpouring, Jesus became transfigured. From His appearance as the bloodied Lamb, He was transformed into a triumphant king. He declared, "The Spirit of the Lord God is upon Me, because He has anointed Me to bring good news to the afflicted. He has sent me to bind up the brokenhearted, to proclaim liberty to captives, and freedom to prisoners; to proclaim the favorable year of the Lord, and the day of vengeance of our God."[161]

Taking the Book of Judgment in His hand, the Father extended it to the Son, and said, "You alone have been found worthy." When Jesus accepted the book, the four living creatures and the twenty-four elders fell down before

Him. The elders then stood and brought the golden bowls of incense to the altar that resides within the great wheels. The incense contained the prayers of the saints[162] that called for the Father's intervention to put an end to pride. These pleas they cast onto the coals of fire under the altar. Suddenly, the aroma of frankincense and myrrh arose before the Father with the fragrance and strength of unconditional love. Michael never imagined that his prayers and affections could have contributed to such a bouquet of scents. He was mesmerized.

Accompanied by musical instruments, the elders sang a new song:

Worthy art Thou to take the book
And to break its seals
For Thou wast slain
And did purchase for God with Thy blood men from every tribe
And tongue and people and nation
And Thou hast made them to be a kingdom
And priests to our God
And they will reign upon the earth.[163]

At that, the Father sat down.

11

DAY TEN:
THE FOUR HORSEMAN

*"Authority was given to them
over a fourth of the earth."*

Revelation 5:8

Jesus turned and stood before all the people with great power and authority. Before Him gathered a strong contingent of
warrior angels who formed ranks with exacting discipline.
Jesus took the Book of Judgment and broke the first seal. One
of the four living creatures declared with a voice of thunder,
"Come!"

Michael's stomach filled with unease as he turned to
look back and beheld a stately white horse that seemed to

be half-spirit, traverse the distance from Jacob's Ladder in just seconds. As it drew closer, he could see that the imperious rider had a bow slung across his back with arrows in his quiver. His features were strong and princely, his eyes sure and his manner resolute and cruel. He galloped with an air of superiority, stopping abruptly with apparent disdain, not once looking down at the crowd.

The living creature that had called him forth descended slowly, stopping in mid-air before it reached the water. Holding a crown in its hand, it placed it on the head of the rider and declared, "To you it is decreed, that you should go forth conquering, and to conquer."[164] Michael heard the rider retort sarcastically, "Now, that wasn't that hard, was it?" But the living creature merely bowed its faces and returned to its place.

Michael turned to Turk who answered him without words, "This is the first of the four horsemen. He is the Antichrist who will rule over the nations of the earth for three and one half years. He will fully appeal to their pride and seemingly earn their trust, but will bring about the death of many."

Then the Son broke the second seal, and the second living creature thundered, "Come!" Michael craned his head around toward Jacob's Ladder and watched as a red horse emerged and crossed over with its blood-soaked mane rising and falling with vehemence. It too moved with unnatural speed, until the rider pulled up before the angelic ranks, yanking the reigns back viciously and skidding his horse to a stop. Michael was visibly alarmed as he stared into the malice of this rider's fierce eyes. He had a blood-red complexion that was accented with black markings, along with jet-black flowing hair. Behind him, rising above his head and down both sides of his mount, were huge, charcoal colored, leathery wings that bore the marks of combat. His whole body was dressed in battle gear with a thick leather belt and an empty scabbard at his side. His powerful hands revealed needle-sharp talons that gripped his reins maliciously.

This brutal fallen angel jerked his ride compulsively about, the sound commanding the moment as the horse's hoofs thudded on the water. Michael could see the rider's hostility and ill-will in every gesture, as he surveyed the ranks of the Heavenly Host. Michael noted with alarm the rider's overt antagonism as he looked about with deliberate contempt as though in search of someone. The horseman then swung his gaze around, turning his torso about on his mount and adjusting his weight in the stirrups to better scrutinize the angelic sentries. Michael was captivated by his membranous wings that unfolded and folded with perfect ease to grant balance and stability. Finally, the rider could bear his disdain no longer, and called out, "Where are you, Turkania? Hiding no doubt?"

The instant Turk laid eyes on this rider, his thoughts were taken back to a battle far removed from this moment. *Turkania's hand desperately clutched his sword. He was in midair, engaged in combat with Babylon, the ruling principality over the Babylonian Empire. Sweat burned his eyes; he raised his forearm to wipe it away. Below him, the armies of man collided in battle, but before him was the spiritual power that commanded them like chess pieces.*

Turkania breathed heavily. He had repelled a ferocious assault from Babylon, who was like a vicious animal. Turkania found Babylon to be battle-trained and astute beyond any he had encountered. Each matched the other, blow for blow. Neither made headway until finally they were flung apart.

Turkania began stalking him again. Babylon just laughed mockingly. "Come and get me, Commander of the Legions," he challenged.

Stroke for stroke, the air hissed as they locked their swords in combat. Neither relented from pressing the fight to its determined end. Turkania parried a downstroke, then pushed his blade forward, only to have it intercepted and thrown left. Babylon whirled to the right and sought to make a reverse lunge at Turkania's blind side. Turkania hurriedly threw his sword back with his right arm and was just able to block the blow. He then countered by planting his right foot and bringing his left foot around to Babylon's midsection, causing a guttural outburst.

Turkania wasted no time gloating, but charged forward, abandoning caution, his sword coming around with bewildering arches. His barreling strategy, overtly risky and unschooled, caught Babylon off guard. Again and again, Turkania's strokes scraped and clanged against Babylon's sword. Turkania disposed several failed counterattacks by Babylon. In response, he lunged and twisted, forcing Babylon's sword to anticipate his next blow.

Turkania thought the battle over when he brought his sword down hard and Babylon fell back. But his enemy countered by thrusting upward with his foot striking Turkania just below the neck, throwing him back. Babylon quickly rolled to his left.

Turkania recovered and continued his eccentric assault with frantic determination, hoping his adversary was as frenzied as he appeared. Step by step he pressed him back, yet found he was making no appreciable headway. Turkania could feel his arms fatiguing and giving way. He had the sinking feeling that Babylon's defensive strategy was working. Time was against him; his blows were weakening.

An intrusive fear jolted Turkania that he might fall short. The cause was in peril. Turkania's eyes betrayed him.

"What, mighty one?" Babylon snapped derisively. "Is your sword failing you?"

Turkania forced himself to draw deeply from a strength not his own. His advantage was slipping away, and his forcefulness was waning, but he was not cowed.

With a bellowing roar, the Commander of the Legions feinted a massive over-and-down attack to Babylon's left. Babylon moved to counter. Rather than completing the maneuver however, Turkania turned his blade flat and pulled it back, leaving Babylon's blade brandishing the air. In that instant, Turkania aggressively stepped forward until he was face to face with Babylon, denying him the needed space to navigate his blade.

With his left hand, Turkania grabbed Babylon's right shoulder and thrust his sword in just below the collar bone, running it clear through.

Babylon dropped his sword. He lost his footing and fell back, shock and disbelief exploding in his eyes. Despite his determined commands, his right arm was useless.

Turkania took up Babylon's sword. "You are dispatched," he said. "Now you will be banished."

The crimson warlord looked at his stricken limb, winced, and replied, "Unorthodox, Commander of the Legions, but effective."

Michael nudged Turk urgently and asked, "Are you Turkania?!"

Turk was startled back into the present, again aware of the Heavenly Host. He stood up, and declared, "I would never hide from you, Babylon. It's been three millennia since you were banished to the abyss. It is a pity your city has risen up from the sand."

"You mean timely, don't you?" replied Babylon. "It is the end of the age. The Mideast War is days away, and Armageddon is fast approaching. The harbingers of destruction are gathering before you."

*   *   *

Damian drew himself to within ear-shot, engrossed in what was being said. His eyes smoldered as he began observing the animosity being expressed toward Turk. He reveled in the taste of anger, an emotion that had been distant for some time.

*　　　*　　　*

"The fun is about to..." ranted Babylon, but stopped midsentence trying to grasp what he was seeing. "What's this? Where's your uniform?" Instantly, Babylon's face lit up, as his eyes bore into Michael with a long, measuring look. "Don't tell me you've been demoted from rank?" he remarked contemptuously to Turk. "Did I not tell you from the beginning that the cherubim would be made lowly servants? Say it isn't so, Commander of the Legions. Is this boy your allotment?" Babylon stared him down with a baleful look and laughed in derision. He mockingly decreed, "You disgust me. Your pitiful decision to trust Him has cost you everything. You brought this upon yourself." At that, he turned toward the Throne in disdain without waiting for a reply, leaving Turk staring at his backside.

*　　　*　　　*

Damian's heart leapt as the rider demeaned and disgraced Turk before the great assembly. When the rider had finished, Damian uttered in a voice eerily calm and almost indecipherable, "What, no witty comebacks?" In that moment, Damien felt empowered in everything he believed, and with a cold aura of malice determined to set his own course.

*　　　*　　　*

Turk stood there feeling naked without his uniform, having the eyes of everyone in the vicinity upon him. Once the bastion of strength, he felt less buoyed-up, with a sinking feeling coming on. Against his will, he found his heart processing his own uncertainties at having been reclassified to civilian work. Babylon's accusations had hit home as more than a verbal slap. Indeed, both he and his peers had wrestled internally with the move, though never verbalizing it. However, in the span of seconds, he determined that trusting beyond himself was the truest expression of love. He lifted his face, made eye contact with the Son, and instantly knew he was right in releasing Babylon's contempt. He yielded without reservation.

As Turk returned his attention to Michael, the second living creature descended before Babylon and declared, "To you it is granted, that you should take peace from the earth, and that men should slay one another."[165]

The living creature handed Babylon a great sword, to which Babylon responded with malevolence, "I'll do your dirty work."

Jesus continued and broke the third seal. The third living creature declared, "Come!" After a meteoric approach, behold, a black horse pulled up whose rider held a pair of scales in his hand.[166] Michael thought his horse showed dark and sinister as it sniffed and snorted about. As it shifted sideways, he could see it was emaciated. Michael was appalled at the rider's countenance, with his eyes unnaturally set back and distant, his bony frame starved and famished, and his skin pallid and pasty. Michael felt squeamish as the rider's rank and foul-smelling odor made the air reek. A voice arose from the center of the living creatures saying, "A quart of wheat for a day's wage, and three quarts of barley for a day's wage; and do not harm the oil and the wine."[167]

Michael inquired and immediately understood that this was the horseman of famine that would cause the world to embrace humility for its survival. The famine would be so severe that a day's wage would pay for little more than a box of cereal.

Jesus broke the fourth seal, and the fourth living creature said, "Come!" Against his will, Michael turned again to see an ashen horse storming up, snorting and sneering with defiance, its eyes wild and seething. The rider's black hood draped over his steely gaze and stoic countenance that seemed to avow unwavering resolve, as he all but ignored his surroundings. Still, Michael could see on its haunted face, a ghost of a smile form as it took note of the gaping onlookers. The evil of the rider's intent revealed itself on a sign that hung from his robe that bore the name "Death".[168] The fourth living creature declared, "Let Hades follow behind you unto great devastation, for the wine press will be trodden outside the city, and blood will flow even up to the horses' bridle for a distance of two hundred miles."[169]

The last living creature commanded the four horsemen, "To you authority is given over a fourth of the earth to kill with sword, famine, and pestilence, and by the wild beasts of the earth."[170] At that, each viciously yanked their reigns to the right and immediately ascended toward the portal with all vengeance.

Jesus stood in silence with the weight of all that had just transpired heavy upon Him. Within moments, all the people affirmed Him by declaring, "Worthy is the Lamb that was slain to receive power and riches and wisdom and strength and glory and blessing. To Him who sits on the Throne, and to the Lamb, be blessing and honor and glory and dominion, forever and ever."[171] Michael kept hearing the four living creatures saying, "Amen," and the elders and all as far as the eye could see fell down and worshipped.[172]

Then the Father said to the Son, "Sit at My right hand, until I make Your enemies a footstool for your feet."[173]

12

DAY ELEVEN:
LOAVES AND FISHES

"And they ate and were satisfied"
Mark 8:8

The next morning, Michael went out looking for his mom and Rachel. Feeling hungry, he had gotten some freshly baked bread and fish wraps to bring for them and their angels. The *aroma*, he thought, was *heavenly*. The chef angel had wrapped it up to go, and Michael was heading off to find them when he came across a man staring at him. After Turk caught Michael's attention, Michael glanced back and found that the man had disappeared. He found it peculiar, but let it go.

"Turk, have you seen my mom and sister? I've got some breakfast for all of us."

"I've been told they will meet us up front in ten minutes."

"Really? Wow! My mom's going up front? That's surprising, but great!"

Within moments, they were below the Throne and Turk was preparing a circular water table, about eight feet across, at which they could eat. By simply willing the water upward, it rose a foot off the surface and was spacious enough for the six of them. As Michael sat on the sea with his feet dangling in the water, he looked down at his reflection in the table and wondered how such a reality could be playing itself out. He could not imagine a more comfortable seat. The water formed perfectly to the contour of his body to provide total support and comfort. He thought that he could probably sit there for hours without fatigue, and smiled at the beauty of it.

Just then, the Son of God descended from the lofty Throne with elegant ease. When His feet reached the water's surface, He greeted the twenty-four elders who congregated about Him.

Michael tugged on Turk's sleeve and asked "What's happening?"

Turk replied, "We are beginning the eleventh day. Those, as you know, are the twenty-four elders. There's Moses on His left and Abraham on His right. He is now speaking with Adam. That's Noah behind Adam, and Job in the back, on the right. Daniel is also in the back, and to his left are Elijah, and then David. As you can see, each of them and several others are already glorified. The other twelve elders are the twelve apostles. Paul is the shorter one on the far right, who replaced Judas."[175]

Just then, Deborah and Rachel arrived. It was evident

from his mom's expression that she was a bit unsettled, but she tried to hide it. "Hi Michael, how are you?"

"I'm great Mom. It's wonderful to be up here together. How are you?"

"I'm fine." Then she thought, checked herself, and said, "No, really, I'm good. I like the table."

"Me too, the water's so cool. Ready to eat? I brought some food. How're you doing Rach?"

"Great! Thanks. I'm starving!"

As they sat to eat, Michael started to open up the bag of food when he felt a tap on his shoulder. Turning, he found a man crouched down beside him who said with a smile, "Hi Michael, my name is Andrew.[176] I was just talking with the Lord, and He asked if we might, well, borrow your breakfast?"

For the briefest of moments, Michael almost allowed a question to form, but chose against it, and with a smile said, "Absolutely. Enjoy!"

"Oh, we'll bring plenty right back. Thank you."

Michael turned to Turk who smiled and nodded ever so slightly in approval. Within moments the twenty-four elders, with the help of angels and those with a heart to serve, started handing out baskets of freshly baked bread and steaming fish wraps. Michael was beaming from ear to ear when he realized that the Lord was coming in their direction with a basket full of food. He noticed Jesus' eyes appeared normal, which allayed any of his concerns about his mom's uneasiness.

"Greetings, Michael. There are many here enjoying breakfast because of your generosity. I'm grateful for your willingness to trust, and I am here to serve you some hot food."

At that point, Rachel couldn't help herself and offered impulsively, "Would You like to join us?" For an instant,

Michael could not believe his ears, and then Jesus responded, "I'd love to, if that's alright with everyone?"

Jesus looked ever so gently at Deborah. "Sure," she said timidly as they all agreed. The table simply expanded as He sat to Rachel's right.

"Would you mind if I raise us up a bit? It would help Me to see above the crowd." With their consent, the table and their water seats lifted easily into the air another ten feet.

"Wow," said Michael, while the others just giggled a bit.

"Well, this food is already blessed, so let's eat," said Jesus. Together they passed out steaming hot bread that had butter dripping from it, and the fish wraps that had the most wonderful sauce.

As they were feasting, Michael exclaimed, "This tastes amazing!"

"Yeah, don't they do a good job?"

"The sauce is great," replied Rachel.

"So, not one fish died, and yet this great multitude is being fed," said Michael knowingly.

"That's true. Nothing is caused to die in Heaven, although every creature willingly gives of itself. We all lay our lives down in love, before taking them back up again.

"So tell Me Rachel, what's been your highlight so far?"

"Well, actually, You being here right now."

"Thank you, I've been looking forward to this."

"Also, last night, I, um, seeing how many people You helped, and hearing what You said. I never realized that a lot of what You said back then, was really spoken prophetically for all of us here. I could never have imagined. When I saw Your willingness to love us, even to the point of laying down Your own life, well, that's when I knew."

"Thank you. Your willingness to welcome Our love

last night touched all of Us."

Rachel fixed her gaze and pondered how far she could allow her trust to go. Without words, she thought, "But what about…?"

Jesus paused, reached over, and touched her shoulder tenderly. He then caught her up in the Spirit as He spoke privately to her heart, *"I was there when your mom struck you, when she cursed ever having you. You were wearing your pink baby-doll pajamas and fluffy slippers. Your hair was pulled back into a ponytail, and you were just getting ready for bed. She had received a phone call from your teacher about you hitting a girl, which gave her the opportunity she wanted. What happened next was very grieving. But I knew that without you being challenged to forgive, you would never truly understand your own need to be forgiven, for the same root of pride resides in both of you. Still, My grace was upon you, and I stayed there in your room, and sat with you while you cried yourself to sleep. Tam and I never left you, nor forsook you."*[177]

In that moment, Rachel leaned to her right and embraced Him warmly. In those seconds, she knew what she'd always longed to know, that she was loved in spite of each and every circumstance. Even though her mom had rejected her, Jesus' love had never waned and was never distant. As He returned her embrace, she softly spoke, "You were there. My angel Tam was there. You never left me. You were there." With tears spilling down her cheeks and awe in her heart, she said, "I love You. I will always love You."

After a pause, the conversation at the table resumed going back and forth, while at the same time Jesus' eyes privately engaged Turk, "Thank you Turkania for not responding to Babylon's verbal attacks, nor for questioning My judgment. Your willingness to embrace your assignment speaks well of your implacable and unwavering resolve. But fret not, soon, you will engage your adversary again." At that, Turk's eyes widened with pleasure, and an almost primitive look came over his face.

During their breakfast, Michael noted the moments when Jesus' eyes would come alive, not as brilliantly as before the larger gathering, but noticeable nonetheless. On a half dozen occasions while Jesus was sharing and laughing freely with them at the table, Michael noticed entire sections of the adjacent crowd turned in His direction. Each of them showed signs of being deeply intimate with Him, as though He were sitting at their table. Jesus attempted on two occasions to draw out Michael's mother, but she remained reticent to allow it to go very far. Michael then realized why the table had needed to be raised. When he casually looked down, expecting a ten-foot drop, he was taken aback to see that they were now hundreds of feet in the air, and that the table was slowly turning.

When Michael wondered to himself how many people Jesus had interacted with during lunch, he heard Jesus' voice within, "Many, Michael. It is important that I am able to give undivided attention to as many as possible." Michael turned to Him and realized that Jesus wanted to say something more. "Michael, I am sending you as a sheep in the midst of wolves. Beware of men. Do not be anxious about what you will speak, for it shall be given you in that hour what you shall say; for it is not you who speak, but it is the Spirit of your Father who speaks through you. And you will be hated on account of My name. But do not fear them, for there is nothing covered that will not be revealed, and hidden that will not be known. What I tell you in darkness, speak in the light; and what you hear whispered in your ear, proclaim upon the housetops."[178]

Michael's eyes grew wide with astonishment as he sought to understand Jesus' words.

Jesus continued, "These words will bring you comfort

in the days to come."

Jesus then lowered the table, and standing up, said, "I want to thank you for inviting Me to share breakfast with you. I know there is a lot in store for each of you, but I am convinced your faith will carry you through to the end."[179] As he was leaving, He shared one more thought with Michael saying, "You will want to take your mom to a safe distance, because in a few moments, Gabriel will once again uncover the Father's glory."

"Oh yes, I understand."

"See about getting her situated, before you come back."

"I will. Thank You."

13

DAY ELEVEN:
THE SEED OF INIQUITY

*"Behold, I have found only this, that God made
men upright, but they have sought out many devices."*
Ecclesiastes 7:29

As Gabriel pulled away from shrouding the Father's glorious presence, light penetrated the Cloud of Covering like the sun's rays at sunrise.[180] The rainbow colorations were beyond magnificent. Love manifested itself in the most glorious array of ribbons that rose and spiraled about the Throne. Songs of worship began breaking out spontaneously. The whole of the congregation, even the prideful cohort, were awestruck at the unbridled love.

By the time Gabriel moved away from the fully illuminated cloud, he himself reflected the Father's glory as the
morning sun.[181] Michael bowed down prostrate, his forehead pressed against the water, with his whole being enveloped in perfect peace. The full assembly was caught up
in the most amazing rapture of love. The only words most
could utter were, "I love you. I love you. I love you!" The
four living creatures were heard to say, "Holy, holy, holy,
is the Lord God Almighty" in such a way that it blended
perfectly into the background, and yet was the soothing
confession of every heart.

Michael lifted himself off the water and smiled in wonderment. In an unhurried moment, his eyes rested on Gabriel as he stood nobly to the side of the Cloud of Covering,
his face lowered in humility, despite his brilliant radiance.
Michael wondered why Gabriel's selfless devotion so appealed to his own heart. The question lingered as he stared
unblinkingly at him, trying to discern what he was seeing.
There was something more than Gabriel's unvarnished
faith and unflinching loyalty. There was purity of soul and
an innocence before the highest ideals of love. More than
that, there was perfect unity with the One who is love.

Mystery swept over Michael, with sudden moisture
filling his eyes, as he asked himself, *Who am I supposed to
be?* He then looked at his warrior angel, Turk, noting he
was sizably larger and more formidable than the other escorts, and asked himself, *Why me? There is nothing special
about me.* As humility took hold of his heart, he saw the
truth of it. There was not a wide swath between selling out
to pride or humbly yielding to love, but only a razor's edge.
It's merely a turn of the heart between sunrise and faith, or
shadow and fear.

Moments later, Gabriel turned, his wings unfurling
with brilliance, as he entered the cloud to cover the expanse.

Suddenly, the music shifted from a soulful requiem to a melody filled with hope and courage.

Jesus came to the edge of the Throne with one of the twenty-four elders at His side, and began to speak. "I hope you enjoyed your breakfast," to which everyone responded with hearty approval. "Good, we have a lot to cover over the next four days before we celebrate the Feast of Tabernacles.

"I am keenly aware that each of you will be challenged to surrender your pride with its conditional acceptance, in favor of a love that is unconditional. Many of your hearts are conflicted on just this point, for reasons that you cannot quite understand. It is My aim, over these next few days, to help you come to the point of releasing your pride.[182]

"As you know, we will be together in this Outer Court for twenty-two days in accordance with the three fall feasts of Israel.[183] For the first nine days, you celebrated the Feast of Trumpets and rejoiced over Our love in the creation of all things. Yesterday, we celebrated the Day of Atonement where the Father's love was demonstrated by My life being laid down, where each of you now knows Our true heart and love for you.[184] Four days from now, we will celebrate the seven-day Feast of Tabernacles where you will revisit your 'wilderness wanderings' so to speak, or more plainly, your time on the earth, and all of your interactions with one another. During this celebration, you will be invited to unify with all those you have known, making amends as needed. Then, on day twenty-two, those of you who willingly reconciled with your neighbor, will be welcomed into the Inner Court of Heaven.

"For some of you, the stakes are high. Your eternal existence still hangs in the balance. I have previously said, 'He who overcomes shall not be hurt by the second death.'[185] Let Me just say, a second death is possible.[186] If any of you choose to hold onto your pride, you will lose your life. As many of you have been made soberly aware, no pride can cross into Heaven, and therefore, it is imperative that you recognize your need to release it. However, your decision to abandon pride must be of your own volition, and as such, it is not one that will be forced upon you. We are pouring Our hearts out to you in hopes of winning your trust and willingness to do so.

"Over the next two days, you will have the privilege of hearing from several of the twenty-four elders. Each of them has walked through trying circumstances and personal failures that have served to grow and build their faith. I believe their testimonies will be crucial in helping your transition into the Inner Court.

"As we begin today, I want to introduce you to your first father. He has served Me well these many years with great humility. I believe you will come to love him dearly. Let Me introduce, Adam."

At that, there was a reticent ovation, as many were unsure whether he had even existed, while others had latent resentments tied back to their propensity to sin. Nonetheless, all joined in giving him a tentative welcome that then surged into a receptive embrace.

As Adam walked to the forefront of the Throne's platform, Jesus embraced him warmly and stepped back. Adam's transfigured body shone brilliantly before the congregation. His luminescent facial and physical features were so striking that the people marveled. His eyes were earnest, his hair sat above his shoulders, and his beard was neatly trimmed. He wore a white tunic that reached to his hips, along with matching white britches beneath, all of which radiated vividly.

As the greeting subsided, Adam began speaking softly and somewhat reluctantly, "I am the last person who should be granted an audience before you. When I think back to the moment of decision, it seemed such a desirable thing, to be like God, to be on His level, to be able to be loved apart from Him."

Adam let the words drift off as he found himself revisiting those former events in a vision. After a few awkward moments, Jesus stepped forward, put His hand on Adam's shoulder, whereupon, He began projecting Adam's vision through His own blazing eyes to the whole of the assembly.

*   *   *

Eve was strolling about the garden when she noticed an angel standing some distance away, near the forbidden tree. It piqued her curiosity. She made her way toward him, but he turned and disappeared in the opposite direction. Still, her bare feet slowly approached the Tree of the Knowledge of Good and Evil. For the first time, she stood beneath it. Her heart skipped a beat when a serpent unexpectedly appeared from behind a limb. "Serpent, what are you doing up there?!" she challenged, feeling startled.

"Let me ask you, Eve, why are you standing down there?" he inquired coyly.

"I, uh…"

At that, the serpent with its spindly fingers picked a piece of fruit from the tree, and held it before its eyes, turning it ever so seductively about. "Beautiful, isn't it?" he said admiringly.

*   *   *

"I didn't know," cried Eve with dismay. "Oh, Adam, the serpent showed me; he ate a piece. He said it was good for food, good to make one wise. I thought…," she started, and then broke into tears again. Eve was sitting hunched over on the grass, her hair thrown forward. "I can't breathe, I can't…" she anguished, gasping for air.

113

Adam moved toward her, reaching down to touch her back. After she settled down, he propped himself back against the tree. He felt numb, but still the tears spilled down his exhausted face. His long, matted hair fell awkwardly over his forehead. For some time, they had both wailed uncontrollably, grieving their loss of innocence.

"We've changed everything," Adam said evenly with a subdued voice. "I can't feel Him. Before, His presence, His love, lived and breathed in me. He was always here. Now, I feel empty, like there's a hole at my center," he wailed.

"I want Him back," sobbed Eve. "I feel cold and naked."

"Even the grass is different," he replied meditatively. "It's like the life is going out of it somehow; the trees, everything. The garden is dying, I can feel it. Look, see these flowers, they're not as illuminated as before. The life is leaving them."

"I know, I know," despaired Eve. "I'm so sorry, it's all my fault."

"No, no darling," protested Adam. "We chose together."

*　　*　　*

"Honey, Cain's anger is intolerable," stated Eve with consternation. "He berated Abel again yesterday for next to nothing."

"It's the heat. Everyone's on edge. The crops need a little more time, but the dew seems to be dissipating by midday. Cain's concerned about the yield, and probably a bit jealous over Abel's flocks. If it isn't this, it's that – sweat and toil, thorns and thistles," conceded Adam.

*　　*　　*

Cain dropped the hoe from his right hand and it fell to the dirt. His eyes stared down at Abel and the blood puddling about his head. Cain's wrath, there but seconds before, had turned to ice. He tried to recapture why he'd felt so justified, but none of it seemed to matter. The scene before him appeared surreal.

As he lifted his eyes, he could see the altar where their offerings had been presented. "How dare the Most High refuse my gifts and accept Abel's," he had just been ranting to himself. "Why are sheep better than vegetables? Why is blood necessary?" But the words seemed distant.

Being jolted back to reality, he turned around in fear to see if anyone was in sight. Instantly, his mind began spinning as to what he would say to his parents. "No, I can't tell," he concluded with haunted dismay.

In trying to formulate a plan, he noticed that a short distance away, beyond the field, a natural gully dipped down. At once, he picked up the bloody hoe and moved to the gully, working feverishly to deepen it several feet. He returned to Abel, picked him up under his arms, and dragged his body to the hole. After covering his body with dirt, he concealed the site further with dried top soil and debris.

Feeling thirsty, Cain made his way over to the stream. While sitting on a boulder with his feet in the water, feeling numb and unsettled, he heard the Almighty drawing close through the trees. Cain tried momentarily to wash the blood off his hands, but realized his clothing was saturated.

Cain kept his head lowered as the Most High approached. For a number of breaths, nothing was said. Then God asked, "Where is Abel, your brother?"[187]

"I do not know. Am I my brother's keeper?" queried Cain.

"What have you done? The voice of your brother's blood is crying to Me from the ground. Now you are cursed from the ground, which has opened its mouth to receive your brother's blood from your hand. When you cultivate the ground, it will no longer yield its strength to you. Instead, you will be a vagrant and a wanderer on the earth."

Cain could not accept what he was hearing. "My punishment

is too great to bear! Behold, you are driving me this day from the face of the ground, and from Your face I will be hidden."[188]

*   *   *

Adam stood there, trying to grasp what he was seeing. Cain was coming toward the homestead, distraught and bloodied. His eyes were wild and delirious, and his words unintelligible, over-wrought with emotion.

"What? What happened?" cried Adam, as he met Cain at the edge of the field.

Cain half-turned, moaning nonsensical words, "He's dead... ahahhah...hidnground...the Most High cursed...losteveryting ... eearrhahha...haftalev..."

"What are you saying?!" Adam yelled. But Cain continued trying futilely to wipe the blood off his hands by using his blood-ied shirt. He stumbled beyond Adam toward the house. Adam be-gan retracing Cain's path through the chest-high wheat to find his other son. Minutes later, he came upon the Most High carrying Abel's dirtied, bloodied body toward him. Adam collapsed hysteri-cally to the ground weeping, pulling dirt upon his head, realizing with horror what had transpired.

*   *   *

Adam's vision ended. Jesus stepped back, and after the great assembly took a few moments to collect themselves, Adam spoke contemplatively. "It is not too much to say that I am actually complicit in the untold evils that have come upon the world. In every way, I unleashed terrible woes upon all of us. You watched Cain and Abel, but the truth is, almost immediately, Eve and I started bickering. When we added the children, it only magnified. I know you know what I am talking about, because I've seen it play out in your lives as well. Even after Abel was killed, I could never have imagined all the human suffering, the wars, and the heartache that would transpire.

"Eve and I were granted what we asked for, and pride left us toiling for love. We hated what we had become. For the rest of our lives, we felt on the outside of love. Pride and fear defined our very nature, but not just ours, we witnessed it in our children and our children's children.

"It spread all the way to you and yours. And yet, anytime any of us quieted ourselves just long enough, we saw that what we truly wanted was to return home to the likes of this garden. We longed for our relationship to be restored with the One who not only created us but loved us. We were desperate for Him. After years of striving, as we got older and perhaps wiser, we came to see our youthful ambitions as nothing but vanity.[189]

"By honoring our decision, along with its painful consequences, the Father showed us the way of humility. You and I are now approaching the time when the Scripture will be fulfilled, 'He shall wipe away every tear from their eyes, and there shall no longer be any death, nor mourning, nor crying, nor pain; the first things have passed away.'[190] He gave us the 'first things,' so we could discover the vanity of searching after love through self-effort. Can you appreciate the magnitude of His gift? If it were not for the pain that we experienced in life, we would likely be blind to our loveless state. We would boast of the very things that leave us empty.

"Please hear me! I have witnessed the death that has occurred because of my choice. There is no love in pride; there never was. Knowing good and evil did not give us the ability to do good and avoid evil. On the contrary, it literally stole the love from our hearts, leaving only pain and death. The tree was never about temptation. It was about our decision to trust His love over every lesser love. It is time for you to give the fruit back. It is time for you to return to the intimacies and joys of being in relationship with the One who truly loves you.

"Please, right now, I beseech you; see that it is I who needs your forgiveness. If you blame your father or mother, or your grandfather or grandmother, then see that their iniquity was passed down from my original sin. I ask you, would you please forgive me?"

Suddenly it all became clear. Michael turned to Turk with his eyes speaking volumes. He was amazed at how it all made sense. He saw his mother's ranting for what it really was. He considered his dad's fearful passivity and unwillingness to stand up to her as falling short of love as well. He recalled his grandfather, how he would throw fits at his mom, always telling her how to think and what to do. He saw how the seed could be traced back generation to generation all the way to Adam. It all flowed from him.[191] With all the weight of his family's iniquity held in the balance, Michael uttered the words, "I forgive you."

When Michael finally looked up, Adam was on his knees bent forward before the people in silence. Some time went by as all contemplated the ramifications of how pride had worked its death into their own relationships and circumstances. As a consequence, many in the great gathering called out their forgiveness.

Then the Son came and lifted Adam up and said to the assembly, "While it is true Adam and Eve's decision brought with it brutal consequences, it has also deepened and enriched your capacity for love. Thus, the tree brought death, but it also invited the possibility of life. Only now are you able to know things you would not have known otherwise. You realize not only the liberty granted in love, but the humility to hold it precious. Our love allows you the horrible freedom of being separated from Us. To be sure, We are the only fount from which love springs, so to walk away from Us means you will be voluntarily calling for drought and famine. Truly, the Tree of the Knowledge of Good and Evil did make you wise. May wisdom lead each of you to surrender your pride in the days ahead."

* * *

After Jesus had lovingly escorted Adam back to the other elders, He returned and began interacting with the assembly in a less serious fashion, and in short order, most were laughing hysterically. They never conceived that He could be so friendly. He chuckled, "Some of you have yet to fully enjoy the amenities of this place. Are you ready to be surprised and have some fun?!" When there was hearty applause and enthusiasm, Jesus answered a bit mischievously, "Great, because I think it would be a terrific time for a swim!"

Suddenly, the water no longer supported anyone and all fell into the sea. As the congregation was laughing, large jets of water began spurting into the air like a child's water park. All over the sea, three and four foot wide jet streams erupted into the air thirty to forty feet high, and then looped back around to the surface. Within moments, young people were throwing themselves into the streams and were launched up into the air hooting and hollering.

Michael could not have imagined having more fun as he was flying through the air, the water at his back, pushing him higher and higher, until he was turned back towards the surface. With pure exhilaration, he went crashing into the water, only to find that it cushioned his landing like a great featherbed. "Wow! Turk, that was awesome!" he said, looking a bit cockeyed with a big toothy grin. Like a child, he declared, "Again!" and all of a sudden, he was off, and Turk could not help but laugh with a throaty chuckle.

After a time, Michael looked about and overhead to see if the coast was clear. Wanting to take it to the extreme, he willed the water to explode beneath him rocketing him high into the air. When he was up a hundred feet, he decided to double it, then triple it, and then he just let loose until he was more than a thousand feet high. Finally, without a care, he released the water and let himself free-fall as though parachuting without a chute. Euphoria overtook him as he hung in the air, face down, his cheeks flapping in the wind, his arms and legs behind him as he spun about. Seconds later, with the eyes of many watching him, he plummeted into the water which perfectly cushioned his landing. When he lifted himself out, having a goofy smile plastered on his face, many clapped, and others followed the new trend.

Across the assembly, everyone was enjoying themselves as the waterspouts were ever changing and adapting to become a myriad of carnival rides. Others went exploring the depths of the sea, being taken on adventures with the varied creatures. It was splendid midday recreation.

14

DAY ELEVEN:
THE TEST CASE FOR
UNCONDITIONAL LOVE

"Have you considered My servant Job?"

Job 1:8

Later that afternoon, the multitudes reassembled, being drawn together by love after Gabriel had lifted himself from the expanse. Michael was embraced by the harmony. To him, it was unbridled joy. It brought meaning and significance, passion and purpose. Everything suddenly mattered. Fully trusting, his experience was one of ecstasy and elation. However some toward the rear of the assembly were impacted differently.

His mother sensed the cleansing side of love, but by resisting it, was left conflicted and uneasy. She felt her pride burning within. Rather than surrendering it, she held tighter, only to feel its intensity welling up even more. Still, love would not force its way, and instead withdrew, and she could feel that as well. She imagined herself exposed, and looked down to check her clothes.

Jesus returned to the front of the platform and, hoping to put at ease those who were reticent, began to share His heart, His head humbly bowed. "I know it can be frightful to feel like you're stripped of love, to feel like you're empty and alone.[192] I am at the very door of your heart. If you will open it, I will come in, and we will sup together at a banquet of love that lasts far beyond this day.[193] This I promise you, I will never leave you nor forsake you."[194]

Jesus continued, "After hearing Adam share with such transparency, you can see that I am not going to downplay the time we have to prepare your hearts. My next guest is a man of whom many of you have heard. He was considered blameless and upright by My Father. There was no one like him in all the earth. He lived in righteousness and turned away from evil.[195] He lived at the same time as Abraham,[196] whom you will hear from shortly, but rather than living northwest of the Dead Sea, he lived to the southeast in a land called Uz.[197] May I introduce you to Job?"

Job stepped forward to a resounding ovation. Michael found him to be a pleasant looking man with a mid-fiftyish appeal, who exuded love through his transfigured radiance. His warm brown eyes, short gray hair and clean-shaven face communicated a sophisticated aura as did his subdued manner. Michael's first impression was that he'd enjoy being friends with him. When he turned to

Turk to smile in affirmation, he found Turk caught up in recollecting past events that had to do with Job.

*   *   *

"Turkania, a new assignment has just come down for you," said Gabriel with deliberateness.

"Sir?"

"Satan is to be escorted from the portal into the Outer Court where the Most High will meet him at 1200 hours."

"Sir, I don't understand. The Throne is moving out there so the Almighty can have a conversation with Satan?"

"Affirmative. Not only with him, but with the other angelic watchers.[198] You're to bring Satan from the portal to the shoreline just opposite the Passage. Then you will return with him earthside to watch over his activities in accord with the Almighty's stipulations."

"Who's the subject?"

"A man named Job, that's all I know."

"JOB... Juliet, Oscar, Bravo?"

"Affirmative."

*   *   *

Turkania arrived at the designated time as Satan exited from Jacob's Ladder. Turkania had not been this close to him since his beauty had been seared off.[199] Turkania's once-over revealed Satan to have no hair, but rather dark-red, leathery skin, almost scaled. He was tall and lean, his muscles and tendons protruding from his long limbs. His burgundy-brown membranous wings rose above his shoulders in a stately fashion, with two noble looking horns protruding from his head like a crown. His strong forehead browed his piercing, snake-like red eyes. He had hardly any nose, with his nostrils being slits cut as furrows evenly into his face, expanding at the base. His mouth showed cruel and lipless, with menacing fangs barely concealed, appearing ominously able to shear whatever they clamped down upon. His massive hands and talons stretched down his sides. His long black robe with draped hood was belted with dark scabbards that held twin swords falling back to each side.

Though Satan's dark-red appearance was profoundly tortured with combat scars and black tattooed markings, it was still possible to glimpse etchings of his former self. Remarkably, even in his present state, he still commanded a regal aura, sharp intelligence, and even attractively malicious features.

"Well, if it isn't Turkania, the turncoat," he hissed.

"Well, if it isn't Satan, the loveless."

"Don't flatter me, I just might..." He then crossed slowly but threateningly into Turkania's space. His approach was carnivorous, as he sniffed vampire-like and extended his tongue as though ravenously hungry. He positioned his salivating mouth just above Turkania's neckline. He grabbed Turkania's arms with lightning speed, clamping down with his powerful talons. He gave a guttural laugh as he drew close, baring his fangs. Just when he might have been expected to sever Turkania's jugular, he felt a sword reaching up his torso tapping ever so slightly on his neck.

"Are you sure you want to play?" bemused Turkania.

Masochistically, Satan pulled his own neck against Turkania's sword, drawing blood. Backing off coyly, he retorted, "Commander, only one sword? You don't want to take on the Strongman, do you? Surely one of my lieutenants would suffice, like your old cohort, Babylon. He'd like a piece of you."

"Are you done?"

"You may escort me now," he replied dismissively, as he turned to cross the Crystal Sea.

The Throne was coming through the fire when Turkania and Satan arrived. After they traversed the distance up to the Mercy Seat, Satan looked visibly squeamish knowing that the expanse of the Father's presence was just inside the Cloud of Covering.

"What, is Gabriel covering today?" Satan sneered inquisitively, to which no answer was returned.

Turkania escorted Satan front and center, his powerful right hand clamping Satan by his left arm. He bowed before the Almighty, pulling Satan down as well. After rising, Turkania stepped back.

"From where have you come?" inquired the Lord.[200]

"Just roaming about the earth," answered Satan.

"Have you considered My servant Job? For there is no one like him on the earth, a blameless and upright man, fearing God and turning away from evil."

"Does Job fear God for nothing?" challenged Satan. "Have You not made a hedge about him and his house and all that he has, on every side? You have blessed the work of his hands, and his possessions have increased in the land. But put forth Your hand now and touch all that he has; he will surely curse You to Your face!"

After a pregnant silence, the Lord allowed, "Behold, all that he has is in your power, only do not put forth your hand on him."[201]

*   *   *

As the assembly quieted down, Turk refocused and heard Job speak with deliberateness saying, "Thank you. Please. I could not have imagined that the Father considered me the perfect test case. He believed that even if my children and possessions were taken away, I would yet choose to love Him. I had no idea that the Father was using my life to ask the ultimate question of whether humanity had the capacity to love unconditionally without self-interest. In other words, could we believe the Father enough, no matter what adversity we faced, to trust Him with perfect love?..."

Suddenly Turk was far away again.

*　　　*　　　*

Turkania noted the other angelic watchers[202] showing up as he and Satan were departing from the Throne. Within moments, they were soaring through Jacob's Ladder.

"So, what, you're my watchdog?" slimed Satan.

"It's amazing how you can bend the rules without actually breaking them," retorted Turkania.

"Watch and learn, big boy," said Satan with cold indifference.

*　　　*　　　*

Turkania followed behind Satan into his inner sanctum, and found they had come through the doorway adjacent to his throne. Turkania's eyes were immediately captured by twelve warrior principalities that stood with rapt attention. He recognized them as former associates, known for their strength and allegiance that was now pledged to Satan. Each however, was driven to submission through Satan's unrelenting intimidation, along with his stingily withheld praise.

Beyond them, Satan's underground lair was illuminated by flames emanating from rock-hewn trenches that bordered all the walls. The immediate room had a tall limestone ceiling that overlooked a secluded throne area. Descending from this small enclave, multi-tiered levels reached down into an expansive cavern that was supported by noble-standing stalagmite columns. Throughout the split-level caverns, there were richly engraved wall murals that told of victorious campaigns, along with ornately chiseled sculptures depicting fallen comrades. From the lower levels, the various attendants were obviously made to look up toward Satan's illuminated throne.

Satan promptly sat himself before his principalities, and ordered,

"At ease. I have a treat for four of you. Sabean, Persian, Chaldea, and Goshen step forward." Satan pulled away in his thoughts, rejecting the remote possibility that a son of Adam might be found blameless and upright. His eyes refocused and he maliciously declared, "We're going to strip the much-boasted-about-Job of his earthly comforts. What he fears most will befall him.[203] The assaults will be ruthless and coordinated to perfection. Sabean, get your ranks to kill his servants and take the livestock. Persian, call fire down on the sheep and their tenders. Make it appear the Almighty is responsible. Chaldea, form raiding parties, steal the camels and slay the merchant riders. Goshen, you're last. His oldest son is carousing with his siblings. I want a wilderness wind to burst upon the house, leaving them all dead. In each of your cases, leave one servant alive to bring news of the devastations. I want the reports coming one on top of the other, like clockwork. I want him cursing God before you're done. Am I clear?"

"Yes, Sir!"

*   *   *

Turkania stood by watching as Job was pummeled. Calamity after calamity assaulted Job's faith, until at last he tore his robe, shaved his head, and fell to the ground, overwrought. After some time, Job resolved, "The Lord gave and the Lord has taken away. Blessed be the name of the Lord."[204]

*   *   *

After days went by, Turkania beheld that Job did not sin, nor had he blamed God. Satan was livid. Fully enraged, he was driven to retribution. Turkania had kept his eyes somewhat lowered while in Satan's abode, being careful to hold his tongue. But there was nothing moderating Satan's wrath this time.

Satan's conclusion that Job's faith was not going to fall left him seething. Perched on his large throne, he gave coldblooded thought to his next move. Possessed by the hot aura of anger, with equal parts malice and bitterness, he sat like a superheated geyser ready to explode. "What am I to do with you?" he bellowed at his subordinates in fury. "Failure is anathema!"

Before him, the four principalities stood statuesque in numb horror realizing what was about to befall them. Behind them, the gallery was filled with other principalities, and numerous onlookers divining a clash.

"You have forced me to make an example of you," Satan said eerily. Before brandishing his swords fully into the air, he began drawing them in and out against the scabbards, causing steel on steel to announce his intentions. "The weakest of you will be executed for your crimes against your master. It's time to pay tribute. Which of you shall it be today? Of course, if you win, you shall be master," he said rife with sarcasm.

Satan immediately yanked out his swords and vaulted into the cavern's center. All four powers instantly separated to stalk their adversary, resolute that they would not fall. As they moved about, several took their swords and sliced them across their own arms, shedding blood in preparation for the pain.[205]

Turkania backed up to the wall, clenching his teeth at the ghastliness of what was transpiring. Like an intrusive thought, he finally realized where the dank and foul-smelling odor was coming from – it was the reek of charred flesh and blood from these sessions. While it was pungent to him, perhaps, he considered, they were invigorated by it. He just grimaced, and pressed back further.

"Blood and death!" shrieked Satan.

"Blood and death!" they returned.

"Aarraghhg," Satan yelled as he attacked. Using both swords, he corkscrewed about as the predator, not the prey. Turkania was astonished at his dexterity and adroitness.

"You are over-muscled," scoffed Satan. "It makes you inept

and ungainly. *Against the asp, you will be bitten."* With lightning speed, he attacked Persian, impaling him repeatedly, but not mortally, in the shoulder, arm, leg and side. Persian fell back reeling in agony.

Just as quickly, Satan fended off Goshen and Chaldea who counter-attacked together at his backside. In a split second, their blurring swords were intercepted when he thrust his swords up and over his shoulders, blocking their blows, and turning nimbly to meet them head-on.

Turkania had an icy chill run down his spine. His eyes were aghast, almost spooked, by what he was seeing. He was nowhere near as shrewd and skilled with the sword. To be sure, he and his compatriots clanked and rattled with honed agility, but this was a tutorial of another kind. His attention was skewered again when Satan dipped himself down with a shoulder roll, ducking beneath Goshen's and Chaldea's swords, and then jabbed them repeatedly in the legs with penetrating stabs. They both collapsed helpless.

In that moment, Sabean sprung on Satan from the side. Meaning to thrust his sword like a dagger into his heart, he ended up perforating Satan's wing instead. Satan cringed and spun about acrobatically, cartwheeling several times without his hands, until he was to the side of Sabean. Deft of hand, he severed Sabean's wings, at which the on-lookers gasped. An instant later, Satan's swords plunged into Sabean's chest.

In Sabean's final seconds, as Satan stood over him, Sabean stammered, "Forgive me."

With a calloused look, Satan answered, "I do," and turned abruptly away, both his swords resting casually on his shoulders, wet with blood.

Turkania stood by in shock, astounded that four worthy opponents were dispatched in mere seconds.

*   *   *

Later, Turkania escorted Satan back to the Almighty, relieved that Job had held fast his integrity. But as they spoke, Satan charged the Almighty, "Skin for skin! Yes, all that a man has he will give for his life. However, put forth Your hand now, and touch his bone and flesh, and he will curse You to Your face."

After a long pause, the Almighty said, "Behold, he is in your power, only spare his life."[206]

Turkania could scarcely believe what he had heard. Everything within him balked at the apparent wrongness of it. Why subject Job to such inquiry? Satan abruptly turned and departed, leaving Turkania to catch up on the run.

*   *   *

That night, Turkania followed Satan into Job's bedchamber. Satan drew himself close and began whispering disquieting thoughts into Job's ear.[207] Satan gave him horrifying visions while in deep sleep, causing dread and trembling to come upon him. Job's limbs began shaking violently as his soul was in upheaval.

Satan positioned himself directly over him, hovering before his face. Turkania could see the hair on Job's flesh bristling up.[208] Stirring wildly, Job awoke, only to open his eyes and realize it was not a dream. Job shook while he tried to discern the presence that was before him. Satan's noxious sulfurous breath threatened to gag him. He jerked his head back and forth in primal fear.

Satan then mocked caustically to Job,[209] "Can mankind be just before God? Can a man be pure before his Maker? He puts no trust even in His servants; and against His angels He charges error. How much more those who dwell in houses of clay, whose foundation is in the dust, who are crushed before the moth! Between morning and evening they are broken to pieces; unobserved, they perish forever. Is not their tent cord plucked up within them? They die, yet without wisdom." [210] Satan then extended his index talon and touched Job's skin, breaking the surface. Immediately, *disease began spreading, until his skin was covered in boils.*

Turkania held his tongue. Satan passed by him, remarking scornfully, "I'm done here, dog."

*   *   *

Michael nudged Turk, "Hey, are you listening?"

Without a reply, Turk refocused, trying to pick up what Job was saying. "...Do you understand what was at stake? The Almighty posed a test for all of humanity, and Heaven itself, to witness. Was it possible for any of us to take one true step in the direction of unconditional love? Could we gain back what we had lost – our childlike faith to know we're loved without measure and without condition? That He even gave us this opportunity was a gift. He owed us nothing. Indeed, if He determined to do so, He could have taken back His Spirit and breath, and all flesh would have perished together, and man would have returned to dust.[211]

"I would like to say that I passed the test, but I didn't. I failed. After defending myself at length, day after day to my friends, who likewise were in the dark as to my ordeal, I justified myself before the Most High. In that crucial moment, I declared, 'Oh that I had one to hear me! Behold, here is my signature; let the Almighty answer me!'[212] I had charged God, and my friends knew it, and therefore ceased trying to console me. I had sinned. When I offered my signature, when I signed the indictment against God, it was over. The Father appeared in the whirlwind,[213] and my arrogance was exposed. I was left with my hand on my mouth, unable to defend myself in the least.[214]

"What God demonstrated through my life was that it was impossible for any of us to stand firm in faith if tested to the utmost. In fact, every single one of us has been put to the test, and each of us has failed. Everyone save the Son, who opened not His mouth, and who never offered a sign proving His worth.[215]

"I don't know what brought on your failure, whether it was refusing to honor a mean-spirited parent, by giving yourself over to rage and violence, or, falling prey to lying, cheating or stealing. Perhaps, you lived fearful of someone you should have loved and stood up to. Maybe you coveted more than was given you. In one way or another, each of us showed the true stripes of our nature, even as Adam has declared. Clearly, our pride produced a mountain of condemning evidence. How much more failure do we need to be convinced of its depravity? When will you see that it left you fearfully working for that which cannot be earned, but only received as a free gift?[216]

"Did we not recognize just last night that all have fallen short?[217] Was any found in all of Heaven who could redeem us, save the Son Himself?[218] Please, this is your hour to believe, to surrender your pride and, through humility, come into faith and love. I bid you to learn from my failure. I pray you will gladly accept His amazing love without condition. May you freely receive, as He has said, that you may freely give."[219]

At that, Job humbly stepped back, and turning to leave, was met by Jesus who gave him a hug and turned him back toward the assembly. A sustained applause broke out, as most of the congregation gave affirmation to his exhortation.

15

DAY ELEVEN:
THE FATHER OF MANY NATIONS

"Be sure that it is those who
are of faith who are sons of Abraham"

Galatians 3:7

Jesus stepped forward again and spoke, "My beloved, let Me say that after Job had failed to trust God unconditionally, this next patriarch was approached by the Father as to whether he would live in accordance with faith, not works. What Job could not prove through obedience, this man proved through faith. Thus, while he was not a perfect man, he was a man willing to trust beyond himself. It was his faith that was reckoned to him as righteousness.[220] Because of it, his children were blessed to multiply into many nations. It is My privilege to introduce to you, Abraham."

If Michael had thought the ovations for both Adam and Job were remarkable, the sustained cheering and adulation for Abraham seemed to go on without end. In all of it, Abraham politely motioned with his hands for the people to quiet themselves. As the acclaim continued, Abraham turned to the Son who just smiled and indicated with His hand to stay put. Michael noted that Abraham's illuminated body had handsome features that gave him the look of a mature and tender grandfather. His eyes were filled with wisdom, his smile was endearing, and his beard hung over his clothing. He wore a well-tailored tunic that reached his knees, along with pants underneath.

Finally when Abraham appeared unable to endure the ovation any longer, the assembly quieted themselves. Moved with compassion, he looked to his left and to his right. Seeing the myriads upon myriads, and thousands upon thousands, he began to speak slowly, only to have his voice break with emotion and wonderment.

"Some time ago, when I first arrived with this great multitude of Old Testament saints, I thought that no one could count them for their great number. However, since all of you belonging to the New Covenant have arrived, I know for certain that the Father's words are true when He said, 'Now look to the heavens, and count the stars, if you are able to count them. So shall your descendants be.'[221]

"I remember distinctly the moment the Almighty appeared before me and declared that soon His promise was to be fulfilled. Sarah laughed, as did I,[222] and I asked, 'Will a child be born to a man one hundred years old? And will Sarah, who is ninety years old, bear a child?'[223] But at that same season the next year, we were holding our new son Isaac in our arms.

"Years later, when Isaac was a young man, the Most High said to me, 'Take now your son whom you love, Isaac, and go to the land of Moriah, and offer him there as a burnt offering on one of the mountains of which I will tell you.'"[224]

Abraham paused, too overcome with emotion to continue, and turning to the Son, asked, "Will you...?" Jesus stepped forward, and with eyes blazing, returned the congregation to experience that moment.

*   *   *

Abraham collapsed limply, then crumpled to one side. For the longest time, he lay absolutely still, his mind trying to reason his way out of the incomprehensible directive. Everything he thought he believed lost its cohesion. His mind fogged, his insides grew cold. After a time, he fell dead asleep, exhausted, not stirring until morning.

When Abraham revived, nothing had changed. He felt brittle now, devoid of life, but he commanded himself, "In hope against hope, just believe."[225] Not knowing what he would say to Sarah, he determined simply to announce that he was called to offer a sacrifice on Moriah. He was sure she would not allow him to honor the Lord's command were she to know the truth.

With a tightly held face, Abraham approached her and said in a neutral tone, "The Almighty wishes me to offer a sacrifice three days journey from here. I'll be taking Isaac and two of the young men."

Sarah held his gaze, looking into his eyes inquisitively, sensing some duress. As she drew closer, continuing to look up at him, he could not endure meeting her eyes, but furrowed his forehead and softened his gaze.

"What? What is it, my Love?" she beseeched.

Abraham smiled fractionally and laid a reassuring hand on her shoulder. He had concluded this would be one time she would

not be able to buttress his faith. "It's three days away, so that's...
We'll make it. It'll be about a week 'til my return. Don't worry,
His angels are with us. I'll be back soon."

"Okay, I'll have some provisions packed for you. Please,
you'll be careful, right?"

"Of course, Dear."

Within minutes, Abraham was striding over to alert Isaac
and two servants. As Isaac came into view, Abraham paused, his
heart wanting it all to be a bad dream. Isaac's countenance, with
his bright eyes, handsome nose and broad and youthful smile,
caused Abraham's cheeks to rise in appreciation. Isaac's adoles-
cent frame was spry enough, and though lanky, his straight car-
riage told of a good spirit.

Abraham informed the three, and a short time later they had
the donkey loaded with supplies and wood. Before leaving, he took
a good supply of wool strips, cord and oil with which to make a
torch and keep it lit. Together they set out over the drab sweep of
forlorn landscape.

The first day's twenty-mile trek did little to quell Abraham's
trepidations, where mostly he stayed ahead of the three, seemingly
to set the pace, but actually to hide his turmoil. He wrestled over
telling, or not telling Sarah, feeling that his decision was right,
and then again, altogether wrong. He blinked away tears whenever he got too absorbed in his thoughts, which seemed to be most
of the day.

By nightfall, Abraham found a small cratered area to set up
camp. He thought it ideal for hunkering down below the cool night
breeze. After they unloaded the donkey, he built a cooking fire to
bake some flat bread. He gave little recognition to the fact that he
was doing the servants' job, but continued forming and flatten-
ing the dough with his knobby-fingered hands. When he finally
backed away from the fire, he rubbed a sheen of glistening sweat
from his brow.

"Can you clean up?" Abraham indicated, gesturing at the

flat stones and utensils. "And maybe find some more brush for the fire later tonight?"

"Yes, sir," they replied, almost in unison.

Abraham then removed himself a small distance from the three who were animated in their conversation. He immediately noted his legs were feeling the trek, and thought he might have overdone it. But his heart had needed him to keep at it until sundown. In the outskirts of his mind, he wanted this thing to be over with. No matter how he reasoned around it, nothing made sense. Having no relief, his mind simply cycled through the same thoughts over and over again.

The next morning, the sun highlighted his aged and wrinkled face as he set out, mostly dream-fogged. Later, they stopped for water, ate lunch, and napped under a large juniper tree to avoid the mid-day heat. Still, Abraham spurred himself on toward the inexorable end of his son's life. By sheer will alone, he held the matter tight, knowing his pangs could not be carried by anyone but God. By day's end, his somewhat barrel-chested torso expanded and contracted vigorously as he crested a final hill. There, Mount Moriah came into sight. He pulled up to take in the whole view. He decided to stay put and set up camp, and then ascend the mount in the morning.

After daybreak, Abraham said to the young men, "Stay here with the donkey, and I and the boy will go, and we will worship and return to you."²²⁶ As soon as he said it, he regretted the deception. "No," he thought, "I will return alone," but said nothing more.

Abraham took the wood for the burnt offering and tied it on Isaac's back, and then took in his hand the knife and a torch with which to ignite the wood. Together they walked on.

After Abraham got a bit ahead again, Isaac called, "My Father!"

"Here I am, my son," he replied.

"Behold, the fire and the wood, but where is the lamb for the burnt offering?" Isaac inquired, perplexed.

"God will provide for Himself the lamb for the burnt offering, my son,"[227] he answered.

When Abraham arrived at the place where God had directed him, his eyes gazed over the superb vista that greeted them. Methodically, he built an altar of stones, and then arranged the wood upon it. In his moment of decision, with his mind reeling, his heart yet professed, "In hope against hope, I believe." He compelled himself and took Isaac and bound him with cords upon the wood.

"Father, I don't understand," pleaded Isaac.

"Quiet, my son. The Most High has commanded it," he retorted, tears spilling from his eyes. "I love you."

Taking hold of the knife, he lifted it into the air. Just when he was bringing it down, the angel of the Lord cried, "Abraham, Abraham!"

"Here I am, Lord."

The Lord said, "Do not stretch out your hand against the boy, and do nothing to him; for now I know that you fear Me, since you have not withheld your son, your only son."[228]

*   *   *

In that moment, Abraham's heavenly vision raced forward in time, even as he was bent over Isaac. Sunrises and sunsets sped by in a blur, seasons changed, years and centuries flew past. Before his eyes, a city, Jerusalem, grew up house by house around the surrounding landscape of Moriah.[229] Abraham's vision rested upon humbly dressed men in sackcloth, who were looking up at the angel of the Lord standing between earth and Heaven, with a drawn sword in his hand.[230] Abraham understood without asking that these men were King David and his elders, as they prostrated themselves before the Lord.

"I am in great distress," pleaded David. "Please let me fall into the hand of the Lord, for His mercies are very great. Please, let it be against me instead. Already, the pestilence has fallen on

70,000 men."[231]

"It is enough," said the Lord to the destroying angel. "Relax your hand."

Then David laid out a burnt offering to the Lord on Mount Moriah, and the Lord answered him with fire from Heaven upon the altar.[232] Then the Lord commanded his angel, and he put his sword back in its sheath.

*   *   *

Abraham's vision again sped forward in time as he beheld the city around Moriah greatly expanding. Jerusalem's plateau was leveled and a wondrous temple was erected. A great gathering of people assembled, as time slowed. Before him was a young king, dressed in royal robes, who prayed with great fervency before the Lord. Abraham muttered his name under his breath, "Solomon."

When Solomon finished dedicating the temple to the Lord, fire again came down from Heaven and consumed the burnt offering and sacrifices, and the glory of the Lord filled the house. Such was the glory that the priests could not enter the temple. All the sons of Israel, seeing the fire come down and the glory upon the house, bowed low on the pavement with their faces to the ground, saying, "Truly He is good, truly His lovingkindness is everlasting."[233]

*   *   *

Abraham's vision sped forward yet again with day turning to night, and night to day, with peoples and wars traversing Moriah's landscape decade by decade. In a matter of moments, he was more than 1,000 years beyond Solomon. There before Abraham, lifted up on a cross, was the Son of God hanging between earth and Heaven. Abraham looked into His face, and upon hearing

Him whisper, "It is finished,"[234] *he finally comprehended the importance of his faith on the hillside of Moriah.*

*   *   *

Abraham and the people were suddenly returned to their awareness of the Crystal Sea. Jesus stepped back, and Abraham concluded, "Please realize, the Almighty overlooked my flawed life, and instead appealed to my faith to trust Him to work out His plan. First, He gave to Sarah and me the miraculous birth of our only son. Then He asked me to go to Moriah to lay Isaac down, but he was not to be the Lamb of God. The Almighty's story at Moriah continued to be told throughout the lives of David and Solomon, where He called down fire from Heaven on the burnt offerings, speaking of the future Lamb who would be slain. It would be on Moriah that the atoning death of His only Begotten Son would win over our hearts in love.

"Listen to me. I am saying to you that Moriah represents your heart. If you will humbly lay down your pride, the fire of His Spirit will consume it as a burnt offering. You will become a living temple[235] filled with His unconditional love, and will rejoice in a restored relationship forever.

"I ask you to join me, in hope against hope, and believe. It is those who are of faith who are my children,[236] though not mine, but the Father's. Please, rather than clap, pray. Pray and prepare yourselves to reach out to every person so that no one should fall short of believing that they are loved unconditionally."[237]

As Abraham stepped back, some applause came forth, but many more raised their voices in prayer and supplication. For quite some time, many interceded for their loved ones, as did Michael, who found himself praying for the softening of his mother's heart.

16

DAY TWELVE:
THE BILLOWING DARKNESS

"For their worm will not die, and their fire
will not be quenched"
Isaiah 66:24

The next morning, Michael and Turk were adroitly making their way through the upper tree canopy. For more than an hour, they traversed from limb to limb, far above the ground, in the Amazonian-type trees whose large appendages allowed them to scamper at a good clip as long as they paid rapt attention. Michael enjoyed pressing the breakneck speed, sensing the palpable air of danger with finding his own footing when going from one tree to the

next. He thrilled at challenging Turk, who was much larger and bulkier, to follow after him through the oftentimes
tight-fitting juggernauts.

"No wings Turk!" he called back. "And no cheating!"

After a time, their monstrous tree-line had reached
the side of a lushly vegetated sheer cliff, from which an
elegant waterfall spilled over. Michael's impulsive determination to careen forward caught up with him when he
found himself passing through some foliage containing
dozens of foot-long parakeets. In the split second his attention was diverted, his long hair became entangled in the
thicket and his feet swooshed in front of him, leaving him
suspended in mid-air. As he dangled back and forth, hundreds of feet up, he grabbed hold of the branches that held
his hair and cried out, "Whoa! Ahhhh! Turkania, h-e-l-p."

Turk caught up and eyed him insufferably, "The name
is Turk to you." He then sassed him like a parent, "'Ahem,
it's all fun and games 'til someone gets hurt.' Let's get you
untied. Hair, untangle yourself." Almost magically, his hair
came to life and began tugging and pulling to free itself.

"Ahhh, that hurts!"

"Hold on, almost there." In a moment, he was free
and Turk pulled him back onto a branch, "See, not too bad.
Come on, let's drop down and cool off."

After arriving at the secluded pool below, Michael
was contemplating the previous day's events as he stood
beneath the downpouring water. He felt moved by how the
three patriarchs had shared their shortfalls and failures
with such transparency. Each of them had confessed their
inability to trust the Father's love unequivocally while in
the midst of their own trying circumstances. Indeed, each
had unashamedly professed their gratefulness for His
faithful intervention.

Michael's reflections turned to wonder why his mother

still had not yielded. With a concerned voice, he asked over the uproar of the churning water, "Turk, what's going on with my mom? Why won't she let go of her pride and just accept His love?"

"Good question. Let's first back up behind the waterfall so we can hear. That's relaxing. It feels like I'm on furlough, simple pleasures. I don't get out here as often as I'd like," he said, thinking out loud.

As they retreated behind the water, Michael saw for the first time that it opened up into a cavern that shimmered with a vibrant luster. He waded further and beheld an exotic turquoise pool with baby turtles, frogs and brightly colored fish. They found their way to a rock shelf upon which to sit, wherein Michael re-focused back to their conversation.

Turk continued, "Your mother believes she'd be loved if only she were allowed to validate herself through you, and given back control over Rachel. She's made it her aim to base her worth on both of you. In other words, she has built up this image of what a good mom she is, and in doing so, has attempted to ascribe love back to herself through her parenting. Even here in Heaven, as she sees you honored on the Wall of Love and having lunch with the Son Himself, she still feels she can validate herself through you. She thinks you legitimize her."

"Me?" queried Michael, his face pinched with an air of disbelief. "How can I legitimize her? I can't even legitimize myself."

"Well said. What she is doing is pushing the question of whether she is loved or not onto you and Rachel. Essentially, she is giving herself the false hope that love would be hers if only you two would return and prove her to be loved."

"I don't understand," he said grappling, his eyes narrowing.

"When you fearfully tailored your life around your mom in order to appease her, she felt intoxicated by it. She deemed it worship. She liked the empowerment and control. In your case, she took credit for your successes, and therefore lived vicariously through you. But in your sister's case, she treated Rachel as the side of herself that she hated. Therefore, she determined subconsciously only to show Rachel love if she met her expectations. In essence, she told herself, 'I will show love to Rachel if she changes *this*, or doesn't do *that*.' But in order for your mom to ensure that she would not be forced to give away the little bit of love she did have, she continually raised the standards against Rachel, to the point where nothing was ever good enough. Rachel could do nothing right. I'm not saying your dad wasn't complicit as well, because he was supposed to have loved your mother enough to stand up to her and protect Rachel. With both you and Rachel, your mom was trying to acquire love, rather than simply receiving it as a gift from God, and in turn, giving it freely to the both of you."

Michael turned back to Turk from the pool with a glint in his eyes, "I understand what you're saying. The truth is, I always knew something was wrong; I just didn't know what. That's why I just tried to keep the peace, and even lied and cheated to keep her happy. The whole thing was screwed up."

"You lied and cheated for other reasons as well, but yeah, it all played itself out."

Michael "Umphed," and admitted, "You're right. My pride was at work too, well, big time. So now what?"

"Soon, she will have to own up fully to all those years of failed parenting. She will have to see that her pride left her loveless, and that her only solution is to begin trusting in the Father's unconditional love. When she does that, she will find apologizing to you and Rachel a desirable thing."

"I hope she turns soon," Michael replied softly. "So, um, what's on the schedule?"

"Schedule? That's a funny way to put it. Actually, let me ask you, what do you feel like doing?"

"I feel like I want to get back to the Throne."

"Why? Aren't you having a great time?"

"Yeah, you bet, this place is amazing. Look at all the baby turtles and frogs. They're so, I mean... wow. I don't know, but I feel like I'm wanted, like He is calling me. I just feel a drawing to get back there."

"Then that's the place we should be. You see, it's not rules and schedules, but the relationships we share that define our activities. Love draws us together – there are no obligations up here."

Unexpectedly, a distant crack of thunder rolled over them so forcefully it rippled the water.

"I think Gabriel just backed away from the Father," said Michael briskly.

"Maybe..." replied Turk hesitantly. "We'd better go. Ready?" As he offered him a hand, they were instantly transported to the Throne. The atmosphere was apprehensive. Dark red and scarlet coloring resonated from the Cloud of Covering with a pervasive fog lurking throughout the assembly.

Michael felt a time-muted press of urgency, sensing the enormity of so many hearts given to indecision. Flashes of lightning and groaning sounds thundered over the assembly, all but bludgeoning the prideful self-confidence of those turned inward. Michael noticed the faces of those about him looking back with consternation. He rotated around and his eyes became glued to great billows of malevolent darkness that were pluming snake-like into Eden's atmosphere. Upon asking, he was shocked to discern that Outer Darkness was coming to make claim on some of the prideful. Second by second, enervating, whirling squalls approached with menacing authority. Alarm filled the air. The cacophony of lightning and thunder from above ignited and reverberated to the point of causing the water to slosh beneath their feet. Voices could be heard, "Save us, O Lord!"[238] Screeching cries descended the amphitheater, as the seawater itself began pulling away from the approaching horror.

Even over the sizable distance, Michael could see his mother's paled face and trembling lips, as she raised her arms over her head as a black, worm-like, tentacle drew close. Michael's chagrinned look, and intention to shoulder his way over to her, caused Turk to narrow his eyes and shake his head. Just as the horrifying darkness was latching on to her and the other prideful discontents, Jesus walked forward, extended His hand, and commanded, "Get back Hades! Your time has not yet come."[239]

Suddenly, with a shrieking "aarragghh," the Darkness retreated, and within moments, there was stunned silence.

Michael stared up at Jesus who was stoic and serious with an air of reserve. His eyes were fully ablaze as He was engaged with many that very instant.

"Turk, what just happened?" beseeched Michael in silence.

"I think you know. Enough people had fallen into a prideful arrogance by dismissing the truth they heard yesterday, that Outer Darkness was drawn into Eden itself. These people, your mother included, mistakenly believe that they have the right to decide what is true and what is not. But there is only one Truth."[240]

Jesus began speaking in a slow and deliberate manner, "Peace to you. These are serious days. Outer Darkness came, because you called for it. This time, I intercepted it with grace. But that will merely forestall the inevitable if you choose to persist in your double-mindedness. Truth does not negotiate with pride. As I have said from the beginning, 'I am the way, the truth and the life, and no one comes to the Father but by Me.' If you would come into life, you will need to come through the way of unconditional love. I AM[241] love, and you know how far I am willing to go to help your hearts to believe.

"We have always respected your right to independence and self-determination, and We will not frustrate those rights for long. Hopefully this moment will help you realize what you will be volunteering for, should you choose to separate from Us. There are only two choices before you – Heaven and its unconditional love or Hades and its conditional judgments. Many of you seem to believe you have the right to imagine a third reality, but such is not the case. In order to encourage your heart to see its way to the truth, let's hear from another of the elders."

17

DAY TWELVE:
MOSES AND OUR EXODUS

"Now the man Moses was very humble,
more than any man who was on the face of the earth"
Exodus 12:3

"Just about all of you know of My next and final witness. He helped Israel exodus from its slavery, and I trust you will allow him to help you as well. Would you welcome please, Moses?"

Michael looked about wondering where Moses was going to come from since he could not see him, when suddenly he emerged from the Cloud of Covering ablaze with the glory of God. The people were at first taken aback at the dazzling magnitude of his luminescence and brilliance, only to realize that he had been face to face with the Father just moments before.[242]

In an instant, the people threw off their trepidation, and there was an explosion of joy, as the congregation roared in astonishment and awe. Michael was struck by the resolute faith in Moses' eyes, even as every part of his transfigured body radiated with beauty. His flowing white hair fell back on his splendorous white robe. As Moses stood patiently by, staff in hand, Michael could not help but see the years of wisdom on his face. He could see no conceit, only gratitude and humility.[243]

After some minutes, Moses finally quieted them down. "Please. Thank you. Thank you. It is my privilege to share my experiences with you. It is a wonder to look back and see how the Almighty intervened on our behalf. I say 'our behalf', because His plan of salvation reached far beyond the nation of Israel, to every people, tongue, and tribe.[244] After the people of Israel had been slaves for 430 years as prophesied[245], where we were made to build many of the great structures of Egypt, God saw fit to hear our cries. As is the case with each of us, God began working in me, helping me to come to a place where I would truly trust His love.

"As you may know, I first met Him at the burning bush.[246] Up until that time, I wasn't sure whether I even believed God existed, let alone that He would willingly identify Himself with a group of slaves. At that time, I had little knowledge of His enduring promises to Abraham, Isaac, and Jacob. But rather than me telling you the story, I've asked our Lord to show you what happened."

In that moment, Jesus who had been standing ready, stepped forward, and opening His eyes, caused light to burst forth across the assembly allowing each to witness and hear the events of the Exodus.

They saw Moses' encounter at the burning bush. They saw the cruel treatment of the slaves, the floggings, the brutal conditions, long hours and endless hardship. They watched Moses' sojourn back to Egypt, and his staff come to life. They witnessed the first nine plagues and the hardening of Pharaoh's heart. They observed the protection God afforded the Israelites in the midst of their harrowing circumstances. They saw the Passover lamb slain, the blood brushed on the doorposts, and the angel of death pass over. They saw the first born of all Egypt die, and the great cry of despair rise up from every Egyptian home. They saw the Israelites leave Egypt through the miraculous Red Sea passage.

Person after person was captivated. No one moved as the drama played itself out and the whole of their vision was filled with the events. In the end, they were disheartened by the grumbling and complaining of their forefathers. *They saw how close the people were to entering the Promised Land, but because of their pride and unbelief, were laid waste in the wilderness over the next forty years. Finally, they beheld how the next generation rose up, and believing God, saw Him perform great signs and wonders to bring them into the Promised Land.*

There was no need for Moses to gain anyone's attention. Every eye was fixed, every face steadfast. "When the Almighty asked us to imagine the impossible, that Pharaoh would let us go, denying Egypt our slave labor, He also asked that we express faith in being ready to leave that very next morning, when as yet, nothing had changed. We were told to eat the Passover meal at nearly midnight, fully dressed for travel, with sandals on, staff in hand, and standing up. What He was asking us, and you, right now is, 'Are you ready?' Are you ready to leave a slave's existence for a promised land of love? Are you convinced, after a lifetime of failure and heartache, that pride has given you nothing but calluses on your hands and stripes on your back?[247]

"Can you see that God used our history to demonstrate humanity's enslaved condition? Are you hearing what I am saying? We are not staying here in Eden's Gardens. This cannot be your home. No one can live on the front porch of Heaven. Your home is behind those mountains in the Inner Court of Heaven. I trust that is eminently clear after seeing Outer Darkness break into Eden's milieu to snatch up some of you in your unbelief.

"The question before you is, are you ready to leave a slave's subsistence for a home more beautiful than you can imagine? Are you ready to say 'Yes' by standing up right now and joining me in a meal befitting our coming departure into the Promised Land?"

In that moment, the elders stood up from their water thrones. Michael and the whole front section did as well, as person after person rose to their feet until the entire assembly was standing. Admittedly, some stood from curiosity as to what was transpiring.

Suddenly, lightning bolted across the foreboding clouds, and thunder cracked with great authority, as the Almighty answered each person's response. Then, with perfect silence, manna began falling like a wondrous blizzard. As the people realized what was occurring, joy broke out on every face, and hands reached into the air. Their gazes turned upward as they caught the food in their mouths.

Michael whooped and howled and jumped about. Turk just fell back and caught the manna on his tongue as it fell lazily through the air. Like children welcoming snowflakes, every person was delighted and amazed. As Michael looked up to the Throne, even Jesus and Moses were enjoying themselves, their faces lifted, and their bodies shifting left and right to catch the flakes as they fell. It was a delightful time. In the midst of all this excitement, Michael pondered how the Almighty had provided a midday meal that tasted like honey, well, honey oatmeal. Looking up, he mouthed the words, "Thank you… thank you for this food."

As the falling manna subsided, and the people turned their attention back to Moses and Jesus, the Throne began descending. Without warning, the water under their feet lowered like an elevator. Michael smiled in anticipation. Angels from above began singing a triumphant melody without words, but filled with emotion. It was literally deep calling to deep,[248] with an inexpressible appeal.

Down the assembly drew, deeper into the depths, until finally, they gently slowed as they came to the sea floor. Michael beheld the coral and rocks that jutted forth, and found each person was situated comfortably in their place. He looked up at the waters that rose in great heaps as tall as mountains on either side like the passage through the Red Sea they had just seen in the vision.[249]

Michael's eyes widened in stark amazement. He could clearly see fish of every sort looking on. As the Throne finished its descent, the thunderous wings of the four living creatures became still.

Michael looked over the mass of humanity stretching across the whole of the seabed. It was stunning to behold. Standing between the two great walls of water with so many people, he was awestruck. Turk's eyes and lips smiled, as he shook his head ever so slightly side to side, as if to say even he was surprised by this turn of events.

After everyone settled down, Moses walked out to the edge of the platform. "The second thing I want to emphasize is that your passage through the sea, so to speak, is the dividing line between a slave's life and a free man's life. A few minutes ago, you could not have anticipated being where you are and hearing the things you are hearing. Just days ago, you were oblivious as to what to expect once you arrived in Heaven, or whether there would even be one. Let me ask you, could you have imagined the fish being on-lookers?" Turning to the great walls of fish, he said, "Fish, let us see your faces!"

At that, sea creatures of every sort, across both sides, stuck their faces outside the walls of water. The congregation exploded in laughter and acknowledgement. After the fish returned to their places, and when things had calmed down, Moses continued, "I wonder if you can appreciate what I am saying? There are mansions prepared for you, wonders which will astound your senses. There is beauty that will enrapture your heart and lift you to transcendent heights. What you consider magical now will pale by comparison. It is true, 'Eye has not seen, ear has not heard, and mind has not conceived, all that the Lord has prepared for you.'[250]

"Let me try to make it clear. There is a passage that you will have to walk through by faith, where only your un-equivocal trust will keep your feet walking forward. That passage leads through Mount Sinai and into the Promised Land. Just as our people did not know whether the walls of water would collapse upon them, you will be tempted to believe your very survival is at stake. Will it be? Of course not. But your pride and fear will try to convince you otherwise. Why? Because that part of you that has enslaved you all your life, will not survive. It will have to be cut off.

"On day twenty-two, your pride will not be permitted entrance into the Inner Court of Heaven. When our people came into the land, Joshua circumcised the entire generation.[251] In like manner, Jesus will cut off your pride in order to free you to be all you were destined to be. Why is this important? Because all fear is actually pride. All anger is pride. All lust is pride. All deception is pride. The problem is pride; the symptom is every form of work, slave's work, which leaves you endlessly striving after love. It is time you rid yourselves of this cancer and return home. It is time you believe beyond yourselves for a love that has no fear. To quote our beloved John, 'Perfect love casts out fear, for fear involves punishment, and the one who fears is not perfected in love. There simply is no fear in love.'[252]

"Finally, consider this. If in the days ahead, you will ask the forgiveness of every person you have wronged, and forgive every person who has wronged you, trusting yourself to God's love each step of the way, you will be ready to walk through that passage into Paradise itself. There is more than milk and honey awaiting you there. There is true relationship with the Father, the Son, and the Spirit, and all the saints of Heaven. I ask you, after everything you have seen and experienced, can you believe there will be wonders beyond your imagination behind that mountain? Do you suppose there will be surprises? Do you believe the Father's love will be awe-inspiring and amazing? Do you think there are rewards and treasures that come with trusting yourself to Him? I am telling you from someone who's been on the other side that you cannot possibly conceive of what is before you---it is far more wondrous than you can remotely imagine. The choice is yours. May God bless you to choose life. God bless you everyone."

18

DAY THIRTEEN: RESURRECTION FAITH

"Now there was a certain rich man"
Luke 16:19

It was early on the thirteenth day since Michael's arrival, when he and Turk were miles to the east riding wild horses through Willow Forest. Michael was fully caught up in keeping ahead of Turk in a game of tag. His face showed a panicked smile, as he drove his heels into the horse's sides, and gripped tighter to its mane. His hair was whipping behind him as he directed and redirected his horse which had unending agility and stamina. Up and down the gully, a hard right at a monstrous willow, a strenuous left behind a tall hedge, then down underneath more willow branches. Michael thought, *I'm getting thrashed to death by this game,* and then laughed, *Oh, I'm already dead!*

All of a sudden, he realized he had run out of path and there was no turning back. Without warning, he and his horse were thrown into midair where they went plummeting down a steep cliff toward a deep pool below. Turk was right behind him. Both let go of their mounts just before plunging into the water.

After coming up unharmed out of the water, Michael exclaimed, smiling crookedly, "Wow! I didn't expect that! I can't believe the trail just ended like that. What if we had fallen on those rocks?" he cringed dubiously with a scrunched face as he looked across at the jagged granite. "Ouch," he remarked, as they moved away.

"You can be sure those horses know their forest," related Turk rhetorically.

As they swam to the bank, Michael shared, "Hey, um, Turk, there's been... I've been seriously meaning to say, I'm sorry for making you endure all my garbage. It makes me feel sick, that you had to be there through all my junk."

Turk held onto the rock face and quietly responded, "It is not for me to harbor ill-will. I have had nothing but love for you. There's been no judgment, no reproach. I fully expected that you would fail your way to a deeper humility. The truth is, I authorized some of your more pronounced temptations.[253] All of your real beauties had to go through me. You see, it was never about you doing good and avoiding evil; it was always about you learning where pride would take you and discovering your profound need for grace. Without these, you would never comprehend your far-reaching need for humility, faith, and love. Does that make sense? I simply loved you enough to have allowed your pride to be put to the test, even to its miserable failure."[254]

"Well, I'd have to give you an 'A.' In fact, I think you did your job a little too well," chuckled Michael with mock indignation.

Turk just laughed.

Suddenly, both felt a wave of love pass over them. "Wow, did you feel that?" asked Michael pointedly.

"Indeed. It's seldom that strong this far out. He obviously has saved the best for last. Ready?"

"Absolutely!"

With the speed of thought, they were transported before the Throne. Michael could see the familiar amphitheater with the rows of water seating rising up towards the back. His ability to be an objective observer however, was immediately removed due to the weight of the glory.[255] He could not help but be caught up in the Spirit as love was poured out, both from the Throne and through the angelic voices that filled the air. Even the saints were singing, not necessarily with words, but with spontaneous intonations arising from their innermost beings. Rapturous harmonies blending with euphoric melodies rose and fell as a great recital of praise. It was as though Michael's very body was designed to interact with the notes and chords, ebbing and flowing in synchronization. Everywhere was love. His very existence seemed to find definition and meaning. Healing and wholeness resonated within, and he felt as though he never wanted to leave.

After some time, Gabriel slipped into the Cloud of Covering to conceal the Father's glory, and the Son of God again stepped forward. He turned His gaze on the assembly and began speaking with a sober deliberateness, pausing between thoughts as each person hung on His every word.[256]

"During these past two weeks, My Father, the Spirit, and I, along with your escort angels, Old Testament Saints, and the twenty-four elders have made Ourselves known. We have offered you Our hearts and unveiled Our innermost love for you. We have shown you how much We delight in you, and how We long to see you come into the fullness of love. For nine days, you witnessed Our creative glory, beholding Our invisible attributes and divine nature in all the living creatures.[257] From the plants and insects, to the birds and animals, you beheld Our love for them not only to function and survive but to flourish. Then, on the ninth day, you called for the demise of pride, at which time the Father asked, 'Who is worthy to open the book?' to bring a final judgment to pride.

"As the Spirit searched out every heart, each of you saw your life flash before your eyes. You also saw My willingness to trust the Father in all things, even to the laying down of My own life. At that point you called for Me to lead you, and the Spirit fell upon Me with great power. In accordance with your intercession, I released the four horsemen of the Apocalypse. They are now at work, and will soon bring the conflict of pride to a head on the earth.

"Over the past two days, we have also been addressing the uncomfortable truth of your fallen nature. In doing so, I introduced you to Adam, Job, Abraham, and Moses, whose lives well demonstrated the impossibility of anyone proving themselves worthy of love through pride. Love will simply not be bought or sold, earned or deserved. You are witnesses that you will forever be offered unconditional love, with all the privileges ascribed herewith, if only you will freely accept it and freely offer it to your neighbor.[258]

"Today, let Me share My heart about the preeminence of love. Our love is the essence of what binds all relationships together. It fully defines the nature of the Kingdom of Heaven that awaits you. The Inner Court is a place devoid of pride, arrogance and judgment, for these cannot coexist with Our love. There is no striving with your neighbor, no jealousy, rudeness, or boasting. There is no lying, gossiping, or nay-saying. There are no angry outbursts, or frustrated reactions, because every person is motivated by the law of love. This is the Royal Law, that you love your neighbor as yourself."[259]

Jesus became still, His eyes penetrating with a long, searching look, His voice dropping down in reflection, "Do you hear what I am saying? There is only love behind that mountain. There is only joy and gladness, gratitude and delight. I bid you, put on love now, for love bears all things, believes all things, hopes all things,[260] and endures all things. Love covers a multitude of sins.[261] In the days to come, cover the nakedness[262] of your loved one. During the great seven-day celebration before you, make friends quickly with those who have held something against you. Reconcile with them as you transition to day twenty-two, in order that they may not deliver you to the judge, and the judge to the officer, and you be thrown into prison.[263] Let Me say it plainly. If any of you should choose not to apologize or forgive in the upcoming seven days, you will be given over to the prison of your pride. Only the humble, who abide in love by faith alone, will be welcomed into Heaven. No one will escape the hold of Outer Darkness until they have paid up the last cent of their pride."[264]

Jesus allowed His irresistible presence to settle on the assembly, His eyes searching the crevices of each person's heart that had yet to trust Him. With a subdued appeal, He said into the silence, "What will it take for you to believe?" Jesus felt the need to drive His point deeper.

"While you were yet on the earth, most of you said at one time or another, that you would believe if only you had enough proof. But the truth is, it's not about proof, it's about self-worship. Let Me illustrate what I am saying."

Then, with His eyes ablaze, He took the assembly back to His ministry days.

*   *   *

It was an hour before daybreak with the light just beginning to cast its shadows, when Jesus awoke. He sat up in silence and quietly strapped on His sandals. He stood, and as an afterthought, He made His way over to the bread basket, reached down, and tore off a chunk from a large loaf that had been given to them the afternoon before. Already His heart was communing with the Father as He made His way in the cool morning air through a grove of olive trees. He found a boulder beyond the trees that presented a nice resting place. It allowed him to look east toward the Jordan. He beheld the horizon slowly brightening and the birds beginning to stir. He placed the bread on the rock, turned Himself about, and lifted Himself up with His arms so he could secure a seat, His feet finding some niches in which to set.

Jesus took the bread in His hand and looked at it, wondering why He felt compelled to bring it, since He wasn't particularly hungry. He broke off a piece and took it to His mouth to savor its timeless flavor.

"They are a spiritually hungry people, Father," He quietly thought.

"Yes, everywhere You go," the Father answered.

"They are so little aware of how the Spirit provides them daily with the bread of Your presence."

"Some see it," observed the Father with subdued recognition. "Yes, some, but We've been revealing the nature of their spiritual hunger for millennia, and yet they're still blinded to the truth[265] that pride has left them in a perpetual famine. From the time of Joseph's seven years of famine, or for that matter, Moses' bleak wilderness surroundings, or Gideon's lack of strength to engage the battle, or even David's flight from his enemy, or Elijah's drought,

We've been telling and re-telling the truth that without Our love, their hearts are left famished. Few have seen it however. Why do We think they'll see it now?"

The Father responded, "It is only when their hearts are softened that their eyes[266] will see. Soon You will open them.[267] Then they will recognize that Joseph's storehouse still welcomes them.[268] They will see that manna still falls each morning, where with a little humility they can gather all the love they need for the day.[269] They will be emboldened, like Gideon, as they discern that You are the huge barley loaf that is rolling into their heart to flatten their pride.[270] They will recognize, like David, that in times of duress, the Bread of the Presence will always be waiting to give them strength.[271] They will see, like Elijah, that when the drought comes, that even then, We will call upon the birds to carry Our love to them.[272] I have sent You, the Bread of Life, and soon they will eat and be satisfied."[273]

"Yes, Father, though I am unsure of their faith to believe, even when I am raised up. It seems it is in their heart to reject Our love, no matter what miracles are offered. Their pride leaves them predisposed not to believe," replied Jesus somberly.

"Then let that be Our topic for today. Let Your heart challenge them, that even if someone is raised from the dead, they will still not want to believe."[274]

"Yes, but where are You taking this?"

"After You challenge their hearts to come to faith, We will then illustrate Our contention by raising someone up and showing them the truth of it."

"But this would require giving them advanced notice of someone's death. It falls too close to offering proof."

"Not if You mask the events in parable form. Tell it as a story containing truth, rather than an actual description of what You are about to do."

"Who are We volunteering for this object lesson?" Jesus asked with hesitancy and concern.

"How about Your friend Lazarus? Let his name be honored among all. He will do nicely."

"I don't think him dying is something he or his sisters would expect from Us."

"No, but there will be grace to see them through. Now, about the bread, can I get You to feed some hungry friends of mine?"

At that, birds of every sort drew in close, landing all about Him, even on His shoulders and hands.

"I'm going to need more bread," replied Jesus with a chuckle.

*　　　*　　　*

Later that morning, Jesus stationed Himself before the overflowing synagogue and began sharing the truths of the Kingdom of Heaven. The Pharisees, however, continued to be verbally combative, and were scoffing at Him. In their arrogance, they considered themselves rich in spiritual things, being situated in their seats of honor, and adorned in their royal robes. After sharing several parables, Jesus began introducing the morning's agenda concerning the raising of Lazarus.

"Now there was a certain rich man, who habitually dressed in purple and fine linen, gaily living in splendor every day." Jesus briefly paused, allowing his gaze to land on the Pharisees, before continuing. "And a certain poor man[275] named Lazarus was laid at his gate, covered with sores, and longing to be fed with the crumbs which were falling from the rich man's table. Besides, even the dogs were coming and licking his sores. Now it came about that the poor man died and he was carried away by the angels to Abraham's bosom; and the rich man also died and was buried. In Hades, he lifted up his eyes, being in torment, and saw Abraham far away, with Lazarus in his bosom. And he cried out and said, 'Father Abraham, have mercy on me, and send Lazarus, that he may dip the tip of his finger in water and cool off my tongue; for I am in agony in this flame.' But Abraham said, 'Child, remember *that during your life you received your good things, and likewise Lazarus bad things; but now he is being comforted here, and you are in agony. And besides all this, between us and you there is a great chasm fixed, in order that those who wish to come over from here to you may not be able, and that none may cross over from there to us.' And he said, 'Then I beg you, Father, that you send Lazarus to my father's house - for I have five brothers - that he may warn them, lest they also come to this place of torment.' But Abraham said, 'They have Moses and the Prophets; let them hear them,' But he said, 'No, Father Abraham, but if someone goes to them from the dead, they will repent!' But he said to him, 'If they do not listen to Moses and the Prophets, neither will they be persuaded if someone rises from the dead.'"*[276]*

Jesus let His words hang in the air, and then He and His disciples left and headed toward the Jordan. Jesus walked ahead of the group to be alone so He could pray...

"Father, how is Lazarus?"

"He's doing as well as can be expected. He's a couple of days away from death. Servants will be sent tomorrow to look for You beyond the river. Stay there, however, and allow some time to pass. On the fourth day, make Your way to Bethany and raise him up. When they behold the truth that a prideful heart is deliberate in its unbelief, no matter what sign is given, then perhaps they will see why only the humble have their eyes opened."

"The religious will not believe, will they?"

"No, not yet, nor will they believe Your resurrection. In truth, they will take counsel on how to put Lazarus to death, being jealous that many will be turning to faith due to his testimony.[277] But in that day, during the final three feasts, when the religious are before Us in the Outer Court, many will believe."

Jesus' head dropped forward, His chin drooping to His chest. "I know My words will not return void, but something more has been happening in Me. I'm losing My objectivity." A sudden moisture came to His eyes as He lifted His face. His voice became *wistful with an unmistakable clarity. "I've seen the seeds of Your love taking root in My friends. Their hope has begun reaching into the veil itself,[278] and their childlike innocence is all I see. It's beautiful. While part of them is always striving, the other part, is longing to abandon itself fully to Us. There are many times when their hearts leap for joy when they encounter even the smallest recognition that they're not alone. They want so much to trust. That makes what we're doing with Lazarus especially difficult for Me. My heart is heavy.[279] I am uncertain as to the cost of this object lesson. Soon, Lazarus will arrive in Abraham's bosom, but I am pained to wait 'til the fourth day, for Mary and Martha's sake."[280]*

*   *   *

As each in Heaven's great assembly observed the tears spilling down His cheeks[281], many thought to themselves, "See how He loved them." As all were digesting what they had seen, Jesus soothed them in a quiet and still tone, "Let Me explain about Lazarus and the rich man. Each of you in this great gathering, who claims to have found love through self-worship, may be compared to the Pharisee in this story. Like the rich man, your supposed wealth is about to be exposed as nothing but impoverishment as you are given over to Outer Darkness. In that place, not so much as a drop of love will be put on your tongue. Even so, your judgments will have you claiming that all you needed was a little more proof, or a little bit bigger sign, in order to trust your heart to Our love. The Pharisee in the story asked that Lazarus be raised from the dead so that his brothers could be warned, but even when I raised him up, they did not believe. They also denied My resurrection, and the miraculous acts of the apostles. Likewise, your un-belief is yet claiming that it is still not enough. This is why I said that whoever does not receive the Kingdom of Heaven in simple faith like a child, shall not enter it.[282]

"Please hear Me, it is necessary for you to lose your life to find it.[283] Some of you remain hunkered down in the dark and feral corners of pride. When, may I humbly ask, is enough, enough? How much more testing of its depravity do you need? When will you see that you are trying to prove the unprovable, that you can be loved apart from Us? Honestly, what will it profit you to gain every lesser love, but lose the one love that matters?[284] As I asked long ago, 'Have you found the pearl of great price, for which you will sell every other pearl?'[285] Or, 'have you found that treasure, hidden in the field, that is worthy of all you own?'"[286]

With a kindhearted expression, Jesus breathed, "Do you want to live in the Kingdom of Love, or waste away in Outer Darkness with pride? Please, I bid you, turn in your hearts, and ready yourselves to enter the Inner Court of Heaven."

19

DAY FOURTEEN:
"WHO IS IN HEAVEN?"

"All the nations will be gathered before Him"

Matthew 25:32

After breakfast on the fourteenth day, the multitudes reassembled with great anticipation. King David and his minstrels were taking the lead in a celebratory time of singing and dancing. Using many of the psalms and a great accompaniment of musicians, David sang with all boldness. Michael found him to be so likable and infectious, that he just let loose, as did the gathering for as far as the eye could see. About the time everyone was winded and laughing, David turned to soulful ballads that reached into every heart. Tears spilled forth and hands were raised, as more and more were making the ultimate decision to trust.

After a time, the congregation transitioned and Jesus stepped forward. "Welcome! Isn't it great to celebrate together?! Some of you think you can dance! I'm sure some of the dance groups from the Inner Court are looking forward to having you. I'm also noticing a number of you are lowering yourselves into the water to cool off. That's a great idea.

"Let Me segue to a topic many of you have asked Me about, and that is, 'Who has been invited to be here in Heaven, as opposed to who has gone on to Hades or Outer Darkness?' Some of you have discovered that people you did not expect to be here are here. For most of you however, there are just too many people to know who's here, or who's not. Also, because all of you look younger and perhaps more visually striking, it is hard to tell at first glance who someone might be. All of this has spurred some speculation that I am now going to address.

"First, let Me remind you of several *separation parables* that I formerly told. Do you recall the parable of the Wheat and Tares? Over the past two millennia, I allowed the wheat and the tares to grow up together, and at the end of the age, I called for the Harvest. All of you were taken up in the Harvest fourteen days ago when you were brought to this place. Thus, both wheat and tares are gathered here now. In the parable, I said that I would send forth My angels, and they would remove out of this kingdom all stumbling blocks and those of you who commit lawlessness.[288] This means that those of you who will not freely receive love unconditionally, and in return, love others unconditionally, will not be allowed into Heaven.

"On day twenty-two,[289] eight days from now, those of you who have humbled yourselves will be considered wheat, and those of you who have not will be known as tares. At that time, you will be separated as wheat is separated from tares. More importantly, those of you who choose unforgiveness will be given over to your pride in Outer Darkness. You had a preview of that two days ago. However, those of you who choose humility will 'shine forth as the sun in the kingdom of your Father. He who has ears, let him hear.'[290]

"The second *separation parable* I told, had to do with the dragnet that was cast into the sea.[291] This dragnet gathered fish of every kind, and drew them up on the beach. This represents all of you who have come from every tongue and tribe and nation.[292] Let Me ask, if a fisherman catches an ill-tasting or poisonous fish, will he not throw it back? So it is that a loveless and unforgiving heart will not be welcomed. On day twenty-two, My angels will go forth and gather the good fish together, but the bad fish they will cast out.[293]

"The third *separation parable* I shared with you was that of the Wedding Feast.[294] I instructed My angels to go into the highways and byways to invite as many as they found, to be with us here. And so they 'went out and gathered together all they found, both evil and good,' so that this wedding hall could be filled with guests.[295] Please note what I said, that both 'evil and good' would be invited. Let Me emphasize it; this is only the wedding hall. I am asking you to marry into Our love. If you will say, 'I do,' then we will be joined together in an everlasting covenant.

"However, if some choose to decline Our love, then on day twenty-two, I will ask those not dressed in the wedding clothes of humility, 'Friend, how did you come in here without wedding clothes?'[296] Then I will give them over to Outer Darkness, where their pride will have them weeping and gnashing their teeth.[297]

"Let Me finish with the *separation parable* of the sheep

and the goats.[298] On day twenty-two, I will sit on the right hand of the Most High, and all the nations present will be gathered before Me. I will then separate you, as a shepherd separates the sheep from the goats. I will put the sheep on My right and the goats on My left. And I will say to the sheep on My right, 'Come you who are blessed of My Father, inherit the kingdom prepared for you from the foundation of the world.'[299] But to those on My left, I will give over to Outer Darkness, where you will be tormented by your own pride, and free to argue your futile case for as long as you will.

"All the while, Our love will be offered freely, hoping to woo you, but even then, it will feel like flames to your pride. Truly I say to you, you shall not come out of there until you have paid up the last cent.[300] If you never turn back, then there will come a time when I will call Death and Hades to give you up, and you will be tried based on your loveless deeds at the Great White Throne Judgment.[301] There you will be found loveless, and as such, you will be cast into the Lake of Fire to perish.[302] This is the Second Death, the Lake of Fire.[303] Since you will not have eaten of the Tree of Life, without immortality you will die.

"Therefore, let Me answer the question, 'Who is here?' Every person who died from the time of My resurrection to the Harvest two weeks ago[304], has been invited to be here, both evil and good. This means every person, no matter their beliefs, no matter what evil they have committed, has been invited to be here to experience Our love to full measure. As you came to see on day ten, all have been 'shut up under sin'[305], and as such, it is all of grace that each of you has been brought to this place.

"Another group now is gathered with us, one that has been raptured up to join us, but before I address them, let Me reiterate what I have said so there can be no misunderstanding. Both wheat and tares, good fish and bad fish, those dressed in wedding clothes and those not, and the sheep and the goats have all been invited to be here in the Outer Court.

"As I share this, some of you know you are on the outside looking in. Still, you are hesitant to welcome Our love, knowing its cleansing side is calling for reconciliation and forgiveness of your past hurts. For so long you've held onto the offenses done to you, convinced that you could never release the wrongdoers. However, you fail to see that your need to nurse and rehearse them has filled your soul with the gall of bitterness.[306]

"Speaking for My Father and for the Holy Spirit, it is Our hope that Our love will win over your heart, to help you surrender these judgments. As One who was despised and rejected, suffered beating and death, I know what you were asked to endure[307], and I grieved with you through it.[308] I appeal to you with all My heart, please, forgive them."

Jesus paused circumspectly, and with a benevolently calm voice, asked, "Do you understand that your very existence hangs in the balance; that your time to choose has arrived?"[309] He then spoke almost inaudibly, "Now that you know that even those who hurt you are here, I want you to trust Me, and let Me heal your heart." At that, His eyes became a flame of fire, as He tenderly appealed to individuals throughout the assembly. The atmosphere changed almost immediately from one of instruction, to one of heartfelt reflection. From both angels and Old Testament saints, deeply moving harmonies, began drawing every heart to revisit their long held umbrages.

Michael looked at Turk with eyes communicating volumes. Everything they were hearing was clearly spelled out; no one could say things were muddied or uncertain. Still, Michael looked back over the great gathering and wondered about the phrase 'evil and good,' and thought to himself, *Well, how evil? Does this include the really bad people?*

Not realizing Turk was listening, he saw Turk motion with his eyes, and then heard, "Everyone who died has been brought here. The answer to your question is, 'Yes,' some really bad people are here, murderers, rapists, warmongers, drug kingpins, you name it. Do you remember what He said? 'He was sent to proclaim release to the prisoners.'[310] People are being faced with forgiving the seemingly unforgivable, with releasing their abuser, and pardoning the murderer. Their pride will scream out that they could never forgive such a wrong, but grace will be given to them, and hopefully they will be freed to abide in a love that is greater than pain, sorrow, or heartache. Even now, some are coming to understand that their great enemy is in this place."

Suddenly, cries of despair arose, mostly from the back, as years of grief were heard in the wailing howls. The Son of God's eyes blazed as He sought permission to heal their wounds. Intercessory voices rose as a reedy, haunting melody, identifying with the despondent souls.

After some time, Michael looked up at the Son, then back toward the outcries. Realizing the cacophony was not abating, he inquired of Turk, who sighed, "Many will not be comforted, but are choosing to grip more tightly to their hurts and judgments. They have for so long reinforced their right to condemn, that they cannot imagine forgiving. You see, it is not only the perpetrator of sin who must ask for forgiveness, but also the victim who must be willing to forgive. Until the victim releases the perpetrator, the victim cannot be allowed into Heaven. Imagine a murderer who deeply beseeched the forgiveness of God and received it, but when walking down the streets of gold is called out by his victim and judged for his former sin. The truth is that the unforgiveness of his victim is equally murderous in its intensity, and therefore has no place in Heaven."

"What are you saying?" pried Michael with consternation.

"If a victim doesn't release their perpetrator, then the Scripture will come about, 'If you do not forgive men their trespasses, then neither will your Father forgive you.'"[311]

As the moment was passing, the Son spoke, "My peace I give to you, not as the world gives. Let your hearts not be troubled, nor let them be fearful."[312] After a time, He shared supportively, "There will be other opportunities for you to release your abuser. Let there be peace for now. These things I have spoken to you, that My joy may be in you, and that your joy may be made full.[313]

"Let Me continue answering your heart as to our topic at hand. Not only was every person who died between the time of My resurrection and the Harvest invited to be in this great gathering, but there is another group of people here as well. They are those who believed in Me, and were yet alive at the time of My coming. These lived humbly dependent through My Spirit in their relationships and activities. They trusted that the blood I shed on the cross, representing My unconditional love, applied to them personally. They accepted My love and the forgiveness that came with it, while still alive on the earth, and as such were invited at the Harvest, or Rapture, to join the rest of you. Let Me compare them to the children of Israel in Egypt, who during the Passover, applied blood to their doorposts[314] believing the angel of death would pass over their abodes. In addition, there are others here who have been taken up, who although misguided in their beliefs, yet trusted Our love and lived devout lives in faith.[315] Let Me ask all of you who were alive and raptured at the Harvest to stand up and declare yourselves."

Then, from across the expansive gathering, a very

great celebration came forth, such that it sounded like rolling thunder from a distance. "We rejoice in your faith, and we're so glad to have you.

"Now there are some who thought they would be here, who religiously believed in Me, but fell short of ever really loving or forgiving others. They were abusive, self-indulgent and bitter of heart.[316] These I have left behind on earth for additional purging, purifying and refining, so their faith would be established in the Tribulation to come.[317]

"As you now know, it is sadly possible in the next week or so that some of you will choose pride over humility, and therefore choose Outer Darkness over Heaven itself. The last thing I would have wanted was to take someone prematurely from the earth who still has plenty of opportunities for growing in humility. It would not have been loving to bring them here only for them to reject Our gift and allow their pride to take them to Outer Darkness. Moreover, I instructed My angels not to reap to the very corners of the field, but to leave those unready for the Harvest, that they would mature and feed the needy and alien.[318] The goal in everything We have done is love. It is love that left them behind to discover the way of humility and faith.

"Tomorrow, the seven-day Feast of Tabernacles will commence. During this time, you will be urged to reflect upon your wilderness wanderings. I say to you, 'if therefore you are presenting an offering of gratefulness at this altar, and remember that your brother has something against you, leave your offering here, and go your way; first be reconciled to your brother, and then come and present your offering.'[319]

"If possible, so far as it depends on you, be at peace with all men.[320] Let Me repeat My admonition. Make friends quickly with your opponent at law while you are with him on the way, in order that your opponent may not deliver you to the judge, that's Me, and I hand you over to My officers, that's My angels, and they throw you into prison, that's Outer Darkness. Truly I say to you, you shall not come out of Outer Darkness until you have paid up the last cent of your pride.[321] At this point I leave you to converse with your angels.

May tomorrow bring healing and forgiveness, and may the celebration of this great Feast of Tabernacles be a true reflection that you have been forgiven of all your sins, and therefore, you willingly forgive the sins of others. Would you pray with Me?

Our Father, who art in Heaven
Hallowed be Thy name
Thy kingdom come
Thy will be done
On earth as it is in Heaven
Give us this day our daily bread
And forgive us our transgressions,
As we forgive those who transgress against us
And lead us not into temptation
But deliver us from evil
For Thine is the kingdom
And the power, and the glory, forever, Amen."[322]

20

DAY FIFTEEN:
THE FEAST OF TABERNACLES

"On exactly the fifteenth day"
Leviticus 23:39

The morning began with Turk suggesting he and Michael have breakfast down at Orchard Falls where fruit trees of every kind graced a cascading, rock-ledged stream. "Let's do it," replied Michael.

In an instant, they were roaming through the trees and vines, picking their favorite fruits. Michael smelled the citrus tang in the air. As he and Turk were looking for a place to sit, he noticed that others were gathered under a nearby tree laughing and enjoying the bounty. As he smiled and

OUR FIRST 22 DAYS IN HEAVEN

went over to join them, he realized it was his former high-school teacher and vice-principal, along with their angels.

"Hi there, care to join us? Hey, Michael is that you?" exclaimed his teacher.

"Mr. Miller, um, good to see you."

"Michael, we were so sorry to hear about the accident, yet so proud of you for the choice you made."

"Um, thank you. I um, wow. I guess I should have anticipated that the Spirit would begin arranging opportunities[323] for me to say what I need to say. Well... I really need to ask your forgiveness for something I did that was very wrong. Will you both forgive me for buying the test scores, for cheating in my math and science classes, and then lying to cover it all up? No, wait..." said Michael, as he swallowed hard, his voice conceding defeat. "I'm ashamed to admit it, but my part was worse than that. I actually went around with Squirrel several times, sneaking from classroom to classroom in the dark with flashlights and his dad's master key. I am so sorry. I never should have stolen the answers. It was wrong. Because I went along with Squirrel, I helped get him expelled, and now as I think about it, I cost everyone a lot of grief to work it all out. I need to ask you to forgive me. Would you please forgive me?"

"Michael, what you did, did in fact cost a great deal of time, money and heartache. But in these last two weeks, we have all come to see our own shortfalls, and as such, we are in no position to judge. We do forgive you."

"Yes, we do. That's all behind us now," agreed the vice-principal.

"So, please sit down with us, and let's catch up on your adventures around here. I'm sure you have some wonderful stories to tell." At that, Michael, Turk and the others partook of a cocktail of fruits and some enjoyable conversation.

In the hours to follow, there were many holy moments

in which Michael revisited his past and apologized to those who had been hurt by him. Moreover, he had a line of people coming up to him to ask him to forgive them. This brought forth a great celebration among all who were releasing old offenses and embracing each other as brothers and sisters.

When Turk beheld a family that had just reconciled, laughing and crying together, he shared with Michael, "Do you see that? Do you see how the Father's love has freed them to humbly release and forgive?[324] This is why we so deeply believe in forgiving and forgetting. Love covers; it's that simple."

During the busyness of the next several hours, on three occasions, Michael again saw a man staring at him from a distance. The man was smart looking, with short brown hair and a clean-shaven face. Each time, he stood statuesque with his arms at his sides. It was not like the man was expressing ill-will, in fact, Michael could see no emotion whatsoever on the man's face. Still, the feeling of being watched unnerved him. When Michael was about to ask Turk about the man, he was interrupted by a former girlfriend who was standing by to apologize, which again sidetracked him.

With reconciliation in the air, Michael was so excited he announced to Turk that he wanted to go and set it right with Damien. Turk appealed, "I appreciate your enthusiasm, but I'm pretty sure Damien is not ready to talk to you."

"I hear you. But I think I need to try to talk to him anyway."

"About what? I mean, exactly what would you apologize for?" asked Turk somewhat challengingly.

"It's not about me apologizing. I just know the Lord can smooth things out, that's all."

"I appreciate that. I just don't think he is ready to hear

you yet."

"Come on Turk, have a little faith. Grab hold and take us to him." Turk reluctantly acquiesced. Instantly, they were in a jungle environment where some twenty-five people were having a heated discussion, their escorts standing to the side.

"I am telling you," declared Damien, "that this whole thing is suspect. Something is wrong with this... Whoa, look what the cat dragged in. If it isn't Golden Boy! Hey everyone, this is my nemesis who shaved fifty years off my life."

"Damien, please."

"What? Are you here to *apologize*? Alright, let me have it."

"Damien, I want there to be peace between you and me. How can we make that happen? What do I need to say?"

"Well, for starters, tell me why you're so sold on this place. I admit, hey, the Son Himself had lunch with you. Did you tell Him about your twit pal Squirrel? You don't really think you'd be His 'boy wonder' if He knew everything? Let me ask you something, Golden Boy. Why is there no sex in Heaven? Where are all those virgins we've heard so much about?"

Michael's eyes suddenly betrayed his ignorance.

"What, you signed up and forgot to read the fine print?" At that, there was raucous laughter. "We heard, and so we checked it out. Jesus said, 'The sons of this age marry and are given in marriage, but those who are considered worthy to attain to that age and the resurrection from the dead, neither marry, nor are given in marriage.'[325] That means no sex. Why would God deny us some booty? Even you, oh man, Virgin Boy, even you can't be happy about that!"

Michael was stymied as he tried parsing Damien's

words to make sense of them. Just as his face was exposing his bewilderment, he heard Turk speak within, "Michael, listen. Sex between a husband and wife revealed the great mystery of love. However here, rather than a few fleeting seconds of rapture, you are invited to stay for as long as you like.[326] The love that the sons and daughters of the kingdom share makes the need for sex irrelevant. Ask him why there are no cars in Heaven either. Why? Because when you can travel by thought, who needs something so archaic? Let's go."

Michael echoed Turk's answer, but as soon as he finished, Damien retorted, "See that, no cars either! What kind of a place is this? Huh? And what about rock and roll? I haven't heard any yet. When are we going to hear our first concert? When are the Stones playing? Do you get what I'm saying?"

Michael started feeling defensive as he replied, "Damien, you're twisting things around. Why are you doing this? Everything you've ever done is forgiven. Why can't you just accept it and be grateful? And why are you glorifying things like cars and rock concerts, things that got us nothing? Or maybe you forget, we never did get any 'satisfaction'. You know it's true. We were lost in the dark, left to find our way home. This is home now, where love reigns, and grace lets people like you and me be friends." Michael paused, hoping for a spark in Damien's eyes.

"Wow dude, nice speech. But you still ended my life early."

"Damien, we will end up friends. I'll see you later." At that he grabbed Turk's hand, and they were relocated to their favorite tree. Turk just stood there looking intently at Michael and said, "Good going kid. The Spirit obviously wanted you there. Your willingness to risk being rejected for love was quite 'soldieresque'."

"He didn't bend. You were right. Why can't he see it?" probed Michael, his brow furrowed and his voice disquieted.

"Only the humble can recognize the difference between unconditional and conditional love. Pride promises the world, but blinds them to the fact that at dinner time, there's not a morsel of love on the table. It's slave labor without reward."

Jesus called out with a voice that traveled to the fringes of Eden, extending all the way to Damien's group. "A blind man cannot guide a blind man, can he? Will they not both fall into a pit?[327] And why do you look at the speck that is in your brother's eye, but do not notice the log that is in your own eye? Or how can you say to your brother, 'Brother, let me take out the speck that is in your eye,' when you yourself do not see the log that is in your own eye? You hypocrite, first take the log out of your own eye."[328]

When Jesus paused, Michael felt hopeful that perhaps Damien might truly hear what was being said.

Jesus soothed, "You have said with your words that I am your Lord, so listen with your heart and reconcile with your brother. If you remain in your unforgiveness, then both you and all those who are with you will be left to grope about in the dark."

21

DAY SIXTEEN:
RELEASING THE PAST

*"Abide in Me, and I in you, as the branch
cannot bear fruit of itself, unless it abides in the vine"*
John 15:4

Rachel and her angel Tam approached her mother, Deborah,
who was lying down in Daisy Field with her knees up. Her
angel, Arrack, was sitting to the side somewhat reserved.
"Hey Mom," said Rachel pleasantly. "Are you enjoying the
Feast of Tabernacles? Have you fixed a little canopy or tabernacle of leafy branches to commemorate the feast? People are
doing it in remembrance of their wilderness wanderings."[329]
"Not yet, dear. Are you having fun with it?" Deborah

replied with indifference, staring unblinkingly toward the undulating clouds.

"Mom, can we talk? I need to apologize. Please Mom, will you look at me? I need your attention." At that Deborah reluctantly rolled over on her side, her eyes coolly distant. Rachel continued, "Okay. I need to ask you to forgive me for not trusting the Lord, and for yelling at you all those times in anger. I wish I would have had more faith, so that I wouldn't have reacted like I did. I just want to say, it was wrong of me not to honor you. If I had known I was loved by God, I would have been able to appeal in a spirit that showed respect, rather than blowing up at you. Also, I wouldn't have talked so badly about you to all my friends. When I gossiped about you, I ended up darkening them as well. The truth is, I created a mess with my attitudes and judgments. I'm here to humbly ask for your forgiveness. Will you *please* forgive me?"

None of them realized that Michael and Turk had arrived and were standing off to the side listening while she was speaking. At that, Michael quietly drew closer.

"Oh hi, Michael," his mom said.

"Mom, please. This is Rach's moment."

"What do you want me to say? This is a new revelation, that she was bad-mouthing me to all her friends. No wonder they wouldn't come around. I told you, it all comes down to honoring, something I keep getting shortchanged on."

"Mom, please! Rach reacted to your abuse. Now she wants to own her part in it, but to deny your part is wrong. More than that, I am here to say that I'm guilty too. I lied horribly to you concerning so many things, especially all the Golden Boy stuff. I lied to your face when you specifically asked me whether I had cheated. I said no, but the truth is, I was in the center of it. Squirrel was my best friend, and I was actively supporting him in all of it."

"I never liked that Squirrel."

"Mom! I was a big fake, not just with the cheating, but with all kinds of fabrications. All the recognition you gave to me was based on a lie. Every negative speech you gave to Rach, comparing her to me, was misdirected."

"Don't you tell me why I did or didn't say anything to her," Deborah countered, her eyes smoldering.

"Mom, listen to me," Michael pleaded. "My whole life was a lie. I was never your Golden Boy. I didn't know God's love. Without love, we're all lost."

Turning to Rachel, Michael softened, "Rach, will you forgive me for living a lie that caused you nothing but heartache? I mean it. I look back and I can see that my lies led to so much grief for you. Really, would you please forgive me?"

"I forgive you, Michael. I love you with all my heart," she responded as she reached out and embraced him warmly.

Michael continued softly, "Mom, Rach was so loyal that she never told a soul that she took my chemistry pencil. That saved me from being expelled. She never let on to anyone, even me. I mean, she didn't even say anything to you. She knew I had used my supposed report card reward money to buy my grades, and she had proof. Still, she didn't say a word. I think you were infatuated with the wrong kid. She is way more deserving than I was."

"I said, don't tell me what I was or wasn't doing. I'm really tired."

"Mom, please, I am asking you to forgive me. Won't you please forgive me?"

"Michael, I know you weren't perfect," she said placidly, smiling mock-sweetly. "But you're still my Golden Boy. You know I love you and your sister. Now, can we please change the subject?"

"Mom, I don't want to be your Golden Boy anymore. This place has given us a new beginning, and all I want is for us to be a real family. I want love to be between us. Mom that means you're going to have to humble yourself, because if you don't, you're not going to recognize your need to truly apologize for all that you've done. Not for our sakes, but for yours. We have already forgiven you, just like Rach had already forgiven me. Mom, you can't make me your Golden Boy any longer, and you can't make Rach your project to fix, but we love you."

"You love me?! Really? Then where's the honor? I am still your mother, and you will listen to me. Do you hear me? Now don't tell me all of your theories. Love for me means you're around, and accessible, and not always doing your own thing. Love means living with the reality that we're not all going to get it like you do. Some of us just want our space, without having to be a part of your little program!" What little tolerance Deborah was holding on to curdled in that instant, her affections souring. "Now if you don't mind, I'm tired, and I'm going to take some time for myself." At that she grabbed Arrack's arm, and they were spirited away.

Michael fell back from his crouched position and pulled his hands to his face in a sigh of frustration, "Do you understand what this means?"

"It means nothing yet," replied Turk, "but it is serious."

"Why can't she see it?"

"I think you humbled yourself, but she's not open," said Rachel. "I do forgive you. Thanks for backing me up. It was only going to get worse if I tried it myself."

"That didn't seem to do any good. She's like, cold," he sighed.

"Michael, pray with me," offered Rachel, as she reached out and took his hands. *"Father you know all things. We ask you to intervene, to win over our mom's heart. Do whatever it takes, in Your Son's name. Amen."*

"Amen. Thanks Rach. Thanks."

Suddenly, they heard Jesus declare from the Throne, "Do not think that I came to bring peace on the earth; I did not come to bring peace, but a sword. For I came to set a man against his father, and a daughter against her mother, and a daughter-in-law against her mother-in-law; and a man's enemies will be the members of his own household. He who loves his father or mother more than Me is not worthy of Me, and he who loves his son or daughter more than Me is not worthy of Me.[330]

"Please hear Me," Jesus continued. "True love does not idolize another, but loves all equally. There are no favorite sons or preferred daughters, but all are equal and valued. When I introduced My love to the world, I knew it would bring conflict. Unconditional love always exposes the counterfeit, where each person is caused to discern the difference. This desire for love, once tasted, will ruin you to every lesser love. You will no longer be willing to call something love that is not love. Instead, you will stand your ground, even in the midst of conflict.

"Even now, many of you are confronting loved ones with the hope that they will turn. In order for your loved one to forgive, they must first accept that they are forgiven.

"Let Me speak to each of you who remain hardened in your heart. I am asking that you receive My love, in order that you may love in return.[331] In the end, if you do not receive My love, you will not be able to receive those I have sent to you."[332]

After Jesus finished, Michael replied flatly, "He's right. If she won't receive Him, she won't receive you or me, Rach. Her fight is really with the Lord. As long as she rejects her need for His love, she will never be capable of receiving our love. It's impossible."

"Through pride, it is impossible, but with God all things are possible,"[333] said Turk encouragingly.

22

DAY SEVENTEEN:
THE STONES OF FIRE

"Our God is a consuming fire"

Hebrews 12:29

Damien lurked in the dark at the edge of Willow Forest with a strong wind blowing eastward. Not far off, Michael and Turk were sleeping under Michael's handmade tabernacle of willow branches. It was clear from Damien's demeanor that he intended evil when he called over his accomplices who carried flaming torches in their hands. Damien whispered with vehemence, "Burn it, burn it all!"

As they set the forest aflame, the wind greatly increased the fire's intensity, where in just minutes it was barreling down on Michael and Turk. Michael's hut burst into flames, and they were suddenly engulfed in the inferno. Michael was thrown into a panic, waving his fiery arms about, trying to escape from the flames. His thoughts were spinning, and for five heartbeats he felt his chest would explode.

Still, his tie to reality felt suspect, which led him to turn his torso violently about to find Turk. Abruptly, in an almost mystical vision, he found Turk before him, his head lowered to the side somewhat, his eyes insufferably serene, if not somewhat quizzical. Turk asked in a coolly modulated voice, "What's all this fear about? What is this flame you have dreamt up? Tell me, are you afraid of Damien, afraid of his scorched earth tactics? Has it escaped your notice that the fires of his malice can never reach you?" After a moment, Turk said evenly, "Michael, wake up and come talk with me."

Suddenly, the nightmare was over, and Michael found himself in a cold sweat beneath the branches of his covering. It took a number of breaths for the ghastliness to fade before he could shake the images. As he stood up, he noticed Turk sitting with his feet dangling in the water as the cascading falls caused ripples to spread across the pool before him. "Good morning. I'd ask, 'Sleep well?' but I know that didn't happen. What was that all about? Why are you so afraid of Damien?" Turk chided.

"I'm not sure. I'm finding that the Spirit is speaking to me in dreams. He tells me things. Most of them have been encouraging, but this one was different."

"Well, let me just say, you have nothing to fear, not from Damien, and certainly not from dying. Do you remember what Paul said, 'If God is for us, who can be against us? Who will bring a charge against God's elect? God is the one who justifies, who is he who condemns?'[334]

If you are afraid of Damien's flaming condemnation, you shouldn't be."

"That's not it, but I'm not sure what it is. Hey, maybe it's time to check in on him, to see what's going on."

"I'm not sure that's a good idea." After a pause, he conceded, "But, I was wrong the last time. You sure?"

"Yeah, I think so."

Instantly, they found Damien holding court not with a group numbering twenty-five, but two hundred and fifty[335] along with their angels standing on the outskirts. Turk's ample frame and ramrod posture made him more than a head taller than everyone, causing Damien to spot Michael rather quickly. "Well, well, well, Golden Boy's back. Are you looking for us to read some more of the fine print for you?"

"Damien, where is all your animosity coming from?"

"Let me ask you, Golden Boy, there's only one way in and out of Heaven, and that's through the Sinai Passage. Right?"

"Yeah, that's right."

"Did you know that this passage is guarded by a Pillar of Fire from above, and the Stones of Fire from below? If any of us tries to go through it, we're fried, baby, incinerated. In fact, if we step one foot onto Mount Sinai, anywhere, we're dead.[336] Fact. Truth is, we're here right now as captives[337], or haven't you noticed your watchdog escort? What, you didn't know? Huh? Ask your angel bud. He'll tell you the truth. Look at you, Mr. Deer-in-the-Headlights. You are so sophomoric! This whole thing is one big joke to con us into giving up our lives in the Stones of Fire.[338] This huge mob is about to experience the biggest holocaust ever witnessed, and you're one of the proverbial sheep about to walk right into it," accosted Damien.

Michael's head was spinning again, trying to get his

mind around what he was hearing. He turned toward Turk, at which point Damien roared in laughter, along with everyone else. Damien then snapped, "Come on Michael, don't look to him. I'll tell you everything you need to know. What's your going rate for buying answers? Give me the forty bucks, and I'll sell you the truth cheap. Anyone got a gold pencil I can write on?!"

At that the crowd went into an uproar and Turk said, "Let's get out of here." As they arrived back at their camp, before Michael could speak, the Spirit moved over them like a wave of cool water.

The Son of God was seated high and lifted up,[339] above the wings of the cherubim, at the right hand of the Most High. He stood and walked to the edge of the Mercy Seat and declared to the dissidents, "I know your deeds, that you are neither cold nor hot; I wish that you were cold or hot. Because you are lukewarm, I will spit you out of My mouth. Because you say, 'I am rich, and have become wealthy, and have need of nothing,' and you do not know that you are wretched and miserable and poor and blind and naked; I advise you to buy from Me gold refined by fire so that you may become rich, and white garments so that you may clothe yourself."[340] At that, He went and sat back down.

Michael turned immediately and asked, "Turk, what does that mean? And what was Damien talking about?"

Turk leaned in and answered, "He is saying that pride boasts of its ability to make one rich and satisfied, but actually leaves one wretched, miserable and impoverished in terms of love. The prideful heart thinks it can see, thinks it is clothed, but instead it is left blind and naked. More than that, unconditional love can never be satisfied with lukewarm romance."

"But what does He mean, 'buy from Me gold refined

by fire?' After my dream this morning, I am a little curious about anything to do with fire, and then there were Damien's remarks. What's going on?"

Turk was caught off guard. Michael had a way of following a thought to its logical conclusion. Turk began, "Obviously the Spirit is bringing this up. Listen, do you remember how I said there was no way for pride to get into Heaven?" Michael nodded enough to acknowledge him, his attention rapt.

"The Son of God was forewarning the assembly that something is coming. He was referring to what Damien called the Stones of Fire."[341]

"What's that?"

"On day twenty-two, everyone who chooses humility over pride will be invited into Heaven. Like Damien said, there's only one way into it, through Mount Sinai's passage. It was the very passage out of which all of the Old Testament saints came onto the Crystal Sea without difficulty. But let me say, the Stones of Fire and the Pillar of Fire watch over its passage. The way is blocked to pride. When you go through the fire, your pride will be burned up, but you will not be harmed. The fire will merely circumcise it[342], and free you to be the person you were created to be."

"What do you mean? I have to walk through fire to get into Heaven?!"

"The Scripture says, 'For You have tried us, O God. You have refined us as silver is refined. We went through fire and water, yet You did bring us out into a place of abundance.' When you were first born, you went through water, now at your second birth, you will go through fire.[344] Remember John the Baptist? He baptized with water, but Jesus who was to come after him would baptize with the Holy Spirit and with fire."[345]

"It says that?" Michael asked incredulously.

"Yes. Remember the instance of the three young men in the fiery furnace?[346] How the king heated it up seven times hotter in his wrath, and then threw them into it?"

"Yeah, Shadrach, Meshach and Abednego."

"What happened?"

"The fire had no effect on them."

"Right," replied Turk, "what did burn up were the ropes that bound them which represented pride. Not a hair on their head was singed, nor was their clothing harmed. They didn't even smell of smoke. Get the picture?"

"I'm starting to."

"In Corinthians it says, 'Now if any man builds upon the foundation with gold, silver, precious stones, wood, hay, straw, each man's work will become evident. The day will show it, because it is to be revealed with fire, and the fire itself will test the quality of each man's work. If any man's work which he has built upon it remains, he shall receive a reward. If any man's work is burned up, he shall suffer loss, but he himself shall be saved, yet as through fire.'"[347]

"I've heard that, I just never thought it was literal. I mean, not really."

"Funny, because the whole of Scripture says you will have to be circumcised of your flesh or pride, for flesh and blood cannot enter the Kingdom of Heaven."[348]

"I can't believe the Father would ask this of us. So what's the gold, silver and precious stones stand for, versus wood, hay and stubble? What's all that?"

"That means that every time you truly expressed love in your lifetime, or even here in Heaven, an actual 'good' deed, it will be returned to you as your reward when you walk through the fire. Gold, silver and precious stones represent the transfigured glory of His love that will shine forth from you after you pass through the fire. Everyone will be clothed in love, some more brilliantly, some less, depending on how they loved.

"The opposite, wood, hay, and stubble, represent pride's attempts to earn love, all of which will burn up in the Stones of Fire. Most of what people think of as good works will be exposed as being deeds turned back to themselves in an attempt to garner love. Selfless deeds do not curve back. But the fire will reveal it. Many will find that everything they ever did was self-serving. Still, they will be saved through the fire."

"Alright, so are you telling me no one has ever been hurt going through the Stones of Fire?"

Turk went silent. "I didn't say that." Suddenly his thoughts went somewhere else.

"Where'd you go? What? What is it?" inquired Michael.

"What do you know of Lucifer?" asked Turk guardedly.

"You mean Satan?"

"That's his name now. I mean, before he was fallen?"

"Not much, I guess."

Turk explained, "Before Lucifer fell, he was the seal of perfection.[349] He was full of wisdom, perfect in beauty. He was in Eden, the garden of God.[350] He was created in such a way that precious stones were actually inlaid into his skin, so that any time God's glory shone on him, the light would burst forth like a rainbow.[351] Listen, he was the anointed cherub who covered the crystal expanse of the Father, protecting all creation from His glory. That means he could withstand His full glory without harm."[352]

"Wow," said Michael, being intrigued.

"Yeah, no kidding. That's why he was called the Star of the Morning, the Son of the Dawn.[353] Every time he left the Father, he'd shine like the sun. But something happened when he realized the Father's love for Adam and the plans He had for humanity. It was hard enough on Lucifer that the Father created man out of the earth, with a self-sustaining ecosystem in which to dwell, but to give man the ability to multiply, that turned the status quo upside down. Even His angels were not entrusted with that gift.[354]

"Lucifer might have been able to handle that, but when the Father revealed His desire that angels were to serve mankind, he was filled with jealousy and violence.[355] Because he was so beautiful, so perfect, his splendor actually worked against him.[356] It corrupted his wisdom.

"For the first time, Lucifer allowed his heart to be lifted up in pride. Believing he could conceal it, he covered over the Father's expanse expecting everything to be as it was.[357] But it wasn't. The Father's perfect love was immediately repulsed by his pride. It took all of the Father's grace for Him not to love Lucifer's pride right out of him by eradicating it then and there. But that would have destroyed him. No matter, Lucifer held on to his defilement, and was cast off of Mount Zion. In revenge, he made his way to Adam and Eve, and seizing the opportunity, beguiled the serpent into deceiving them.[358] When they fell, Lucifer had all the justification he needed to make his case before the host of Heaven on the Mount of Assembly."

"So you're saying; Lucifer used the serpent to do his dirty work, because he was jealous of man?" asked Michael in wonderment.

"Yes. Lucifer, filled with venom, challenged the Father's very willingness to create man in the first place. He was very coy in his approach, arguing that a righteous God, who foresees all things, who is omnipresent and all powerful, could not possibly create unrighteous man. On and on he went, twisting the truth of love to serve his own ends. When he finished his ranting, the entire host of Heaven was thrown into dispute.

"One third of the host agreed with Lucifer and turned

against the rest," stated Turk sourly, pausing, his eyes looking off. Suddenly he was far away again.

*"Turkania, what are you going to do?" chided Babylon. "Lu-
cifer discovered that humans have fallen. They are flawed. Things
could not be any clearer. The Most High wants us to serve them[359],
to follow them around day after day. Don't think that our leader-
ship position will save us, because sooner than later, we're going to
be relegated to following one of these humans around. I guarantee
it. And I'll tell you this, I'm not waiting around. So what are you
going to do?"*

*Turkania looked away uncertainly, "I don't know. None of this
makes sense. Why would He create man with the potential to fall?
If man can fall under condemnation like he has, what else is he
capable of?"*

"That's what I'm saying. It doesn't add up."

*Turkania lowered his eyebrows, drilling his eyes into Baby-
lon. He raised his hand to put a stop to the conversation, and then
turned to leave.*

*"Hey, everyone is meeting up later, don't miss it. Lucifer's got
an update. The fireworks are about to fly," called Babylon after him.*

*That twilight, Turkania was standing in his noble attire, un-
sure why he was even in attendance. He felt uncomfortable validat-
ing this unauthorized gathering. He knew many under his authority
trusted him explicitly, which made it that much more troublesome.*

*Most all of the host of Heaven was in attendance, including
a number of the elite seraphim, who were most intimate with the
Father. Lucifer's supporters continued pressing the point that the
truth demanded they leave and never look back. The seraphim sided
vigorously against Lucifer making reasoned appeals that swayed
many. In the end, the issue came down to trust. Those loyal to Lucifer argued the Father was no longer worthy of trust. He was asking
too much of them to become the servants of fallen man. However,
those trusting the Father maintained that mankind's fall was the
work of deceit, and the Father's love could not be questioned. The*

Almighty would bring forth a solution with time, they asserted, and the end would be more glorious than the beginning.

Turkania was uncertain as to what to believe. Back and forth the argument waged until, when it reached a fever's pitch, Lucifer stepped up and declared, "What more do we need to hear? The Most High has blasphemed against love. He has called for each of us to become equally complicit by suffering with fallen man. Let me ask you, what will you do when man outright lies or commits fraud, or worse, murders? What will you say when ten men fight against ten men, or, and you know it will happen, armies of men come against each other? What then, those of you who claim right-standing? Tell me, will this evil set ablaze even our ranks, where we will war against each other? Will you, with your own hands, fashion some weapon to strike your brother? Will it come to that?

"How far will you let your loyalties go before you confess the Father has erred? The seed of sin is planted; the reaping is coming. Ask yourself, will even the Most High be able to endure man's rebellion? Or..., will He turn against them, destroy them, and shrug His shoulders, all the while taking for granted your grief-stricken service? If you don't take your stand now, the blood will be upon your head. Which of you, with your eyes wide open, will allow yourself to see the holocaust that is before us? Which of you, before the blood-bath begins, will hold high the standard of love, and will say right here and right now, enough is enough?"

With the dark, fiery clouds smoldering and resounding from above, and a bedlam of voices breaking out below, Turkania was unable to resist Lucifer's reasoning. Everything about serving fallen man felt anathema. Like a singularly woven cloth being torn asunder, two sides began to separate. With self-righteous vehemence, one-third of the angels set out to leave Heaven, Turkania among them.

Michael jarred him back, "Hey, are you okay?" Seeing Turk was focused again, Michael asked, "You're saying Lucifer persuaded the angels to rebel by throwing into question God's trustworthiness?"

Turk slowly reengaged the conversation, his eyes staring down, and his voice mirror smooth. "I lost some very good friends through his lies. You have to appreciate that he was perfect in beauty, and full of wisdom. He was the bright shining one. There was no one, save the Son, who was more esteemed than he, and when he sided against man, many bought into his reasoning. I mean, on the face of it, his logic appeared sound. Mankind had just fallen and was exposed as impure and unjust. If the focus is limited to only that, and you are given the mandate of serving those who are unrighteous in all respects, it is not hard to see why many angels balked at their newfound calling.

"But that wasn't the whole story," Turk continued. "Lucifer was culpable in Adam's fall, and therefore, all of us were rightly called upon to love mankind despite their fallen state. Still, his great lie was insinuating that the Father's perfect and immutable adherence to love could be challenged. With that, he became the father of lies."[360]

"So what happened?"

"He called together all who would join him, and together they set out to leave Heaven thinking they could just pass through the Stones of Fire. They'd done it countless times, why would anything be different? But everything was. The Father's love could not be passive and yet remain love. It sought to purge the pride, knowing the toll it was wreaking, but Lucifer and his legions would not yield. They had made it a third of the way through the Stones of Fire, when suddenly the fires of love began consuming them from the inside out.[361] Fire literally arose from within, seeking to cut away their pride like a surgeon cutting out cancer. However, their pride was centered in their splendor and glory. When they fully resisted love's cleansing, all that could be considered love in them was removed, turning their beauty into ashes.[362]

"Still, they would not relent. What once was love, turned into hatred. This hatred drove them beyond the Stones of Fire. Lucifer was no longer the Star of the Morning, but a scarred and wretched beast. By holding onto his pride, he almost killed himself and all who were with him. The truth is, Lucifer did die spiritually[363], and Satan was the only thing left. Still, the Father loved them, and allowed them to be banished to the earth. Despite all that Satan had done, all the treachery, all the sedition, the Father granted them asylum. It is only when they violate mankind's freewill that they are confined to the abyss."[364]

Michael protested, "Wait, I need to back up. If a person tries to hold onto their pride while walking through the Stones of Fire, it will…?"

"Destroy them. There is a good reason the Stones of Fire are the one place angels fear to tread. God's love will not force someone to give up their pride, but He also cannot embrace it, even in the least. Therefore, His love will either cut out the pride, or tragically, love will remove itself completely from the person. Because everything that is good in you, and all that makes you beautiful is love, to take love away is to strip you of your humanity. Going through the Stones of Fire without humility is ill-advised. If you do not let go of your pride, love will let go of you—love and pride cannot co-exist in Heaven."

"Wow! So tell me, how'd you make your decision?" solicited Michael.

Turk was not prepared for this question. "Why are you asking?"

"I don't know," said Michael. "It seems you have more to say."

With some hesitancy, Turk conceded, "I followed along with Lucifer and his cohorts. I was uncertain from the moment I left the Mount of Assembly. I was trailing toward the

OUR FIRST 22 DAYS IN HEAVEN

back. By the time I got into the Stones of Fire, I could already hear the screams. Within minutes, the Father's love was so intense that I began violently shaking. Rather than resisting the Spirit, I turned back in my heart and repented. As I did, the love became a healing balm, and I was able to recover with time. Many of Lucifer's rank felt profoundly betrayed when I turned back, and have hated me ever since. You've seen one of them – Babylon. Instead of destroying me, the Stones of Fire saved my life. They rescued me from a life of hatred and rebellion. I am eternally grateful to the Father."

Turk lifted his head, and straightened himself. With renewed surety, he offered pointedly, "Isaiah once declared, 'A highway will be there, a roadway, and it will be called the Highway of Holiness. The unclean will not travel on it, but it will be for him who walks that way, and fools will not wander on it. But the redeemed will walk there, and the ransomed of the Lord will return and come with joyful shouting to Zion. With everlasting joy upon their heads, they will find gladness and joy, and sorrow and sighing will flee away.'"[365]

Michael sat there stunned, processing all that he had heard.[366] He was suddenly so aware of the life and death ramifications of what was being spoken.

"You okay?" asked Turk.

"Not really. I never realized how at risk my mom is, or really everyone, for choosing pride over His love. There could be, I mean, a lot could, well, convince themselves to not want to go through the fire. That group of Damien's is growing."

23

DAY EIGHTEEN:
OUTER DARKNESS

"In that place there will be
weeping and gnashing of teeth"
Matthew 13:42

"Turk, come on, something's happening," Michael called. "Come on! There's some kind of commotion. It sounds like protestors."

"It's just the religious. It's not something to get worked up about," Turk interjected dryly.

"What do you mean? Come on! Let's check it out."

In the blink of an eye, Michael and Turk were standing adjacent to a mob of people who were making their way toward the Crystal Sea, marching toward the Throne. Michael urged Turk to follow to the side of them, so they could observe from a distance. Michael was taken aback by their fervor and zeal,[367] and wondered what complaint they were bringing to the King. It was surprising how many people were adding to the march as it progressed.

Michael turned to Turk, "What's this all about?"

"Irrelevant."

"What do you mean? Look at this!"

"Boring. I told you; it's a sludge-tide of religious bigotry. We could be doing something fun. I thought you wanted to hit the lower plateau, see the dinosaurs?"

"Later. I can't believe what I'm seeing!" said Michael animatedly, as he scrambled along the twisting path.

Soon, the large group of protesters had reached the Throne, causing many who were interceding in prayer to relocate. Michael stood off to the side, finally realizing that some staunch 'believers' had taken offense that people, even after they had died, were being given a second chance to believe. Not only that, but the religious were resentful that those same people also had the promise of being richly rewarded for the good they do during their first twenty-two days in Heaven. This seemed entirely unfair. It felt prejudicial against all of those who had made their choice while still alive, and who had sought to live righteously, doing good deeds in an attempt to acquire merit.

Jesus stepped forward. Having read their thoughts[368], He declared, "For the kingdom of Heaven is like a landowner who went out early in the morning to hire laborers for his vineyard. And when he had agreed with the laborers for a day's wage, he sent them out into his vineyard. He went out about the noon hour and saw others standing idle in the marketplace, and to those he said, 'You too go into the vineyard, and whatever is right I will give you.' So they went. Again he went out about the third hour, then at the sixth and ninth hours, and did the same thing. About the eleventh hour he went out, and found others standing; and he said to them, 'Why have you been standing here idle all day long?' They said to him, 'Because no one hired us.' He said to them, 'You too go into the vineyard.'

"And when evening had come, the owner of the vineyard said to his foreman, 'Call the laborers and pay them their wages, beginning with the last group to the first.' And when those hired about the eleventh hour came, each one received a day's wage. And when those hired first came, they thought that they would receive more, and they also received each one a day's wage. And when they received it, they grumbled at the landowner, saying, 'These last men have worked only one hour, and you have made them equal to us who have borne the burden and the scorching heat of the day.' But he answered and said to one of them, 'Friend, I am doing you no wrong; did you not agree with me for a day's wage? Take what is yours and go your way, but I wish to give to this last man the same as to you. Is it not lawful for me to do what I wish with what is my own? Or is your eye envious because I am generous? Thus the last shall be first, and the first last.'[369]

"Certainly, you recall this parable from the Scripture? I can see it in your eyes, that you're making the connection. Let Me elaborate. Many of you came to believe at a young age, and as a result, enjoyed the benefits of Our love throughout your lifetimes. Some of you came to faith in your middle years, while still others, later on in life. Still some, at this eleventh hour, even though they had died, have come to believe during these last eighteen days. Thus, whether you came to believe early or late, all are welcome in Our kingdom."

Jesus continued speaking to the crowd, "Hear Me.

Everyone who has left houses or brothers or sisters or father or mother or children for My name's sake, shall receive many times as much, and shall inherit eternal life.[370] Every genuine act of love, even a glass of water given, will receive its reward.[371] Now, go your way."

At that the crowd began dispersing until only one man was left. Jesus then dropped down from the Throne, and walked up to him and spoke softly, "It always starts with one angry person. What would you have Me say? On the one hand, you were fearful year after year that people would unexpectedly end up in Hell. Now, you are mad that a way of escape[372] has been provided.[373] Let Me ask you, was your witness so perfect that I should hold them to it? Could I rightfully base their salvation on your testimony, choices, and lifestyle as My ambassador?[374] I think we both know the answer. It is not humility that has conceived this thing in your heart.[375] It's time to let it go.

"Did I not say I would harvest the wheat and tares[376], good fish and bad fish[377], those dressed in wedding clothes and those not[378], and the sheep and goats?[379] I have brought to this place the evil and the good, that by all means some would be saved.[380] Does not Scripture say, 'For the gospel has for this purpose been preached *even to those who are dead*[381], that though they are judged in the flesh as men[382], they may live in the Spirit according to the will of God.'[383] We are providing a perfect witness so that all have an opportunity to turn. That includes you. Is it not true that you have never taken one step towards Me without My help? Turn from your religiosity, and go apologize to those that you have misled. Okay?" asked Jesus softly. The man humbly nodded and withdrew himself.

As Jesus turned and began walking back to the base of the Throne, He stopped, and looking off to the side at Michael said, "So Michael, what have you learned?"

Michael replied, "That Your grace knows no bounds. That You are the Lamb of God who took away the sin of the world.[384] That You overlook times of ignorance.[385] That everything brings us back to humility and love---especially our failures. That You hid the message in a mystery,[386] providing all a way of escape.[387] That Your main purpose in our lives back on earth was to humble our pride to the point where, when we arrived here, we would let You circumcise[388] it in the fire."

"I tell you Michael, flesh and blood has not revealed this to you,[389] but My Father has, in order that you would testify before many."

As Jesus left, Turk turned to Michael and said with subdued affirmation, "You were right again. We were supposed to be here." As they soberly strolled away, feeling the weight of all that had transpired, Turk commented, "The Spirit really spoke through you back there."

"Suddenly, everything became clear. That's all I can say."

"Hey, I'm in the mood for some lobster wraps. How about you?" offered Turk.

"Sounds delicious!"

*   *   *

After relocating to Willow Forest, they sat and ate without saying much. Michael was contemplating all that had transpired. "So tell me Turk, how far will His love go? If He gives people a second chance, will He give them a third, and a fourth[390]? Won't the chances have to end at some point?"

"Now isn't that a topic? Interesting. Where should I begin? Do you remember our experience with Outer Darkness and what the Son said about it?"

"Yeah, but I'm not sure how that relates."

"Outer Darkness is a place of great anxiety at feeling loveless, as well as a tirade of bitter judgments at feeling controlled. That's why there's weeping and gnashing of teeth.[391] It's the worst panic attack imaginable, and the most furious argument contrived.[392] The bitter of heart will gnash their teeth not only against God, but against every person with whom they refuse to be reconciled. Then the Scripture will be fulfilled, 'They will go forth and look on the corpses of men who have transgressed against Me, for their worm will not die, and their fire will not be quenched, and they will be an abhorrence to all mankind.'[393] Obviously, it's not a place anyone would want to be.

"There are two things Jesus reported about Outer Darkness that are crucial to remember. First, the amount of grace you and everyone else presently feel to turn from your pride will not be the same there. Do you recall Him saying, 'to the one who does not have, even what he has will be taken away'?[394] That means that people in Outer Darkness are not as inclined to turn as they are here. Secondly, He said, 'you will not come out of there until you have paid up the last cent.'[395] Thus, to be released from the hold of Outer Darkness, a person will have to fully humble themselves to be welcomed back into Heaven."

Michael queried, "So you're telling me that even after they are cast into Outer Darkness, He invites them to return?"

"Of course. That's why it says, 'The Lord brings down to Sheol and raises up. He brings low, He also exalts. He raises the poor from the dust heap, to make them sit with nobles, and inherit a seat of honor.'[396] In fact, His love, though less pronounced than here, will yet wash over that place beckoning[397] with unending fervency. Still, the prideful will judge His love to be as fire. It will be like flames to them, causing them to argue against it continuously. Many will drift further into the thick darkness where they will exist like blind men trying to get away from the love."[398]

Michael turned his face staunchly back to Turk, and asked with alarm, "What, they can't see in Outer Darkness?"

"Think about it, Outer Darkness, the name implies an absence of light. Actually, they can see somewhat if they look towards Heaven[399], for the Sunrise from on high will visit them, to shine upon those who sit in darkness and the shadow of death.[400] Whenever they look away, the thick darkness will leave them blind, even as it says, 'They did not see one another, nor did anyone rise from his place.'[401] This means Outer Darkness isolates a person."

"So what will they end up doing?" inquired Michael.

"That depends. If they wander far enough away from Heaven's love, a meaningless gloom will overtake them, which in most cases will drive them back to the light[402]. Thus, they will return to the love that feels like fire, hating it and loving it, as their only source of life. Even as it says, 'A day of darkness and gloom. A fire consumes before them, and behind them a flame burns. The land before them is like the Garden of Eden, but a desolate wilderness is behind them.'"[403]

"Is there any hope for them?" asked Michael grimly.

"Of course, Sinai's passage shines upon them as a beacon of hope. All they need to do is humbly accept His love, and their angel will immediately arrange for them to reconcile with all who have been hurt by them. Then they'll be welcomed into the Stones of Fire where their pride will be circumcised, and they will be on their way into the Inner Court. But until they do so, their soul will sob in secret, consumed from within, and their eyes will weep bitterly."[404]

"Wow, that sounds like purgatory."

"No, not at all; not if Purgatory is understood to be

a place where a person is made to pay for their earthly sins. We know Christ fully paid the price[405], so any sense that divine retribution is expected is misconstrued. Outer Darkness, or Hades, is the last refuge granted to the prideful. Outer Darkness has nothing to do with punishment although it may seem like it. Rather, it is a place where the prideful are permitted to be self-absorbed, to experience the torment of self-worship, until and if they relinquish their pride. Even as the Scripture says, 'There were those who dwelt in darkness and in the shadow of death, prisoners in misery and chains, because they had rebelled against the words of God. Then they cried out to the Lord in their trouble; He saved them out of their distresses. He brought them out of darkness and the shadow of death.'"[406]

"How long will they stay in Outer Darkness? Um, I'm not saying, but if my mom, well…" asked Michael, his eyes narrowing slightly.

"Outer Darkness will have a hold on them as long as they throw off humility and remain unforgiving, or until the Great White Throne Judgment, whichever comes first," replied Turk.

"Wait a minute, what's the Great White Throne Judgment?"

"Scripture prophesies that at the end of the thousand year reign, the Lord will sit on a Great White Throne, from whose presence Earth and Heaven will flee away.[407] Literally, Heaven and Earth will dissolve into nothing and be gone.[408] Then Death and Hades, or Outer Darkness will give up their dead, and they will be presented before the Lord.[409] Then the books will be opened, which include the Book of the Law and the Book of Deeds.[410] The former will reveal how love was to have expressed itself in every circumstance, and the latter what the person actually did that was contrary to love. By this standard they will be judged.

However, there will be a third book, the Book of Life,[411] where if a person comes to have their name written in it, they will be welcomed into the kingdom."

"How's that happen, getting their name in it?"

"Very simple. They freely receive His love, recognizing their need for forgiveness, so they can freely offer it to others."[412]

"Am I going to be judged at the Great White Throne Judgment?"

"No, like I said, the Great White Throne Judgment is the final judgment reserved for those who have never turned. After those who have not yet repented are brought out of Outer Darkness, Death and Hades will be thrown into the Lake of Fire.[413] That means there will no longer be an underworld for them to exist in, so to speak. Remember what Paul said, "That at the name of Jesus every knee should bow, of those who are in Heaven, and on earth, and *under* the earth.'[414] Ultimately, the abode of the prideful will be taken away and thrown into the Lake of Fire. Still, it is important to note that if anyone's name isn't written in the Book of Life, and if they still won't turn before they reach the Great White Throne Judgment, then for them it is the end.[415] I think it is likely that Jesus will appeal to them one last time, as He did with the people of Noah's time.[416] However, that will be their last chance."

"And if they still say 'no', after a thousand years of living in Outer Darkness with their pride?"

"Then they will experience the Second Death,[417]where they will perish in the Lake of Fire. Without having eaten of the Tree of Life, they will not be immortal, so their time will be done.[418] Recall the end of John 3:16, 'that whosoever believes in Him will not *perish.*' Jesus called it the second death for a reason."

"Alright; but why would anyone reject eternal life?"

"It's like the proverb said, 'A dog returns to its own vomit and, a sow, after washing, returns to wallowing in the mire.'[419] It's where pride takes them. It's where they choose to go by not humbly accepting God's love."

"Wow. I've got to check in on Damien. He's really at risk for not seeing that he could end up in torment."

"It's not about you making him see it," replied Turk, reprimanding him mildly. "It's never been about that. He is already arguing his case, the very words he will repeat umpteen times in Outer Darkness should he not turn. Damien's heart has to decide whether he wants to accept unconditional love as a gift, or grope around in the darkness of pride."

"Come on, Turk, don't pooh-pooh it. We need to go," persisted Michael.

*   *   *

At that, they found themselves far to the west where an immense group was gathered. Thousands upon thousands of people were united in their common cause. Michael could not believe his eyes. Damien's group had expanded exponentially. Michael looked at Turk, feeling aghast. Everything inside him wanted to run away, but he couldn't. He had to do something to stop this madness. Suddenly, with a resounding voice he called out, "Damien!"

It took but a moment for silence to fall upon the assembly. "Well, if it isn't Pencil-neck, come back for some more tutoring. Hey everyone! Let me catch you up on Golden Boy." In seconds, they all understood Michael's every shortfall, which resulted in mocking laughter.

"Here's a question that's just come up. Why can't God trust us to live in this place and set up our own laws?[420] Why make it all or nothing? Why is it 'His way or the highway'? Seems like He has a need to run the show. Huh, kid? Cat got your tongue?" parried Damien stiffly.

"Damien, He'll never sell out to offering half His love to this group or a quarter of His love to that group. Not forever, anyway. His love has given us chance after chance to see the stupidity of our pride. The funny thing is, you know what I'm talking about. And still, you settle for crumbs, when the banquet table is set before you."

Raising his voice, Michael proclaimed, "All of us have experienced His love to a good measure, that's been pressed down, shaken together, 'til it's running over. It's been poured into our lap.[421] Love is the one thing that we've desired all our life. Even our lame attempts to act like we were 'bad,' with our 'you won't control me' attitude, were us rejecting any form of conditional love. Love's the one thing we've fought for with our every waking breath. Scratch that – even when we were dreaming, our nightmares were our attempts to work through the stuff that was making us feel loveless. You don't need to believe me; believe your own history. Each of us knows what it's like to sell out for years to striving after conditional love."

Focusing on Damien, Michael said, "Damien, I am asking you to let it go. Let the fact that your life was traded for little Katie's be enough."

Damien retorted with a jocular air, "Oh, my God, I get it now! Kid, you've...Here, give me a hug!" Damien approached Michael with open arms, and just as he drew close, he spat in his face. Michael did not move, but held his gaze. Damien finally turned and said caustically as he was leaving, "Dude, I'm never going to forgive you."

At that moment, the Spirit washed over their assembly, and His love was so pronounced that the pride of many withdrew its arrogant boast. Person after person stood there wondering what they had been so worked up about.

Then the Son spoke, His voice carrying over them

with authority. "For this reason the kingdom of Heaven may be compared to a certain king who wished to settle accounts with his slaves. And when he had begun to settle them, there was brought to him one who owed him some ten million dollars. But since he did not have the means to repay, his lord commanded him to be sold, along with his wife and children and all that he had, and repayment to be made. The slave therefore falling down, prostrated himself before him, saying 'Have patience with me, and I will repay you everything.' And the lord of that slave felt compassion and released him and forgave him the debt.

"But that slave went out and found one of his fellow slaves who owed him a day's wage, and he seized him and began to choke him, saying 'Pay back what you owe.' So his fellow slave fell down and began to entreat him, saying 'Have patience with me and I will repay you.' He was unwilling however, but went and threw him in prison until he should pay back what was owed. So when his fellow slaves saw what had happened, they were deeply grieved and came and reported to their lord all that had happened.

"Then summoning him, his lord said to him, 'You wicked slave! I forgave you all that debt because you entreated me. Should you not also have had mercy on your fellow slave, even as I had mercy on you?' And his lord, moved with anger, handed him over to the torturers, until he should repay all that was owed him. So shall My Father also do to you, if each of you does not forgive his brother from your heart."[422]

When Jesus stopped speaking, Michael caught Damien's eyes from a distance, pleading for his concurrence. Damien, wrestling within, nearly yielded. But from the crowd, someone yelled, "Come on Damien, let him have it!"

In that instant, Damien's gaze hardened, and he retorted, "Nice try, favorite son."

24

DAY NINETEEN:
THE CRYSTAL CAVERNS

"The day passes like the chaff"
Zephaniah 2:2

Michael and Turk spent the morning on the Lower Plateau, fascinated with the prehistoric wildlife. Turk's ability to transport Michael and himself about the grounds at will, gave opportunity for extremely up-close viewing. Michael was enthralled.

As a sizable dinosaur was charging toward them, Michael joked, "This ain't no zoo!" Turk laughed, and then waited longer than necessary to relocate, at which Michael cried, "Come on!" and then, "Ahhhhh!" After a split second, they arrived back to the lookout. Michael scolded Turk, "That's wasn't funny!"

"No? I was just giving you a taste of your own medicine," Turk said mischievously. "Remember the sign?" he chided, gesturing with his eyes, pointing with his head to it, *"Enjoy, Please Avoid Pestering."*

"That wasn't pestering, sort of. That thing almost ate me! I mean, can you say snack food? Besides," he responded wryly, while raking his hand through his tousled hair. "It would seem wrong not to *personalize* our visit."

"That *thing* was just joking with you," corrected Turk. "He eats plants, not skinny hors d'oeuvres."

"Funny, I didn't notice either of us laughing," he remarked engagingly, as his smile spread all the way up to his amused eyes. "What do you want to do now?"

"Hungry?"

"Absolutely," Michael said with gusto. "Hey, I've got an idea. Let's grab some food and go find my mom. Today is the day!" he boasted, perking up his eyebrows and drawing a grin across his face, having a renewed enthusiasm for winning her over.

"Yes it is."

"You don't even know what I'm talking about," replied Michael squarely.

"Since when don't I?"

"Well, I just know things are going to turn for the better. My mom's gonna see the light."

"Sometimes things get worse before they get better."

"Perhaps, but it seems I'm the one who's been getting a read on things."

"Surprisingly, I'd have to agree," admitted Turk.

"Ready? First, let's get a picnic to take along with us, and then go and find her."

When they finally located Deborah, Michael was

shocked to hear his mom was holed up in a cave. "What? She's in there?" he questioned warily.

"It's worse than you think," said her angel Arrack, his voice low and strained. "These are the Crystal Caverns that run along and under the Crystal Sea. The large crystals amplify whatever you're feeling to a pronounced degree. That may seem a desirable thing when your love level shoots up, but if you're holding on by a thread, it can throw you off the cliff. Understand?"

"Yes. My mom's bitterness has intensified," Michael replied heavily, his quiet misgivings beginning to gnaw at him.

"That's correct. She's not doing well. She wants to leave now. I mean, leave Eden's Gardens. She's pressed me for two days. I got her to stop off here, because the caverns insulate her from His presence somewhat, but that's not a great reprieve. She's changing, but not for the better. What I mean is, she is becoming less herself as the hours pass. It has to do with the caves. They can work for you, or against you, depending on your disposition."[423]

"Leave Eden's Gardens, why? Who would want to..." countered Michael with consternation, his confidence beginning to fissure.

"She feels she's being pressured to let go of something without her consent, namely, her ability to control. Unfortunately, Eden's Gardens is a difficult place to be if you want to be self-absorbed. The love here is always wooing and doing its work, but it can feel like fire if you resist it. I knew you would never want her running away without being able to express your heart, so I offered her this cave. She's down the tunnel, but she's not going to be happy to see you. I'm sorry. I've tried my best to engage her. I've appealed to her numerous times, but everything is met with apathy. I'm so sorry."

As Michael was about to move forward, Arrack grabbed hold of both his shoulders. "Be careful, these caves will amplify your fears as well." Arrack held on, searching his eyes, seeing if the warning was appreciated. "Whatever you're feeling will be magnitudes more intense."

"I understand. Turk, you'd better stay here. I don't want her feeling ganged up on."

Michael had an eerie feeling sweep over him as he lowered his head to enter the narrow corridor that was damp and cold. The passage descended rapidly causing him to put a hand on the wall to steady his downward progress. The slightest sound reverberated like an echo chamber.

"I hear you! Stay out, do you hear me, stay out!" his mother hysterically cried from still some distance.

Michael paused, leaning against some tree roots that protruded from the tunnel wall, unable to quell his fears. He remained absolutely still, feeling a chill run up his spine as he heard unsettling echoes. He worriedly moved his eyes side to side, suspicious that someone was stalking him. He saw no one, though his vision was obscured in the dark and ominous corridor, leaving him to focus on a dim light further down. He could faintly make out her snapping, "Don't tell me what to think. I'm not your little puppet."

As Michael drew closer, she screamed out catatonically, "You little bastard, you exposed me to everybody!" He stopped mid-stride as the spitting venom spewed up the rocky corridor. He tried to steel his courage, but his resolve felt frozen, his hands clammy-cold. Her bitter tirade felt like a slap across the face. She seemed too close now, which frightened him, reawakening his most primitive childhood fears, old fears. Suddenly, insufferable memories brought him back to his twin-sized bed, his boyhood body curled up in his pajamas, his heart racing, as he listened to his mom screaming and striking Rachel in the bedroom next to his. He could hear Rachel sobbing hysterically through the wall.

"Stop it," Michael said to himself, as he tried to compose his amplified emotions and rapid breathing. Forcing himself forward, he continued down the tunnel until he arrived at its end, his hand and chest pressed against the rock wall, as he craned his neck around the ingress.

Michael's vision opened up to a large limestone cavern, where he beheld a forest of luminous crystals that looked mysterious and other-worldly. The crystal beams stretched high and wide, some thirty feet long by three feet square. Many lay across the cavern floor, while others crisscrossed diagonally connecting the forty-foot tall ceiling to the ground. Michael was profoundly taken with the beauty of the massive white beams that glistened from within. He had the fleeting thought that this wondrously tranquil cathedral could be an intimate sanctuary under different circumstances.

It took Michael a moment to get his bearings as to where his mother was, until he heard her insanely whisper, "What have I to do with you? Have you come to torment me before my time?"[424] Emotionally charged memories rushed upon him, causing him to stop and press his back against a crystal beam. Unwanted images of his mother standing over him invaded his mind. "Get out! I tell you. Get out. Listen to your mother!"

Michael raised his hands and grabbed hold of his head like a vice. "No, no, I won't leave!" he uttered. He took a deliberate breath, pushed off the wall, and commanded himself to forge on. He looked, but there was no easy way to get to the back of the cavern. He stepped onto a long slender beam in hopes of scaling it upward to get a bird's-eye view. He then transferred to another beam as he climbed his way toward the back where she remained hidden out of sight.

Reaching out to gain some purchase, he pulled himself over a final crystal beam. There she was, half sitting, half crawling in an area with a small patch of dirt. She was looking down with her matted hair falling forward. From her silhouetted face, he could see her eyes were wild and irrational, fixated on nonsensical detail. He realized she was completely unaware that she was covered with dirt, her clothing disheveled, and her mind vacant.

"Mom, what's going on?" he asked guardedly.

At that, Deborah turned her face in a single curt jerk, her eyes all but impaling him. Cryptic laughter and arcane gibberish spewed forth as she lowered her head. Michael forced himself to sidle around the final beam to cross into her space. He moved forward with what little confidence he could muster, tentatively reaching to grab hold of her shoulders, hoping she would not whirl about on him. He lifted her up and moved her over to a flat crystal beam. Then he started pulling her clothing back into order, and began fixing her hair. "Mom, this is pitiful. Look how you're getting yourself worked up. Can't you see? A lot of people love you and are rooting for you. Everybody wants you to come back and find your way. Mom, are you listening to me?"

Michael stopped trying to clean her off, and looked her squarely in the eyes. "Mom, listen to me. Don't you know Rach and I need you? What do you think? You suppose we'd be happy with you running off? Mom, the more you pull into yourself, the more we lose you. Don't you see? Pride is having you crawl on the ground like a lunatic. Don't you think Dad is going to want to see you when he gets here?"

Deborah turned her head down, and with a somewhat guttural and morose voice, hissed, "Your father didn't believe, and that's why he got left behind. After the accident, he turned around and married a control freak! So much for loving me!"

"Dad will believe, Mom. He has time to sort it out. But our time is running out. And what you're doing, well, even you know it's wrong." Michael's eyes queried, the skin furrowing between them, "What, you asked Arrack to take you away from Eden's Gardens? What about us? Huh? Don't we matter? You're our mom. You raised us. You got up every morning and made sure we got on our way. You bought the groceries, made us dinner, car-pooled us to school, got us everything we needed. I'm not saying you were perfect, but you're our mom. That's enough. Don't abandon us now."

But Deborah remained unmoored, dislocated in time. Her thousand-yard stare jolted Michael. Suddenly, he broke, the tears spilling down his cheeks. Grabbing hold of her, he insisted, "Mom, listen to me! It's time you let go of your bitterness. It's time you forgive those who hurt you. Who was it? Grandpa?"

Deborah pulled away, "Don't you tell me what to do boy! Don't you tell me! I will not be pushed! You will not control me with your religion!" she countered acidly.

"Religion? I hate religion. I'm only about relationship. Mom, you're the religious one. You're the one with all the rules. You're so hard on yourself that love can't get any-where near you. The truth is, you put all your self-loathing and standards on Rach too. If it wasn't this, it was that. She never had a chance to be accepted in your eyes. And why, why'd you do it? Because you knew that you could never let her be okay, because then you'd have to love her. You knew you didn't have the love to give to her. Let's just pull the mask off that charade."

For the briefest of moments, Michael saw a spark. She

looked up, her eyes seeming to clear, and then she said with a voice dreamily sad, "Goodbye Michael. Tell your sister I love her. I love you too. But I'm leaving."

Michael felt like the wind got knocked out of him. Everything inside rejected what he had just heard. Just before he felt like he was going to throw up, he shook his head in denial, his eyes transfixed. As though years of buried grief suddenly erupted, he began shouting at her, "What kind of a monster are you? You witch! How dare you make it all about you. You would rather crawl off into some corner and die, than be with us. You've got to be the worst person in Eden. My God, what a lunatic!" At that he reached down and, grabbing handfuls of dirt, began heaping upon her the sum of all his fear. "You want to crawl around in the dirt, let me help you! You miserable wretch! Heaven will be a happier place without you!"

Michael could no longer continue, but flopped down, and began sobbing uncontrollably. As his face was pressed against the ground, he pulled dirt over his own head as his soul was wrenched in agony. Deep, long wails burst forth, as his heart rejected his mother's inevitable end. He became frozen, utterly spent, the tears spasmodically spilling forth.

After several hours of complete numbness, he picked himself up. His face showed no emotion as he made his way over to her. She was propped up on the crystal beam, her eyes staring catatonically beyond him. He took the time to crouch down and brush off the dirt he had thrown on her, and to pull her hair and clothing back into place.

While he was still on his knees from attending to her, with his hair and clothes still covered in dirt, his face showing the streaking lines from his tears, he conveyed in an even voice, "I'm sorry Mom, for saying what I did. I didn't mean it. I just couldn't bear the thought of losing you. You're right; you should not be pressured. Obviously

I'm more fearful than I imagined. I'm sorry. I'm really sorry. Please forgive me. Mom, if you are really asking Rach and me to let you go, we will, because we love you that much. But I hope you won't do it. Please Mom, don't go where we can't follow.[425] Dad will join us soon. I'm sure of it. You know I love you. I'm going now, but I hope you'll come back soon."

At that Michael arose and made his way out of the cave. When he reached the entry, Turk approached with muted empathy, and for the first time, embraced him. Michael began to sob again. When he finally regained his composure, Turk took him back to Willow Forest. There they sat in silence for some time, Michael's mind beset by grief. Then Turk got up and, without a word, walked over to the water and got in. Minutes later, Michael followed after him, and began cleaning up. Afterward, he went and lay under his hut and fell hard and fast asleep, exhausted.

25

DAY TWENTY: THE UPRISING

"Because they have taunted and become arrogant"
Zephaniah 2:10

Michael woke uneasy, feeling engulfed by a gray fog. Though dry-eyed, his faith seemed ground down to a hard nub. He allowed his eyes to take in the setting, even before lifting his head. Pulling himself up to a sitting position, he rubbed his forehead and temples in a vain attempt to sooth his sick heart.

Turk had timed breakfast perfectly to greet him as he climbed out of the hut and sat down on the rock shelf that overlooked the water. Michael offered a subdued, "Thanks," and began to eat. "You knew, didn't you, that she was that bad off? You were trying to tell me. I just didn't listen. You should have heard what I said. I'm so ashamed," he said woodenly.

"I know what you said."

"How could I? How could I lose it like that, especially when she needed me to be strong?"

"Everything is as it was meant to be."

"What's that supposed to mean? That she was predestined to choose pride? No, I can't accept that."

"I didn't say that."

"I feel sick. I never even said that kind of thing when I was earthbound. What in the world?! I've pushed her away. I don't know what to think. It's like I'm dead inside."

"It's time we return to the Throne."

"No, no, I don't want to be around Him right now. I couldn't. You don't understand. I made a fool of myself. I mean, I swore at her!"

"Can I be honest? You sound a bit like your mother. Do you really think your outburst was a surprise to Him? Do you imagine He thought, 'Oh no, Michael lost it in the cave?' You know He didn't. Let me ask you, are you listening? If your mom turns right now, will Jesus accept her? I mean, without making her grovel or beg her way back in?"

"Of course, in a second."

"Then what would make your return any different? If there is grace for her, then there is grace for you. Right?"

Michael added it up and replied, "Yeah, I guess," and taking a final bite of food, said to himself, "For sure."

"Then let's go."

At that they were off. Michael had not known what to expect upon their arrival, but found himself in the company of the Son. "Welcome Michael. I'm glad you're here. Can I get you to come with Me, please." Jesus then gently placed a hand on his shoulder, guiding him forward. They began strolling under the Throne, past the twenty-four elders who all raised a hand of acknowledgement or nodded in greeting.

With upturned face, Michael beheld the enormous wheels of the cherubim. They suddenly felt so alive, leaving him exposed. He realized their eyes were following his every move. He could not help but look up in awe at the four living creatures as they towered overhead atop the wheels, their wings spread out below the Father's expanse. Jesus sensed Michael's hesitancy and welcomed it. Then one of the living creatures spoke in a subdued voice just to him, "Holy, holy, holy, is the Lord of hosts, the whole earth is full of His glory."[426] Then all of them repeated it, and the water foundation below trembled.

When Michael heard them say "Holy, holy, holy," it shook him to the core, and turning to face Jesus, he said by the Spirit, "Woe is me, for I am ruined! I have unclean lips, and I am part of a family with unclean lips. My eyes should not be looking at the King, the Lord of Hosts."[427]

Jesus looked up, and a moment later, one of the four seraphim descended with a piece of burning coal, taken from the altar with tongs.[428] He approached Michael, and though towering over him, he bent down and reached out slowly with the tongs holding the coal. Sensing his trust, the living creature touched it to Michael's lips and said, "Behold, this has touched your lips; your iniquity is taken away, and your sin is forgiven."[429] Instantly, his shame was removed. In a timeless moment, everything became clear. It was as though fear had lifted, his doubt fled, and Michael suddenly found himself looking into Jesus' eyes with complete trust. "I believe You. I trust You above all others."

Jesus turned to the twenty-four elders and asked, "Whom shall We send; who will go for Us?"

Then Michael, unable to contain himself, replied, "Here I am. Send me!"[430]

"Yes. We shall," replied Jesus contemplatively. "You will stand in the midst of the assembly, and you will speak for Us. Do not concern yourself with the words, for the Spirit will give you utterance."[431]

Michael was then embraced by a number of the twenty-four elders who introduced themselves. "Michael, I'm David."

"Michael, My name's Noah. How 'bout a hug?"

Again and again they came, until Elijah laid his hands on him, and suddenly the Spirit of prophecy came upon Michael, and he declared, "Multitudes, multitudes in the valley of decision, for the day of the Lord is here. Proclaim this among the nations, prepare for the conflict, rouse the mighty men. Let all My warriors draw near, let them come up. Hasten and come all you surrounding nations, and gather yourself here. Bring down, O Lord, the mighty ones. Let the nations be roused, for the Lord will sit in judgment. Put in your sickle, for the harvest is ripe. Come, tread, for the wine press is full; the vats overflow, for their wickedness is great. Multitudes, multitudes in the valley of decision, for the day of the Lord is here."[432]

When Michael finished prophesying among them, he realized each of the elders was focused intently, with the Son and Elijah standing close at hand. Jesus smiled and remarked soothingly, "You now have clean lips, My son. We have chosen wisely," and they all nodded in agreement.

Michael felt as though he were enveloped in love. Jesus lifted His hand and summoned Turk to join Him and the twenty-four elders. "Gentlemen, our appreciations to Turkania, My faithful servant." At that they all applauded, and joined in showing their affection.

As Jesus pulled Turk and Michael away from the

OUR FIRST 22 DAYS IN HEAVEN

group, He said to Turk, "Thank you for holding onto him. I need you to take him to visit the gathering. There he will see what is occurring."

"Yes Sir, right away."

"Thank you. Off you go."

At that, Turk reached for Michael's hand and asked, "Ready?"

"Yes, let's go."

*　　　*　　　*

In the blink of an eye, they relocated to the hillside overlooking a vast gathering. It took several moments for Michael to take in what was happening. There were literally millions of people stretching out for as far as he could see, all clad in blood red tunics. He extended his right hand, and without looking, gripped hold of Turk's arm. "Look what has become of Damien's twenty-five. From one voice, so many have turned. The lukewarm have found a refuge."

Within seconds, Damien recognized Michael. "If it isn't Golden Boy, our pitiful, true believer. You still dogging me? Let's introduce you to my new friends." Damien again projected Michael's shortfalls[433], and scornful chuckles broke out across the assembly.

Ignoring Damien's sarcasm, Michael walked to where a rock ledge jutted out, and standing firmly, prophesized, "Blow a trumpet in Zion, and sound the alarm on My holy mountain. Let all the inhabitants of the land tremble, for the day of the Lord is at hand; a day of darkness and gloom, a day of clouds and thick darkness.[434] Wail you who stagger about drunk in your sleep, for your field is ruined and your land mourns, your wine is dried up, and your oil fails.[435] Alas, for the day of the Lord is upon you."

Damien's retort came quickly, "Those were mighty

powerful words. Something about you has changed," he relayed guilefully. "You seem..." at that Damien moved his head back and forth trying to get a read on him. "I'd say you are now a worthy opponent; stronger, no longer the Boy Wonder.

"Guess what I found out, that up here, faith moves mountains. I think it's time you were humbled and brought down to our level," and at that, he extended his hand out with authority and commanded the rock beneath Michael's feet to collapse. What Damien had not expected was that Michael would not fall with the rock, but instead, remained situated in mid-air until Turk drew him to an adjacent ledge.

"Are you done?" replied Michael calmly, being unflappable.

Damien lifted himself into the air to meet Michael face-to-face on the rock outcropping. "Tell me, what do you think of our new fashion statement?" he probed creepily, his eyes widened. "Do you like their color? We thought that standing out would best communicate our protest. How about it everyone?" At that there was a great shout of agreement. "Let me tell you, we are not so easily intimidated by your threats. You come here, and you don't even have the courtesy to hear us out. You haven't even asked why we're all here!" Turning westward, he called out, "Did you hear him ask before he lambasted you with threats?" At that, a great shout came forth, "No!"

"By the way Golden Boy, there's someone here I think you might be interested in, the newest member of our group. I think you know her, ladies and gentlemen, will you welcome with me, Golden Boy's mother, the honorable Deborah." Pandemonium broke out as the crowd shouted their affirmations. Damien then retorted insultingly, "Over here GB, we honor those who deserve honor." There his mother stood, her eyes icy and her face like granite.

Michael showed no surprise, his resolve remaining un-moved. Turk looked on with visible consternation, tempted to give Damien a reminder visit to Outer Darkness, but instead, contained himself.

With little fanfare, Michael called down, "Hello Mom, the Lord hasn't given up on you. He still loves you." Some laughed mockingly, but most grew silent. Michael then raised his voice to be heard over the din. "Apparently, Damien's complaints have touched a chord with all of you," he offered with gentleness. "By pulling away, you are isolating yourselves from the very One who can answer your heart's cry. I am here to bring you back to the Throne. There you can voice your grievances to the Lord. 'Yet even now,' declares the Lord, 'Return to Me, rend your heart and not your garment, for I am gracious and compassionate, slow to anger, abounding in lovingkindness, and relenting of evil.'[436]

"See about you, the army of the Lord approaches to escort you to His presence." Suddenly, the terrifying sound of feet striking the ground in unison was heard. Michael declared, "Like a mighty people arraigned for battle. They each march in line. They run like mighty men. They climb the wall like warriors. They don't deviate from their path. When they burst through the defenses, they do not break rank. They rush on the city, they run on the wall, for great is the army who carries out His word. Before them the people are in anguish, and every heart pales. The Lord utters His voice before His army. The day of the Lord is great and awesome, and who can endure it?"[437]

As Michael paused, the Host of Heaven crested the surrounding hillsides with great authority, and with singularity of step, came to a halt. "Blow the trumpet in Zion!" declared Michael. Suddenly, from every side, angels blew trumpets declaring their presence. "I am consecrating a fast, and proclaiming a solemn assembly. You will gather yourselves before the Throne, sanctifying your hearts. Let all the congregation say, 'Spare Thy people, O Lord.'"[438] Suddenly, from all about them, the angels declared, "Spare Thy people, O Lord." As the irresistible love of the Spirit washed over the assembly like a mighty wind[439], Michael declared, "Let everyone say, 'Spare Thy people, O Lord.'" Then, again and again, as though thunder was rolling over the gathering, the people shouted their declaration.

Damien could not believe how fast the multitude fell into line. He just stood there baffled, his face mildly irked. After a moment, he cautioned Michael, "The mob is fickle my young rival, one minute they're with you, the next they're throwing you under the bus. My, my, a few angels with their little trumpets, oh, and the wind…can't fight that wind. It even got to me."

"Let's go," said Michael to Damien evenly, "You, too." Together they walked back, as foreboding clouds hung low, and every heart was sobered.

"I could tell that you had changed," remarked Damien wryly. "You're a force to be reckoned with; formidable, I give you that. I like your little prophetic declarations. I might include some of that in my approach. It really sells. Even I was touched. Begrudgingly, I'd have to say this round goes to you.

"By the way, I've got a boatload of requests for cigarettes. I don't suppose your side has a stash?"

"Damien!"

"Hey, don't freak, kid! I've got a slew of requested items – meds, all kinds, alcohol, all kinds, even porn, you get the idea. Many want their tattoos back. They feel naked without them."

"What?!" barked Michael incredulously.

"Don't be self-righteous, GB. This comedy of intolerance is exposing itself," dismissed Damien with a catty tone.

"I could use a double Stoly martini with a peel of lemon myself." Damien extended his fist to Michael and jibed him, "What? No knuckle-bump? What'd you think, people could get by without some modern amenities? Some are begging for the next two days to get over with, so they can hit the road."

"What d'you mean? You of all people know what that's like," Michael countered testily.

"Oh right, the black horde, beady little eyes, well, we pitiful ingrates have our destiny."

"Oh, I get it. Always searching, never finding, always striving, never achieving, and in the end – no love. As long as you're their beloved leader, it's on to the Promised Land – Outer Darkness."

"Bad karma will kill you. So about that drink…" he said with a terse tone.

"You know, there's plenty of wine in that direction," Michael indicated looking toward Mount Sinai. "You can have as much as you want."[440]

"Hell, yeah! Let's you and me take a couple long pulls. What's your fancy? Oh, I bet you're a Red Bull and vodka kid?" Looking at him sardonically, he mocked, "Damn, that's right, you didn't have enough testosterone for that yet."

Damien turned and walked ahead, leaving Michael to follow. Keeping his gaze forward, he deadpanned, "Dude, drinking in Heaven is like sex in marriage – do it as much as you want to, but nobody wants to. But make it bad, call it fornicating and people can't help but dive in. It's all about the chase – wham, bam, thank you ma'am. Cop to it, Boy Wonder. And let's cut the pretense of civility. This is all too palsy-walsy for me. We're mirror opposites – yin and yang, or haven't you noticed? By the way, I'm still waiting for your *mea culpa*."

26

DAY TWENTY-ONE: SOLEMN ASSEMBLY

"Choose you this day"
Joshua 24:15

It was the noon hour, but all about the Throne was darkness and gloom. The entire congregation, standing on the sea, had aligned itself, one side against the other. Those who had returned from Damien's gathering were emboldened by the fact that the Throne was completely shrouded by a thick cloud.[441] With outspoken intent, they willed their tunics back to a royal red, feeling empowered by this sign of protest. Damien was back in his element, making authoritative declarations, even ones that sounded prophetic, always challenging whether the Lord could truly be trusted. So careful was he in mincing his words, that his rancor never quite crossed the line between innocent inquiry and rebellious accusation. This appealed greatly to the people, enticing their ears to flirt with rejecting authority, though not explicitly. Between his declarations, there arose powerful and compelling military anthems which excited and thrilled the throng.

Juxtaposed to this group, those who made up the other great assemblage were interceding with all the force of love. Old and New Testament saints were resolute in their desire to see the Lord intervene. With unyielding fervor, they issued forth requiems and laments that called to the deep in every person. However, the opposing crowd just chanted their refrain all the louder.

Michael was all but overcome by the foreboding elegies sung in a heavenly language as he pressed toward the center of the crowd to find Damien. He could barely keep focused due to the music penetrating his very being with its cryptic intercessions and soulful pleas. As he pushed forward, the music shifted from a requiem to a symphonic pronouncement, responding to his faith. Up ahead, he heard the distinctively militant, techno-beat of the pride faction which grew stronger as he drew closer. Its agitated melodies, deep horns and seductively pounding rhythms enticed him, rousing a part of himself that he wanted to remain dormant. He felt stirred in his passions as he reached the dividing line between the two groups. Both were clashing feverishly against the other as two voices, one pleading for love, the other declaring independence.

Michael pressed forward as the saints behind him avowed in full chorus, "For God so loved you He gave. For God so loved you He gave..." In contrast, pride thundered back with the refrain, "We will not be made to worship. We will not be made to worship..." Along with the group anthems, both sides had individuals who sang forth their opposing pronouncements. With great reverberation and intensity, the two sides stood against one another with all passion and purpose.

Never could one have conceived it would come to this: Pride's red garments against humility's white ones; pride's independence against humility's surrender. In every way the conflict had come to a head, while lightning and thunder echoed from above with fury. Michael pressed past the front and headed toward the opposing side. In that short distance, rain drops began striking the sea. He was halfway across when Damien saw him and called out condemningly, "Golden Boy!" Michael stopped and waited for Damien's approach, his face eerily lit with a stony facade. The rain fell harder. Instantly the attention of the surrounding rows of people caused both sides across the Crystal Sea to form an arena about the two.

"Dude, you just don't get it?" cried Damien as he circled him as if to fight. The rain poured, and the music hushed. Damien accused, "It was never about me speeding. God could have intervened any time He wanted, but He just didn't want to. We're all mere pawns, pieces on a chess board, expendable. Underneath the niceties of this place, all the perks, you know there is one question being asked, 'Do you believe Him?' Let's not make this about saints and sinners, this is between you and me. I want to know, do *you* really believe the gobbledygook, Golden Boy? Huh? How far is your faith willing to go? Far enough for you to love me unconditionally? Huh?"

At that Damien uncoiled his arm and violently punched Michael square on the jaw throwing him backwards to the water where he twisted, landing on his face with blood spurting from his nose. The reverberations literally passed through humility's side, at which pride's side whooped and hollered. Michael slowly pushed himself up and returned to face him. "Yeah, that's what I want to see," cried Damien. "So you think you have enough love for me to take it to you? Turn the other cheek?!"

Michael replied, "Damien, I'll love you no matter what."

"Huh? The secret's out Bud, you're a counterfeit; you're just like the rest of us, flawed to the core, Mr. Pencil man, the Golden Boy of Rockford High. Everybody knows your dealings. No secrets remember?"

"Secrets?" responded Michael as he wiped the blood from his mouth with the back of his hand. "I have nothing to hide. I know I am a flawed person. My pride kept me lying and denying the truth my whole life. I am perfectly imperfect. How about that? I'm done trying to be good enough, smart enough, accepted enough. It's all a game. Pride had me begging for crumbs. The joke was on me. Is that what you want to hear? That I was the joke? Right again. Worse than you think? Yep, but loved anyway."

At that, the people behind Michael started chiming in, "Me too." "Yeah, me too!"

"Do you hear that?" cried Michael, "No one over here is judging anyone, even you. No one has the upper ground. No one can defend themselves in the least. We've been defeated by pride. We're done with its charade. We lose! Is that what you want to hear? No, we don't deserve love. But we are loved nonetheless!"

"Really?" asked Damien hawkishly. "Because I think God uses guilt as a primal and elemental force to con people into submitting. He lets our own words and actions beat us up, and then steps in and promises relief. But what's in it for Him? Huh? What's He want? Everyone is motivated by something. What's His end game? Do you really think there's hope on the other side of that mountain? Do you think you'll find meaning and purpose in being His robot? Your servitude to the company line is so, lapdog. It's all too good to be true, too easy. You, and all the lackey's behind you, almost sound like you believe it. I think we're all convinced over here," he ranted sarcastically as laughter burst out.

Michael was suddenly far away in his memories, realizing the ramifications of his lies. "It's all true," he started, speaking more slowly and deliberately as the rain streamed down his face and splashed about his feet. "I was so afraid to accept myself that I lived a façade. Right now, my lies and hypocrisy have contributed to my mom being disillusioned, where now she's dressed in red with you. Mom, if you can hear me, I'm so sorry for my part, for selling out and living a lie. I was a joke. I'm also sorry Mom, for not loving you enough to confront the abuse, for not risking everything and standing up for love. It was wrong. I was wrong. I'm sorry. I love you." At that he broke and fell to his knees, with the rain pounding about him, his hands raised to conceal the sobs as his chest heaved.

Damien wanted nothing of it. "What a wus! What the hell kind of opponent are you? What happened to the manly, whup-ass prophet we were liking? This is pathetic!"

After several moments, Michael composed himself and stood, and said deliberately, "Yes, I do believe that He loves me unconditionally. What's His motivation? Isn't it obvious? He's the pure manifestation of love. He is love.[442] He loves us, that's why He's calling for the end of pride. Heaven is a place without pride and fear. It's that simple."

Damien was agitated because the truth was gnawing at him. Without thinking he barked out, "All you'll find there, Golden Boy, is the delusion that the Father will love you if you live up to His expectations."

As the rain continued to fall and the water was rising to their ankles, Michael responded, "Is that what this is all about Damien? *Your* father? Is that where your anger is coming from? Did he hurt you? Did he beat you?"

At that, Damien jumped on Michael, throwing him to the water. He began striking him. "You want to talk about my father? He'll teach you to mouth off. *'Don't you make me change my tone, boy! You volunteering for a lesson, boy? I'll show you what respect looks like, boy!'"*

After a number of unrequited blows, someone caught Damien's arm, and he looked up in a rage. Suddenly, he was face-to-face with his own father, dressed in white. Michael recognized he was the same man he had seen standing back on several occasions watching him.

"Son. Son! That's enough. If you need to punch someone, punch me. I deserve it, not him." At that Damien's father lifted him off Michael.

Damien yanked his arm away, and backed up, startled. "Don't you come near me, old man. I want nothing to do with you. You aren't my father anymore," he yelled, holding his hands out as if to protect himself.

Still the rain fell. His father spoke, "I know I violated every form of trust possible with you. I know it! Thinking about it sickens me. There isn't a day that goes by that I don't regret the perfectionism I leveled at you. You were right, you didn't need to become an architect and take over the business. The whole thing was upside-down. I was obsessed with my standards. It was all about me – not you. I know it now! Everything you said, is true. I failed you. I am asking you right now, will you please forgive me, son?"

"Wait!" cried an older woman coming up from behind him. "Damien, I am your grandmother. I cannot let your father take all the blame. If you had seen how many times I raised his hackles, you would understand why he was so jaded. Poor dear, there was hardly a day that went by I didn't irk him with my bitterness, provoking him until he reacted. Then I'd sit back drinking my sherry, and acting the saint. It was disgusting how much I drank. That's why he pulled away, and you and I never met, because I lost the right to be in your life. You don't... you don't know how many times I've thought about you." Moving forward uneasily, she beseeched, "Sweetie, we've all failed you. I've had a number of my older relatives apologize to me. Do you see this whole large group behind me, they're all your relatives. That's right, all of them. We're hoping you'll let it all go. The truth is, grandson, you were on your way to vexing other people, just like me. We're all guilty. Will you please, will you forgive me?"

Damien's hair was matted down by the rain, his clothes soaked. He stood there trying to emotionally grasp their words. His facial contortions revealed his internal conflict. His eyes questioned everything he heard. He was deeply afraid to accept it, to open his heart, but felt compelled to want to. As he was teetering between the two opinions, his father began walking toward him. "No! No!... Stop!" Damien cried. But his father didn't stop, and instead, reached out and embraced him as the sobs of both burst forth unashamedly. They fell to their knees holding onto each other, and wept aloud as they finally let go of all the judgments. It was in that moment, overcome by love, that Damien surrendered his pride, and came to believe.

As Michael raised himself to his knees, he realized his mother was making her way over to him. Her eyes conveyed a softness that he had not seen before. As she knelt down beside him, Michael noticed Rachel to his left, and then his mother threw her arms around both of them and pulled them close. She spoke into their ears, "I'm sorry, both of you. I never saw it. I defrauded you in the worst sort of way, just like Damian's father. I tried to be loved,

Michael, by using you. Everything you said was true. And Rachel, I'm so sorry for always finding a reason to strike out against you. I abused you – verbally and physically, but also by not accepting you, and appreciating you. I never even got to know you, my own daughter. I made it all about me." Deborah paused circumspectly, "I never allowed myself to see it, that I hated myself; that my pride left me loveless. Wow, there I've said it. It's true. I'm so sorry. I was terribly wrong. I'm sorry for all of it. I am. Please, will you forgive me?"

"Yes, mom," responded Rachel, grabbing hold tight. Michael extended his arms around them.

"I love you both dearly. I will always love you," offered Deborah as she gladly released years of pent up tears.

All over the great assembly, people were moved to press the issue of love even more boldly with their loved ones. Fathers and mothers, sons and daughters, were compelled to confront the ramifications of their prideful judgments.

Within minutes, the rain slowed, and the red and white groups were blending together as millions of people were changing from a prideful red to a humble white.

Nevertheless, there were some that still would not bend. Instead, resolving to stand their ground, they cursed and condemned the humble as weak and pitiful. Even so, their family members appealed all the more for love and forgiveness. Some were physically struck, while others were verbally assaulted[443], but none were truly harmed because of the protection afforded them in God's grace and love. They were simply willing to face down pride without fear, and to take whatever came their way. Love proved itself against its great adversary.

None who were choosing pride in such a moment could claim ignorance as to the decision they were making. Many family and friends, who appealed with all their hearts, witnessed the horrible freedom of those who were rejecting God's love. They saw hearts hardening as they argued pride's position without a reasoned defense, succumbing to name calling and baseless innuendo. Those who remained in their darkness pulled back and removed themselves from the sea.

In those final hours of day twenty-one, the cloud about the Throne gave way to the Father's glory, causing the rainbow of colors to shimmer and dance forth against the clouds and sea. Joy arose throughout the assembly, as the truth of love dispelled pride's twisted logic. It was enough for everyone that no one was left deceived, and each person knowingly made their decision. The haranguing was over, and love left those of faith buoyed up. The atmosphere was electric, as singing and dancing broke out that captured the whole of the white-robed congregation.

> You shall go out with joy
> And be led forth with peace
> The mountains and the hills
> Will break forth before you
> There'll be shouts of joy
> And all the trees of the field
> Will clap, will clap their hands...[444]

22

DAY TWENTY-TWO:
THE SEPARATION

"He will separate them as a
shepherd separates the sheep from the goats"
Matthew 25:32

Michael stood there beaming, with his mother and sister at his side, and several generations of extended family nearby, along with all their angels. Joy and hugs were all about, with dancing and singing and pure elation on every face. Angels were catering the celebration with a variety of tasty finger-foods that had people chasing after them for third and fourth servings. Everyone knew the celebration was just beginning, as they were about to cross the threshold into their new home.

On numerous occasions, people greeted and hugged Michael, telling him how his faith had opened the way for either themselves or a loved one to cross over. But none was so special, as when Damien approached Michael. The entire surrounding crowd paused from their jubilations to witness them fully embrace. This was what love had done for them, and suddenly there arose a prolonged applause. Damien could not help but say, "I'm sorry, dude. I'm sorry for all of it. Thanks for blowing it off when I kept trying to one-up you. Really, thanks for helping me get back with my father."

Damien leaned in to speak into Michael's ear. "And, uh, thanks for pressing me to avoid the hellish limbo of Outer Darkness. I knew the reckoning was coming. I just couldn't put it together to turn. That place would have been vile. Truth is, your buddy, Turk, and his little look-see, had made its point. Are we cool?" asked Damien warmly, as he backed his head away.

Michael nodded in acknowledgement, and said, "Yeah, cool. Hey, because of it, my mom ended up turning. So thanks! That which was meant for evil, God meant for good.[445] Thanks, I mean it."

As the celebration continued, Michael turned to Turk and asked, "How'd you know it would all work out for good?[446] I mean, you never freaked."

"I know the Father. I know the way of love. One thing you discover here is that He tells love's story through our lives. What we most fear, oftentimes becomes the starting place for His love to win out."

As through matured eyes, Michael said, "I believe it. Thanks for holding on to me."

"You're welcome."

Minutes later, Michael sensed the people congregating,

filling in every available place. Michael held his hands out to his mom and sister and asked for the first time, "Join me closer up?"

Rachel looked at her mom cautiously, and inquired, "Shall we?" to which her mother enthusiastically responded, "Certainly!"

Around the Throne, the seven pillars of fire began burning brightly as the expanse of the Father's presence was uncovered, penetrating the cloud about it with great glory. With awesome authority, the four living creatures and the twenty-four elders exploded in song along with the whole congregation:

Holy, Holy, Holy, is the Lord God Almighty!
Early in the morning, our song shall rise to Thee
Holy, Holy, Holy, merciful and mighty,
God in three persons, blessed Trinity![447]

Michael looked up, and could see the Cloud of Covering thinning somewhat, releasing the Father's glory to shine forth with great acclaim. His breathing increased as he lifted his face and arms, caught up in the ecstasy. Joy and rapture overtook him with love that was more pronounced than he had ever experienced.

Still, the prideful were profoundly conflicted, deeply yearning after the Father's love, but convinced that they were justified in not releasing those who had sinned against them. The Son's eyes, however, blazed at full strength as He sought to draw in each person.[448] With unreserved abandon, He pressed the issue of humility as never before, holding nothing back. Through the Spirit, He appealed to each heart, searching out experience after experience from their lives to help them see the depravity of their own choices. Many turned, as great clarity burst upon them.[449]

Holy, Holy, Holy, all the saints adore Thee
Casting down their golden crowns around the glassy sea
Cherubim and seraphim falling down before Thee
Which wert, and art, and evermore shall be.

Michael saw the Father stretch out His hand and lay it on His Son's shoulder. Jesus then turned, and for a long moment, gazed into His Father's eyes which caused their glory to blaze with even greater brilliance. Such was the majesty that the very foundations of the Crystal Sea began to tremble. Above, there was something like a mighty rushing wind[450], as unbridled love exploded across the congregation, bringing all to their knees.[451] Still they sang:

Holy, Holy, Holy, Lord God Almighty!
All Thy works shall praise Thy name, in earth and sky and sea
Holy, Holy, Holy, merciful and mighty,
God in three persons, blessed Trinity.

Michael felt as though his body could transform at any moment.[452] Just when he was feeling like his hand was transfiguring before his eyes, the intensity began to dissipate. He realized that tongues of fire[453] had alighted on people throughout the assembly. Many sons and daughters rose up and were prophesying, and young men were speaking forth visions.[454]

Unexpectedly, Michael felt distracted as thoughts spilled over him of how Damien had raised a bevy of challenges against the Father's trustworthiness. But somehow, in the middle of it, he began laughing at the assertions that had been made. Each fearful objection spurred more humor, as laughter overcame his ability to contain himself. Suddenly, every fear became a hilarious joke. He literally could not keep himself quiet, but turned over and began howling at the ridiculousness of it all. Soon, others were tuning in to his merriment, and laughter began spreading to those about him. Tears of joy were running down his cheeks as he was trying to hold his stomach with one hand, and wipe his cheeks with the other.

When the Son looked on, even He began to chuckle, and then unexpectedly, He burst into full laughter.[455] Being unable to contain His response, He pointed at the Father knowing He had brought it on. That was all it took to send the whole assembly into holy mayhem. People everywhere began rolling over in uncontrolled fits of mirth as the absurdity of their pride came to light.[456]

As things began to settle down, Rachel's spirit stirred within, and she could not help but prophesy, "When the Lord brought back the captive ones of Zion, we were like those in a dream. Then our mouth was filled with laughter, and our tongue with joyful shouting. Then they said among the nations, 'The Lord has done great things for us. We are glad!' Those who sow in tears shall reap with joyful shouting. He who goes to and fro weeping, carrying his bag of seed, shall indeed come again with a shout of joy, bringing his sheaves with him."[457]

Jesus stood up, and making His way to the platform edge, shared, "Thank you Rachel. Truly, truly, all of you who have gone forth humbling yourselves, have helped to restore many of your loved ones, caught in their pride, to a place of trusting Our love.

"If you had asked Me about what today would have involved, I'm sure I would not have imagined this," Jesus conceded, as He strained from losing his composure again. "He..." gesturing back, and barely able to contain Himself, "is a free spirit... And laughter is good medicine, isn't it? Amazing!

"I want to welcome you on this our twenty-second

day. We have been through a lot together. When you first arrived, many of you still thought it was a dream. But little by little, the ground began feeling firm, the fruit tasted authentic, and you realized there actually was life after death. Then you met My Father in all His creative glory.[458] You came to understand creatures of every kind as they made themselves known. With your perfected mind, you appreciated their instinctual patterns and inbred functionality that He instilled, allowing them to survive and flourish.

"As your hearts were filled with the knowledge of the Lord, you recognized your great enemy, pride.[459] You saw its evil ways and loveless end.[460] You then interceded, beseeching the Father's intervention. After the Spirit's examination, you raised your voices and called for Me to be crowned your King. I then introduced you to Adam, Job, Abraham and Moses, who uncovered the conflict that has raged in all your hearts.

"Then we shared the Feast of Tabernacles, where most of you revisited your wilderness wanderings and reconciled with each other. Oh, I know there is a group of you toward the back, and even some mixed in among us, who have not yet made amends. Still, you know enough to fear the separation that's about to occur. I'll come back to you in a moment.

"Today, with overflowing joy, we will enter into the Promised Land.[461] Each of you who have trusted Our love and humbly reconciled with each other will be welcomed to cross over with Me. There, you will discover more than beautiful dwellings with your names on them; you will find your Heavenly home.[462]

"Remember the words of Isaiah when he said, 'Your eyes will see the King in His beauty; they will behold a far-distant land. Look to Zion, the city of our appointed feasts. Your eyes will see Jerusalem, an undisturbed habitation, a tent which will not be folded. Its stakes will never be pulled up, nor any of its cords be torn apart. But there the majestic One, the Lord, will be for us. And no resident will say, "I am sick." The people who dwell there will be forgiven their iniquity."[463]

"As I mentioned earlier, there is yet one more step of faith to come. This involves the circumcision of your pride. As many of you have come to understand, I am going to invite you to follow Me through the Sinai Passage where the Spirit's love will burn away the wood, hay and stubble without hurting you in the least. However, Our cleansing love will do more than take away the dross, it will amplify and magnify the gold, silver and precious stones that are resident within you already. Your natural body will be transformed[464] into your spiritual body. When your perishable body puts on the imperishable, and your mortal existence takes on immortality, then you will say, 'Death is swallowed up in victory. O Death, where is your victory? O Death, where is your sting?'[466]

"It is time. Will you trust Me?"

"Yes," answered most of the assembly with a great shout.

"Good. First I need to separate this great gathering into two groups, those who have humbly accepted My love as evidenced by your willingness to reconcile with each other, and those of you who have not. Would all those who have fully forgiven everyone in their lives move to My right, and all those who have not, to My left?"[467]

Michael sensed something foreboding behind him, and instinctively turned his head. He beheld the billowing black clouds of Outer Darkness churning as a distant malevolent storm. He slowly looked back up to the Throne.

After several moments, Jesus spoke a bit more softly, "You will notice that some of the prideful are intent on staying with the humble.[468] That I am afraid cannot happen for your own sakes. Still, those of you who desire to join our passage into Heaven are welcomed, if only you will humbly reconcile. It is that simple. If I allow you to go forward without making peace with others, the Stones of Fire will burn you up. So you see, I am forced to ask you to decide, right now. It is not too late. What is your choice? We will pause just a few more minutes. Now will come about the saying, 'There is more joy in Heaven over one sinner who repents, than ninety-nine who need no repentance.'"[469]

Suddenly, one person bowed to his knees, then two, then fifty, then a thousand, then tens of thousands. The congregation erupted in joy, as family after family received back their loved ones. Even in the end, grace and mercy were winning out. Michael just shook his head in astonishment. With a smile, he looked at Turk. "Amazing," he mouthed.

Jesus continued in a celebratory tone, "Well, well, well. Welcome to our new friends! Welcome home."

Jesus paused. A glint of sadness showed on His face. His eyes reached into each person's heart that even yet held fast to their pride. He asked with all gentleness, "Friend, how did you come in here without wedding clothes?"[470] And they were speechless. "Alright, angels if you will assist Me, there are some still mixed in with the saints who need to be given the disturbing freedom that their pride is demanding. Please separate them out.[471]

"To those on My left, I say to you, you will not get out of your prison until you pay the last cent of your pride.[472] Your decision is voluntary, one of your own choosing, and now you will be granted your wish in Outer Darkness. Even there, My love will never wane. Let Me leave you with these words, 'Come unto Me, all you who are weary and heavy-laden, and I will give you rest. Take My yoke upon you, and learn from Me, for I am gentle and humble in heart, and you shall find rest for your souls. For My yoke is easy, and My burden is light."[473] If you should turn like the Prodigal's son, know that there is a home waiting for you here. May these words visit you in your darkest hour. Farewell," He said solemnly. At that, all those to His left suddenly disappeared, and Outer Darkness receded.

"Let it be said, that the Royal Law[474] of Heaven is that We love you as We are loved, and We ask only that you love your neighbor as you are loved. This is the Golden Rule. You too will be transformed by it as you follow Me through the fire. This is My gift to you."

Suddenly, trumpets sounded all around. The Old Testament saints divided, allowing the Ark of the Covenant to pass between them leading the way[475] toward Sinai's Passage. Michael was spellbound as he watched the great wheels of the four living creatures turning majestically. Then the Old Testament elders followed in procession, with the Old Testament saints behind them, all singing with great joy as they proceeded.

Michael remarked to Turk as he witnessed the glorified saints go on ahead, "It truly is a highway of holiness, and they are singing unto Zion.[476] Wow. But I have to admit, to follow after them, well, I'm a bit squeamish."

"Don't be, it won't hurt. Death has lost its sting. The closer you get, the more love you will feel. Trust me, or rather, trust Him! Okay?"

"Got it."

Jesus stood between the passage and the people and called, "Come forward!" With each step, the Pillar of Fire grew greater until it crested above Mount Sinai itself. If Michael was nervous before, he all but became alarmed. He questioned Turk immediately, "Why did it do that? Why has it gotten so great?"

"Because the Glorified Saints did not need cleansing;

they were already clean.[477] Remember the story, 'seven times hotter?'[478] The fire you see is the manifest love of God."

Michael noticed that some people stopped walking altogether, but Turk grabbed hold of his arm and said, "I think you're the bravest kid I've ever come across. Don't let a little fire put fear into you. Steel your faith!"

Then the Son spoke forth as the sound of many waters, "Do not fear, for this day, you shall see the salvation of the Lord, which He will accomplish for you!"[479]

Michael felt emboldened, and began walking of his own accord. Soon, he found himself walking directly behind the Son toward a wall of fire. Because it was so dense, he could not see into it. Still, he pressed forward with Turk at his side.

Michael had a fleeting thought race through his mind, "Maybe I should go into the fire, and come out again, to show them it's okay?" But the Son looked at him, and without words, said, "Michael, a wicked generation seeks a sign, but a sign will not be given to them."[480] He then shook His head ever so slightly, and Michael understood. Without hesitation, Michael followed Jesus into the fire[481], although for his last few steps, he closed his eyes. Turk just smiled.

Rather than the heat of fire, Michael felt enveloped in love. He was quickly lifted off the ground as the tongues of fire caused him to spiral into the air, whirling him about like a great ballet dancer. It was as though he were as light as a feather being blown about by the winds of love. Without any pain, his innermost being began transforming[482] with luminescent brilliance, taking on the image of the heavenly. His skin morphed; flesh and bone ignited with radiance. He watched as light burst from his fingertips, and his hands were transfigured before his very eyes, taking on a bronze hue like Turk's. He instantly realized he could feel far more than he had with skin. His new body was fully alive and interacting with the very winds that moved him through the air.

Within moments, Michael realized that up ahead, and still some distance into the air, the Father's Throne had situated itself in the midst of the Stones of Fire.[483] He found himself drawn toward the Ark of His presence, being lifted higher and higher into the air. All about him was fire, but even it seemed dull compared to the brilliant light radiating from the expanse just ahead. Michael was pulled upward, as if lifted as a child by his father. His every sense was ignited in love. He knew he was about to come face to face with the Father's expanse. There would be no Cloud of Covering, no veil of protection. He felt a yearning come over him, as though each second's delay were too long. As he rose before the Throne, he noted the four living creatures directly before him, so close he could touch them, but his eyes desired only to look on the Lord of Life. He could see His unrestrained glory as it pressed past the cherubim's wings. Then Michael's face came into the light as a sunrise crosses the horizon.

Instantly, love encompassed Michael entirely, pulling him into the expanse. Time stopped. For what seemed a lifetime, he floated in the midst of the Father's presence, having, as if it were possible, thousands of conversations simultaneously. He saw his life lived out, as though there had been no accident. He beheld his wife, watched his children grow, and came to know things about himself that showed forth his profound need to be restored in relationship to the Father. His very personhood was joined in perfect harmony with what could have been, but for his willingness to lay down his life.

In another instant, Michael touched the Father's omniscience and beheld his future as though innumerable paths could be taken, each offering a unique vision of how love could express itself. Out of Michael's innermost being arose the words, "I trust You. Please, You choose for me, You guide my way. I love You." Everywhere was peace. All fear was absent.[484] Nothing was hurried. For a long cherished moment, Michael basked in the love as though he would never leave.

Michael then found himself floating beyond the expanse, his eyes glistening, his heart full. He continued in the updraft that lifted him higher into the air. Minutes later, Turk joined him. He too was basking in the intimate union he had shared with the Father. Neither spoke, but lazily rose as though lying on a thermal.

The assembly had entered the Stones of Fire as a great company. Deborah and Rachel, along with their angels, also passed through His presence which had expanded across the passage. After a short time, they caught up with Michael and Turk who were drifting up the mountain.

When Michael saw Rachel, he could not help but declare, "Wow, Rach! You're beautiful, truly beautiful. You look amazing! Doesn't she Tam? Amazing!"

"So do you my brother, so do you!"

"Mom, you look great, too! Hey, you're bronze is blushing! Arrack, can you believe it?

"Hey you guys, we're going to the top of Mount Sinai. Turk says that from up there we'll be able to see the whole of the Inner Court.[485] Come on!"

The Son waited patiently for the last person to cross the threshold. After pausing, He looked back beyond Eden's Garden to the boundary of Outer Darkness, where He saw the faces of many pressed against it. They were yet unwilling to come.

28

DAY TWENTY-TWO:
THE INNER COURT OF HEAVEN

"He who overcomes, I will make
him a pillar in the temple of My God"
Revelation 3:12

Michael and the others arrived at the top of Mount Sinai.
There before them was the most picturesque and breathtaking view they had ever seen. Below them, shining as
a diamond from all facets, was the holy city Jerusalem. It
radiated the glory of God as a very costly stone, as a gem of
crystal-clear jasper.[486] Michael's eyes were captivated, and
his mouth hung open in awe. Never before had he seen
anything so beautiful. Its walls were great and high, and

as he looked, he could see three gates facing them.[487] As his eyes followed the wall downward, he saw three of the twelve foundation stones supporting the three gates, each one named after one of the apostles.[488]

Michael immediately began to realize he had new abilities. "Wow, look how far I can see! It's like my eyes automatically adjust with perfect acuity. No matter how far I look, they zoom in and out. I can see all the way across the city."

"You'll find your hearing is just as great. All your senses have been enhanced. Wait 'til you taste our favorite fruit."

As Michael beheld Jerusalem, he found his heart interacting with its beauty. He said to Turk, "I can feel it, or sense it, oh, I'm not sure what to say. It's beautiful. How big is it? It looks huge! It goes on forever."

Turk responded, "Jerusalem's length and width run for fifteen hundred miles in both directions. And it's just as tall, sitting as a perfect cube.[489] The walls themselves are seventy-two yards thick, according to human measurements,[490] which are also angelic measurements. See how the walls are not only crystal-clear like jasper, but the foundation stones supporting the gates are like the colors of a rainbow? Each of these hues represents a different precious stone and one of the families of Israel. The first foundation stone corresponding to the first gated area is jasper, a reddish-yellow. Then, sapphire blue, chalcedony – a milky-translucent, emerald green, sardonyx peach mix, sardius red, chrysolite olivine green, beryl yellow, topaz greenish-yellow, chrysoprase light green, jacinth reddish-orange and amethyst purple.[491] If you look around, not everyone has bronze skin like you and I have. Do you see that? Different families have different pigments based on the precious stones. You've been seeing those varied colors in the angels all along."

"Every color is remarkable," amazed Michael.

"I agree. Peter called you 'living stones.'[492] Wait until you see what you look like when you're resonating with His love in the assembly."

"I can't wait... Wow! Look at those huge pearls!"

"Each of the twelve gates has been cut out from a single pearl. From up here they don't appear to be that large, but they're actually enormous.[493] At some point, we'll visit Oyster Bay in the Eastern Sea to see the giant oysters that produced them. If you look now, you can just make out the Throne as it's going through the middle gate; and you know how big the Throne is! Do you see that? The gates are proportional to the wall height, which makes them immense. Also, the walls are clear, like glass. In fact, you will never feel closed in when you're in the city, because everything in it is transparent. When we descend, you'll see that each gate has an angel standing beside it, bearing the name of one of the twelve tribes of Israel."[494]

"So the Throne is passing into the city? Is the Temple there?" asked Rachel.

"Actually, the Lord God Almighty and the Lamb are its temple. The city has no need for a sun of any sort, because the glory of the Father illuminates it, as does His Son.[495] That means there's no night here, no need for sleep. You will never get tired again.

"Okay, a couple more sight-seeing tidbits before we head down. First, you will notice on your right the Eastern Sea, and on your left the Western Sea.[496] These two bodies of water are fed from the Rivers of Life that proceed from the Throne at the center of Jerusalem. Also, you can see that Jerusalem's Gardens run from the city to the base of this mountain along with the one to the north, Mount Zion[498], as well as to the seas on the east and west. The landscape rises and falls throughout, creating breathtaking waterfalls and wondrous getaways. There are mansions that spread out in all directions. You're welcomed to stay in any one dwelling for as long as you like, and about the time you're ready for that next amazing place, someone else will be hoping for yours.[499]

"There is much to be enjoyed. The truth is, you can't imagine how much there is to embark upon. One last thing, ask me what my favorite day of the week is?"

"What is it?" asked Michael directly.

"The Sabbath. My favorite is always going to be the seventh day, and I'll tell you why. That's the day we all join together on the Mount of Assembly, or Mount Zion, which you can see towering to the north above Jerusalem. It is spectacular in the truest sense of the word, with wonders beyond your imagination. There are many places where the Scripture, 'Eye has not seen, nor ear heard, nor entered into the heart of man'[500] applies, but the Mount of Assembly sits atop them all as the crown jewel. In six days, after we get settled into Jerusalem, we will be invited to share the Sabbath with the Father on Mount Zion. You can't imagine. Well, alright, let's head down."

Michael could not believe the ease with which he could fly. He merely had to will himself, and he could lift or dip, speed up or slow down. He also noted the overwhelming sensitivity of his skin, and though its texture was different, he found himself reveling in the delightful sensation of the wind softly caressing it. He wondered to himself as to its strength, *Could I take a bullet?* he thought.

Turk replied without words, *Think Superman.*

No way! Can I go faster than a speeding locomotive? he thought back.

What do you think?

"Michael, we can all hear you," replied Rachel. "Our

thoughts aren't hidden anymore," and she just laughed. Then she threw her arms in front of her, and pulled ahead a bit, "Super Michael, zoom zoom!" And they all laughed.

"Funny Rach, but you would have asked too. Admit it."

Rachel then turned over and declared "I'm Wonder Woman! Wait..." and broke into hysterics. "I forget what her powers were. Did she even have powers?" and the others laughed. "Maybe we can ask her, she's probably here."

"Rach, she was an actress. You're losing it."

"I meant her character," but by then everyone was chuckling.

Turk asked, "Alright folks, how about a flying lesson? Everyone take hands. Ready?" At that, Turk increased their speed a hundred times and the distance to Jerusalem flew by in mere seconds. He then slowed to give everyone a bird's-eye view of the middle gate through which they would pass. Each of them suddenly felt the power emanating from the city.

"I can feel the love. I can feel Him. It's like He's here with me right now," commented Michael.

"Wait until we get closer. You have no idea. During the past three weeks, the expanse of His presence was shrouded for your protection, but you don't need protecting anymore. Just wait. Everything He promised is about to come true."

"Like what?" asked Michael intrigued.

"He promised special things to those who overcome.[502] But I'll let Him introduce that to you. Day twenty-two isn't over yet!"

Soon they were all gliding to the ground a short distance from the gate. Multitudes of glorified saints[503] were making their way into the city. From up close, the transparency was stunning. Each could see through the multicolored walls with crystal clarity.

They now saw many more people with their multi-hued array of skin tones, and remarks were made as to how beautiful each person was. Michael again took notice that he could still see his sister's and mother's natural features, and yet with greatly enhanced elegance.

Everywhere he looked seemed to him a wonderland. As much as he tried to take it all in, it was too much to absorb. As they approached the gate, Michael could not believe the enormity of how high the wall rose before them. His vision lowered to see a gloriously embroidered silk banner draping down from the high-arching pearl entrance, and the verse came to him, "His banner over me is love."[504] Then they heard the angel Simeon[505] at the gate declare, "Blessed are those who washed their robes; that they may enter by the gate into the city, and may eat of the Tree of Life."[506]

Turk leaned over, and smiled as he said, "That means you three," and they all grinned.

As they moseyed their way through the resplendently vaulted pearl tunnel, Michael was taken with the lively atmosphere filled with music and the singsong chatter of all the people. It seemed impossible not to smile. He then stepped into the vast openness of Jerusalem.[507] His eyes were immediately struck with the city cube's recognizable pattern that ran around the perimeter.

Michael swirled about to see twelve pillars protruding from the side walls that encircled the great hall. As he looked up, Turk stated, "To him who overcomes, I will make a pillar in the temple of My God."[508] Michael noted that each pillar was made up of rows of suites that ascended to the top of the cube. It was perfectly designed to give balcony views of the center Throne from every vantage point. He could now see how each house of Israel had a pillar that rose from both sides of its gate, creating the vast lower seating. It then narrowed as it climbed toward the cube's middle height, and then greatly enlarged towards its upper reaches.

Michael saw that the higher the suites went up, the more they converged toward the center.[509] He realized that anyone looking down on the city would see the twelve-sided snowflake pattern where the family sections jutted in toward the cube's upper center.

Michael looked and saw the Throne stationed atop the Hill of the Lord at Jerusalem's center, which meant the entire city rose from its base. He quickly recognized the atrium effect, where all sides of the city focused on the Throne. He could also see that the great open aviary allowed for birds of every sort to fly freely throughout.

Michael was taken by the translucent gold that adorned all the structures both high and low. As he looked down, he smiled when he saw that the street actually was paved in gold.[510] He had always heard about it, but now he was seeing it with his own eyes. Each of them was moved, and Michael put his arms around them and kept moving forward.

After a time, Michael looked through the northern wall and beheld the Mount of Assembly reaching up to the sky. He then turned back around and saw Mount Sinai which also towered over the city. As he looked back and forth several times, he realized that the mountains served to create an intimate backdrop as though they were standing guard over the city.[511] The thought occurred to him that, from every direction, each person in Jerusalem had an incredible view.

Turk turned and faced them. "In a little while, we will meet up with our family group and be introduced by the Son to His Father and the angels. We are part of the spiritual house of Israel called Judah that is represented by our skin color of bronze. If you look out at the city right now, you can see the foundation stones that match the various skin colors. All you have to do is follow our color, which is up on the right. Feel free to roam about any place you desire.

As you can see, there are numerous amenities above and around you, whether dining, shopping or unlimited attractions. Oh, with the shopping, everything in Jerusalem belongs to you, so if you see something you want, consider it yours. Remember, you don't have to walk or fly if you don't want to, you can think yourself to any place you like, so, happy travels."

Deborah and Rachel headed off to the garment district. Michael decided he wanted to see the city from higher up, and together with Turk, soared northeast as the crow flies. Turk said, "I bet you would love Solomon's Porch. Interested?"

"Absolutely. Where's that?"

"It graces the ascent leading from Judah's gate to the Throne. It's our front yard, so to speak."

"Great, let's use some of that speed you talked about." At that they blazed across the lower landscape without difficulty, passing over magnificent terrain and structures before they pulled up.

"Woohoo! What was that, twelve seconds? We're flaming!" said Michael beaming.

Michael was immediately struck by two enormous angelic statues that stood boldly in the center of an adroitly designed complex. As they drew closer, Michael saw that the cherubim figures towered some one-hundred stories into the air. Both cherubs faced each other, their heads bowed and touching, and their wings spread out so that the tips of the wings of the one were touching the other at full extension. The length of their wings equaled the cherub's height.[512] All of it was made of transparent gold, so that Michael could actually see through it. As Michael alighted to the ground, he looked up and all but forgot to breath. It was as though the anointing and love that went into their craftsmanship conveyed itself directly to his heart. He had never before witnessed such beautiful workmanship.[513]

"Welcome to Solomon's Porch," said Turk in a subdued voice. Michael was then taken with two statues of majestic lions depicting the Tribe of Judah which stood nobly on pedestals to the right and left of the glorious pearl gate.[514] His vision climbed above the pearled gate where he viewed intricate carvings[515] of cherubim, palm trees, and flowers[516] that stretched all the way to the protruding suites that hung over their heads.

"Awesome! Unbelievable! I don't know what to say. It's so beautiful…" Michael collapsed on the grass, and turned his face toward the Throne. Then, to his amazement, as though his eyes raced across the landscape, he was suddenly before the Son, who turned, and said, "Greetings, Michael! I see you're enjoying Solomon's Porch. All of this has been prepared for you.[517] Welcome home. The adventures that lie before you will be spectacular and wondrous beyond your imagination. Welcome to the Inner Court."

"Thank you…" Feeling tongue-tied, he shared, "I'm so grateful. I just… it's all… Thank You."

In a moment, Michael's eyes refocused, and he was back with Turk. He could not help but say, "You didn't tell me that the old idea of sightseeing doesn't apply here. There is hardly anywhere I look that doesn't overwhelm me!"

"It gets easier. You learn to, how shall I put it, breathe it in and out. Amazing huh? Alright," primed Turk, "check this out. Each family has its own unique voice and expression when it comes to their gate and section. Judah's lead designer is Solomon who, as Scripture indicates, was given 'wisdom and very great discernment and breadth of mind, like the sand that is on the seashore.'[518]

"As you turn about, you will see that the carvings of the golden cherubim serve as the entry for Ascension Way. It weaves all the way around the Hill of the Lord, passing by each of the other family areas. You might remember that a number of Psalms were written as 'Songs of the Ascent.'[519] When anyone travels up the Way of Ascent, it is impossible not to be inspired to worship. Each of the tribes offers their own unique inspiration in this regard. For example, some offer singing and dancing, others drama and production. When the angels dance, you'll be astounded."

As they stood beneath the glorious cherubim, Michael looked to his left and right and estimated the width of the ascent between the cherubim's great feet as spanning some one-hundred yards. He smiled as the thought occurred to him that Ascension Way, which was paved with gold, might be thought of as the Yellow Brick Road. He then looked up the ascent and saw a colonnade of emerald pillars that were cut into the left landscape to support yet more lofty terraces. From high above, small waterfalls fell with elegant ease to pools below. Michael was left a bit choked up.

Turk paused before he continued, "Our house introduces the people to Ascension Way through Solomon's Porch. Solomon initiates the celebration by emphasizing God's glorious creation of both the plants and animals. You'll see wonderfully prepared verandas with such exotic plants as myrrh, cassia, saffron and nard, and also a spice garden with everything from cinnamon to cardamom.

"The Queen of Sheba once remarked, 'I have reached the myrrh-terraces. It is a glorious region of God's land.'[520] Wait until you smell the incense rising from the Hanging Garden Spas. When you lay back in the hot water with thousands of little bubbles rising about you, you'll feel *like you're in Heaven!*" And then he chuckled, but Michael just cocked his eyebrows and smirked. "Wait 'til you get out of the spa! It's like your skin is gilded with electrum. You'll be glistening. And then there's the fragrance of the myrrh; well, everyone will know where you've been, that's all I can say.

"That's just a tiny snippet of the pageant of blooming hills that greets you up the ascent. Ascension Way runs 1,500 miles in that direction, and then around the city, which makes for 6,000 miles of rapturous adventure and loving interaction, whether with activity, dining, or what have you. With the creative spirit of so many in play, by the time you finally finish the loop, much of it will be re-imagined and re-worked, making it impossible for it to become routine.

"What I think you'd really enjoy on Solomon's Porch is to view the vast array of diverse animals and birds and creeping things.[521] Don't think zoo with cages, although you will see habitats. They don't eat each other either. The lion has no problem lying down with the lamb.[522] Even so, these animals are up and about, interactive; you'll see."

Unexpectedly, they were interrupted by a group of children who all but tackled Michael as an honored hero. They all wanted to hug him, and be touched by him. Several shared that their family members came to faith because of him. During this, Michael knelt and fully embraced each one. It struck him how mature and well-spoken they were despite being in children's bodies. There were high-fives and jesting, and all were laughing as they went on their way. Michael just looked up at Turk who looked like a proud parent.

Michael and Turk took their time appreciating the exotic animals and creatures of every kind. Michael quipped,

"Any one of these creatures could have made a great pet back on earth. In fact, they redefine the meaning of pet. Some of them are so smart, they could have taken care of me. I would've been the pet!"

Turk just laughed. He thought to himself, *I love this kid. I never thought it would get to this point...*

Suddenly, in his memory, he was far away taking Babylon through the Bronze Mountains on his way to the Abyss.[523]

"What are you thinking Turkania?" decried Babylon. "That they will suddenly throw off their selfishness and become lovable? It's in their nature! They crave for power. It's everything they're about."

Turkania held onto Babylon's garment with his powerful vice-like grip, and retorted, "Do you actually believe your propaganda?" and squeezed Babylon's right shoulder that had been speared.

"Augh!"

"They say pain helps us rethink our arrogance. Any luck?" questioned Turkania.

"Are you telling me you think there's meaning to your service? You're as big a joke as the humans. Everything you give yourself to is for naught."

"The Almighty has a plan. It's been foretold."

"Don't give me that line. Tell me, I want to hear you say it, that you think you will actually come to trust a human; that one of them will be your friend! Tell me! Say it! I want to hear it!"

Turkania paused with uncertainty. It was the question he had never answered. For three millennia, he had skirted the issue. He had justified his indifference by assigning such questions to the civilian side of things. As a military officer, he did not have the luxury to care. Still, something in Babylon's question struck home, and he knew the pat answer would only bring ridicule and derision. This was his moment of truth.

As Turkania positioned Babylon over the Abyss, about to cast him in, he replied, "I believe I will call a human my friend. I will come to trust a human with my life."

At that Turkania cast Babylon toward a swirling black hole where he was caught and imprisoned in its infinite gravitational pull. As Babylon accelerated backward to its event horizon, he yelled, "It's all a waste, and you know it. I will see you again. Prepare yourself; you will feel my blade enter your body. I swear it!"

"Hey Turk, where'd you go?" asked Michael.

"Far away...far, far away," answered Turk. After pausing, he turned to Michael and asked ever so softly, "Kid, no... Michael, may I call you my friend?"

Michael replied intimately, "I would be honored. May I call you Turkania from time to time?"

"That you may."

29

THE KINGDOM PROMISES

*"There shall no longer be
any mourning, or crying, or pain"*
Revelation 21:4

Trumpets issued forth, resounding across the city from all directions, calling for the saints to assemble. Turk relished the welcome. "Oh, it's been a while since I've heard..." but his voice trailed off, his spirit being enraptured. With symphonic overtures, their melody captured the heart of every person, stopping all activity, pausing all conversation. Each person wanted only to listen, to savor the moment.

After the trumpeters concluded, Turk swallowed hard to collect himself. He turned to look at Michael and found him wiping his eyes. Turk replied quietly, "There's nothing like the clarion call of the Trumpets of Jerusalem. They announce the Year of Jubilee[524] when all debts are forgiven and all bondage is removed. You know, the word Jubilee actually means trumpets."

"They...I don't know how to say it, they reach all the way in..."

"I know," managed Turk, and then said, "Okay, let's gather to our seats."

After Turk led Michael to their places, Michael looked about and saw that every spot was filled. As he turned his head, he could see people his same shade of bronze extending up the rows, which then turned to balconies, extending far above their heads. He gazed about the great assembly and saw the multifarious coloring of every family as they depicted a glorious rainbow. Again he was awestruck with wonder. Turk put his arm around him and whispered, "Your sister is up on the left, and your mother higher up on the right."

Michael looked up, his eyes glancing across the people until he found Rachel smiling and waving, and he waved back. He did the same for his mom, and suddenly he realized that his thoughts could span the distance as well. *Mom, isn't this amazing?*

My favorite so far is the trumpets. With a brief pause, she said, *I just can't stop crying.*

It's freaking me out, too, he laughed.

Thank you so much for fighting for me. I am so grateful.

You're welcome, he responded humbly. *I love you.*

Michael's eyes focused on the Throne at the center of the great city cube with the four living creatures standing upon their great wheels. Their wings extended above their heads to form the Mercy Seat platform. Above them, the crystal expanse of His presence was shrouded at the moment by Gabriel. Between the four living creatures was the golden altar of incense with the coals of fire, from which the cherubim had anointed his lips. Above the expanse, the Father and Son were clothed in glory and arrayed in beauty. About the Throne, the seven pillars of fire burned brightly with the Spirit's presence. He noted that there was no longer a Cloud of Covering, so he could see Gabriel wrapping his wings about the expanse.

Turk leaned over and cautioned, "Get ready, Gabriel's about to pull his wings back. There's going to be an explosion of love, magnitudes greater than we experienced in the Stones of Fire. You have no idea." Michael gripped Turk's arm just as Gabriel withdrew with boldness, and love burst forth upon the assembly.

Feeling like he might pass out from ecstasy, he closed his eyes and breathed deeply. After a few moments, he began to adapt somewhat, at least enough to be present. Turk whispered, "I saw the Lord sitting on His Throne, high and lifted up, with the train of His robe filling the temple."[525] Michael immediately understood as he saw the rainbow configurations streaming from the Throne, which were like great ribbons floating carelessly on the wind. They were like an elegant train of a bride's gown.

Michael's eyes were taken with the ribbons wherein each time they touched one of the twelve pillars that entire section would explode with vivid brilliance. It was a color extravaganza. At least that's how he thought of it until one of the ribbons washed over his section and he was raptured in bliss. Instantly, his whole being became a conduit of love, and his bronze hue ignited with the most gleaming and dazzling light imaginable. His whole section broke into cheers, and immediately stood up hoping for the next go around. This went on for some time as the rainbow ribbons expanded and multiplied, filling the entire hall, until there was unbridled brilliance and unrestrained glory emanating from the whole of the assembly. The cheers turned to worship, with every hand raised, every mouth speaking ecstatic utterances, and every body radiating the luminescence of His love.

Then the Son stepped forward, His eyes a flame of fire.[526] The brilliance of His gaze turned about in every direction, allowing Him to speak to both the corporate body and each individual simultaneously. Michael found it incredibly intimate.

"Welcome, each of you, to Jerusalem, the City of Peace. Twenty-two days ago, you were asleep in waiting and now you have been welcomed into the Inner Court." At that He paused, and being so moved with emotion, lifted His hand to His face. His compassion rippled across the assembly and up the pillars as He collected Himself.

"I often feel these emotions, but as I stand before you now, they are at a crescendo. Maybe I'm the one who'll be smiling for a week. If you think you feel overwhelmed, I'm center-stage receiving all your love, and I can tell you, it's overpowering."

Jesus continued to elaborate, "As you can see there are twelve great banners under which you are assembled. Each of you is part of one of the twelve spiritual tribes of Israel. Your family groups are made up of angels, Old Testament Saints, and New Testament Saints. At the head of each house, there are three overseers. First, there is the angel who bears your family name.[527] I would like each of you to stand." At that, Michael recognized the angel Judah, who was several seats away, as he stood up in all his glory, his wings unfurled. Judah bowed his head in appreciation of the remarkable ovation.

"The next overseers are represented by twelve of the twenty-four elders, who you know and love so well. Would you please stand?" Michael looked to his right again and saw David stand and lift his arms graciously.

"The final overseers are made up of My apostles, My friends and co-laborers. Would you please stand?"

Michael saw a man stand on the other side of Judah, and as fast as the question formed, the answer came---he was John the Apostle. "Oh my," was all Michael could utter. He looked at Turk, and without words, said, "What a team!"

Jesus continued, "You will discover that each of them will use their ministerial oversight to your great benefit. Underneath their care, you will be released to fully express your latent gifts.[528] There are many facets of love, and you will uniquely shine forth as a diamond for the benefit of both your house and this great assembly. Heaven is a place where your contribution is greatly valued. As you will come to appreciate, there are many members, but one body, with each part being vital to make up the whole."[529]

And turning to the Tribe of Benjamin, Jesus said, "Let me ask Paul the Apostle, what is it that you said in this regard?"

Michael looked straight ahead to the pillar directly across the assembly and saw the Apostle Paul stand, and raise his voice saying, "For we are His workmanship, created in Christ Jesus for good works, which God prepared beforehand that we should walk in them."[530]

Michael turned to Turk and whispered, "So each of us has a part to play! I'm amazed that I could hear that." Turk just smiled.

Jesus continued, "It is time for Me to express Our gratefulness to each of you. Your humble willingness to freely receive Our love, and to offer it freely to your neighbor is the Royal Law of Heaven. There is nothing more precious, more treasured, than the gift of love freely given.

"At this time, I will be dividing each of your family groups into smaller units, so that I can reward[531] you individually with My promised gifts. Obviously, there are many millions of you who make up your house, but you will see that as I honor large numbers of you individually, the others who know you will be fully involved. Then, as I honor them, you'll be sharing in their celebration as well."

Jesus then walked to the side of the platform, and with His eyes ablaze, began speaking through the Spirit with countless individuals, and their loved ones who looked on.

Suddenly, Jesus stood before Michael. As though he were the only one, Jesus said, "Michael, you are My friend.[532] You did not choose Me, but I chose you, and appointed you, that you should go and bear fruit, and that your fruit should remain, that whatever you ask the Father in My name, He may give to you."[533]

Jesus then turned and extended His hand, at which time, Gabriel arrived with a piece of fruit taken from the Tree of Life. With a long look shared between the two of them, Jesus turned and said to millions simultaneously, and to Michael individually, "Michael, here is My gift to you, the fruit of the Tree of Life, take and eat."[534] At that Jesus extended His hand and Michael grasped hold of the fruit.[535]

Insight flooded over Michael as he realized he was about to take his first bite of immortality. Staring at the fruit in his hand, his innermost being trembled and he almost collapsed for joy. As he lifted it to his mouth, he felt the presence of his family and loved ones all about him, and then he took his first bite. For the briefest of moments, he considered its culinary attributes, until love shot through him like bolts of lightning. Every cell in his being was filled with the glory of love, and he began radiating with great brilliance. Everyone around him shouted and cheered at the spectacle. Before he could finish the fruit, his eyes were fully transfixed on the Son, where in perfect communion, they leaned together, forehead to forehead.

After they pulled back, Jesus said, "To you Michael, I give the crown of life.[536] You will never be hurt by the Second Death.[537] As Michael bowed his head, Jesus placed an exquisitely jeweled crown upon his head. Michael immediately felt the physical sensation of authority being bestowed upon him, and he was deeply humbled.

"Michael, I also give to you some of the hidden manna.[538] This will bring healing for all of your memories in the wilderness, where every fear will forever be done away with in My love." At that, Michael opened his mouth, and Jesus placed on his tongue the manna of love. In a moment, love rushed upon every memory, reinterpreting them with grace and triumph, and removing all shame.

Jesus extended His hand, and said, "Michael, to you I give the White Stone which bears your new name, which only We will know, for it is a name of intimacy.[539] In our most cherished times on the Mount of Assembly, I will call you by name, for you are Mine. This is the name I have given you, which means 'one who lays down his life.'" Michael looked down, and holding the stone close, turned it over and read his new name. Again he felt the trembling sensation start to take hold.

Jesus drew Himself closer in, taking Michael's right shoulder in His left hand, and bringing His face to his right ear. His voice, unrushed and engaging, questioned, "Michael, what ministry would your heart desire? What would you most enjoy being a part of?"

Suddenly, Michael's heart returned to something Turk had talked about, the Writings of Truth, which foretell all future events.[540] "I would like to work with the Writings of Truth and the Scriptures to serve people in accordance with Your will."

"Then you shall, for to you it has been determined,

you will serve under Elijah the prophet as his liaison to the 144,000 witnesses in the days to come.[541] You shall go to and fro from My temple, bearing news as My messenger. Stand tall, and let Me introduce you to My Father and His angels!"[542]

At that Michael straightened, his body permeating with love, his head crowned in glory, his memories healed, and his calling secure. Jesus turned to His Father and privately introduced Michael by his new name. Then to all, He declared, "You have seen his valor on the Wall of Love. You have witnessed his bravery on the Crystal Sea. You have seen him fall and you have seen him rise. Well done, My good and faithful servant, with whom I am well pleased. You were faithful with a few things, I will put you in charge of many things; enter into the joy of your Lord!"[543]

EPILOGUE

Turk, Michael and Damien stood watching over the festivities and merriment. They were regally dressed in formal attire, showing forth their resplendent state. Michael's demeanor communicated a new aura of sophistication and maturity. From the moment he had received his commission, his heart had changed to become more focused, more serious.

While relishing in the jubilation of the celebrating saints, Turk interjected soberly, "I'm afraid our time to play is limited. We are needed. The world has come to the brink. All authority and power are coalescing to the Antichrist as we speak. The hair-trigger that was poised over the Middle East has been pulled. Nation is rising against nation, and kingdom against kingdom. Soon the world will be in full travail.[544] In just ten days, the Antichrist will be given emergency powers, and he will decidedly end the Middle East War with a nuclear barrage.[545] Soon he will sign the Seven Year Treaty with Israel.[546] The Tribulation countdown has begun. Time is short. Tomorrow, we will go down to Earth and deploy as a three-man infiltration team."

"Three-man?!" retorted Michael, crooking his neck deliberately to the right. He gave Damien an inquisitive look.

Damien responded, "I requested my assignment to be with you. I couldn't let you have all the fun."

"Welcome aboard," returned Michael simply, his demeanor exuding trust.

*   *   *

After enjoying some delicious Cornish hen with all the fixings, Michael felt a messenger tapping him on the shoulder. He was being summoned to rendezvous with Elijah the Prophet at his private quarters. As Michael headed over, he felt a bit jittery at the prospect of working alongside Elijah, sensing him to be somewhat eccentric. When he arrived, Elijah was waiting.

"Gates! Good, you're here," said Elijah in his throaty, commanding voice. Michael took note of his weather-beaten face with his penetrating gray eyes and beaklike nose. His long frizzy white hair was unkempt, his clothing disheveled, and his sheepskin vest torn. Michael smelled something a tad pungent, but before he could bury the thought, Elijah just garuumphed.

Elijah then eyeballed Michael and appraised, "Spry enough. You'll be in the middle of it. Fire and blood son, so listen up. Can't have you being some neophyte down in that grisly hell-hole.

"When you're on my team, you're a free thinker. Trust your instincts. I'm not sending you in to clean up the dregs and vermin. Copy? No nickel-and-dime assignments. Mission-worthy only, use your head. Souls are dangling precariously. I need you to flesh out the big picture. Belay that, the Writings will key you in. Just avoid doing things other people can do. Do it once, hand it off. You're to go here and there. Keep moving. Others will settle in, not you."

Michael was having a hard time not looking bug-eyed. Elijah's rapid-fire, manic mannerisms, and back and forth pacing, unnerved him. Elijah seemed somewhat unglued, though not explicitly. Several times, Michael found himself backing up to get out of his way, while trying to focus intently on what he was saying. Elijah's passionate tone and high-strung quirkiness left Michael off-balance, and on the edge.

Michael's thoughts fixated on Elijah's torn vest, and as he pondered *what a little command it would take...* Elijah wheeled about and sputtered, "Come on Gates, get your mind in the game! Turkania will show you the ABC's of clandestine incursions.

"The Book of Truth is going to make you privy to events before they happen. It'll take some getting used to, living through the very events you've already seen. The important thing - mum's the word. 'Talk about it, change it'; that's my motto.

"Rule number one, no fraternization with the girl. No sordid affections! Don't make me come down before my time! I did not like what I saw. Got it? Shoot. See that, by talking about it, I've changed it." Elijah gave him a baleful look, and repeated himself, "Stay emotionally detached, no friskiness. She's going to see you, what were her words, 'as a whole lot of happy.' Copy? Keep your distance."

"Yes, sir," responded Michael, though he was entirely

baffled as to what he was talking about.

Elijah lumbered over to the transparent outer wall. "Come over here. Take a good look at the Mount of Assembly. You're going to spend a lot of time there."

Michael strode to the wall, and before following Elijah's gaze up the face of Mount Zion, he looked down and was briefly unsettled that they were miles above the ground. After refocusing forward, he felt his eyes were tricking him. He quickly realized that unlike Mount Sinai's stateliness that was fixed and unchanging, Mount Zion's radiating landscape seemed to be in flux. Like lava that slowly descends, so Zion's land and foliage appeared to be drifting down ever so gradually toward its base.[547] When Michael asked about it, he realized that the Father's creative persona is constantly renewing the surrounding panoramas so they are brimming with new life. He smiled with expectancy.

"Within Zion's interior, the Mount of Assembly is ever changing as well," interjected Elijah flatly. "It's astonishing, I give you that. I've asked you to join me, because I need to take you to the Inner Sanctum, and introduce you to the Hall of Truth. Let's get over there."

In a split second, they arrived at a long translucent hallway that bore not sculpted Seraphim, but live Warrior Sentries standing at the ready. Their swords extended down from their hands, touching the ground between their feet. "This is as far as anyone can transport themselves," Elijah commented. "And few ever get this far."

Elijah pressed forward with his unbalanced stride, their footsteps echoing down the corridor. "Lickety-split, Gates, keep up," he harangued. He paused deliberately before the hallowed entry, and turning to face Michael, he fixed his gaze upon him. He then took hold of Michael's arm and squeezed it as if to say, 'Don't cross this line flippantly.'

Elijah entered into one of the Inner Sanctum's of the Holy of Holies. Michael followed behind as they moved to the right. As they were doing so, he noted that on the other side of the room there were three golden pedestals with the Great White Throne books sitting on top of each.[548]

Elijah stepped forward to the Table of Truth, and motioned for Michael to draw near. "Before we look into the Writings, I'm to entrust the Stones of Truth to your keeping." Michael sensed a distinct change in Elijah's temperament and tone. He was more subdued, more reverent. He then watched as Elijah stretched out his knobby-fingered hands and pulled back the lid of a small rectangular box made of hand-carved acacia wood.[549] Inside, he saw two glimmering oval stones, each one-and-a-half inches long, resting in their furrows.

In a quiet but serious tone, Elijah said, "These are the Stones of Truth, the Urim and Thummim.[550] When anyone with a righteous heart asks a *yes* or *no* question, these stones will give an answer." Elijah drew out the stones from the ornate box, and swiveled carefully to face Michael. Holding them out before him, he asked, "Am I to consign these stones to Michael?" Instantly, both stones illuminated, and Elijah carefully handed them over.

Michael gasped slightly.

"There you go. Practice. It'll take days before you're skilled enough to use them instinctually. Keep them safe. Keep them hidden. They'll guide your path. You'll know when to turn right, left, do this, do that. These stones have raised up kings, and led armies into battle.[551] Guard them. There isn't a soul alive who wouldn't crave their power. Do you understand?"

"Yes, sir," he responded soberly.

Elijah shifted back and extended his hand, as he tentatively said, "Alright, you have the Stones of Truth, now let's look into the Writings of Truth." He slowly lifted the book's large cover and the light of a thousand candles burst forth. Then as if gravity took hold, the light pulled back and became a swirling vortex that descended into its pages. Elijah stood back and said to Michael, "Come, look into the book, and see what will transpire. Please know, it is highly possible for your actions to change the events as you see them. That can be good or bad. Take caution."

Michael took an uneasy step forward, and looking down, found himself peering into the churning vastness of time. Within the spinning whirlpool, faces and images materialized – his father appearing haggard, the landscape of the earth being forlorn and bleak, the moon showing like blood.[552]

The scene shifted and he beheld a beautiful young woman, with her wiry auburn hair pulled back, who seemed panic stricken. She was looking away, when suddenly she turned and stared directly into his eyes, "Michael, where are you? Where *are* you?" she cried in desperation. Michael swallowed hard, and muttered, "Katie?"

Ominously, the image darkened, and there appeared the four horsemen of the Apocalypse driving their beasts, their hooves thundering with malice and spite. Michael beheld them storming forth to kill a quarter of the earth with sword, famine, pestilence and wild beast. As he looked on in horror, behold, Death was trampling on to reap a stern reckoning, and the dark clouds of Hades followed after him.[553]

ACKNOWLEDGEMENTS

I would like to express my profound gratitude to several people for their valued contributions. To Drew Berding, my close friend, for your unswerving enthusiasm and keen editorial eye. To Kim, my loving wife – beyond your skilled editorial prowess, which is considerable, your belief in this book has been life-giving. You both are amazing! Other generous thanks go out to Florentine Cobb, Lauren Orlowski, James Edgar, and Natasha Bartinelli.

Dr. David Orlowski, D-Min, LPC, is doctorally trained in both theology (King's University) and psychology (Northcentral University). He received his Masters of Divinity from Fuller Theological Seminary. He has served as a senior pastor for 15 years, and is a Licensed Professional Counselor. David, age 50, is married to Kim, and is the father of five grown children Rich, daughter-in-law Khristy, Tyler, daughter-in-law Erin, Mark, Lauren and Macy, and three grandchildren, Anne, Josh and Brian.

THE FEASTS OF ISRAEL

SPRING FEASTS (Fulfilled)			SUMMER FEAST (Fulfilled)
Passover	Unleavened Bread	First Fruits	Pentecost
Blood on Door-posts	Purging of Leaven	Wave Offering Of Sheaf Of Barley	Wave Offering Of Wheat Loaves and Sacrifices
Jesus Becomes our Passover; His Blood Shed	Jesus' Love Cleans Out the Leaven of Our Pride or Sin	Jesus and Old Testament Saints Raised as First Fruits at Barley Harvest (1st Resurrection)	Jesus Gives the Spirit to Prepare Us for Future Wheat Harvest
1st Month, 14th Day (March/April) Lev 23:5 Based on Sacred Calendar	1st Month, 15th Day for 7 days Lev 23:6-8	1st Month, The Day After the Sabbath	50 days After the First Fruits Feast

FALL
FEASTS
(Twenty-Two Days yet to be fulfilled)

Day 1-9	Day 10	Day 15-22
Feast Of Trumpets Rosh Hashanah	Day of Atonement Yom Kippur	Feast of Tabernacles (Booths)
Trumpet Blown for the Ingathering Rev 4	Atonement made by Lamb of God – Rev 5	Revisit Wilderness Wanderings and Reconcile
Jesus Brings in the Wheat Harvest (Rapture) and Start of 22 Days – Rev 5. Jubilee – All debts forgiven	Jesus is Presented as the Slain Lamb – Rev 6	Jesus unites Humanity by Calling for Forgiveness thru His Love
7th Month (late Sept each year), 1st Day Lev 23:23-25. First Month based on Civil Calendar	7th Month, 10th Day Lev 23:26-32 It is a Sabbath	7th Month, 15th to 21st day. Then Holy Convocation on 22nd Day Lev 23:36

ENDNOTES

CHAPTER 2
1 Ephod: Exodus 28:4-29:5;
  I Samuel 2:18; II Samuel 6:14
2 Isaiah 26:19
3 Psalms 139:16
4 Hebrews 1:14
5 John 1:51; Genesis 28:12, 16, 17
6 II Peter 3:8; Psalm 90:4
7 I Thessalonians 4:15;
  Revelation 4:1; 14:14-16
8 I Corinthians 15:18;
  Acts 7:60; 13:36; 11:30
9 I Corinthians 15:20
10 John 11:11-14
11 I Samuel 28:15
12 Daniel 12:2; I Samuel 28:15;
  John 11:11,14; Matthew stated
  emphatically, "many bodies of the
  saints who had fallen asleep were
  raised, Matthew 27:52
13 I Corinthians 15:51-52
14 I Thessalonians 4:14-15
15 I Thessalonians 5:10
16 Ephesians 5:14
17 I Peter 1:5, 7, 13. Please note that our
  inheritance is reserved in Heaven,
  and will be revealed at the last time,
  at the revelation of Christ.
18 Revelation 4:1; Most theologians
  agree that this is a rapture text
19 Matthew 13:30, 39; Revelation 14:14-
  16; Ruth 2:21-23 alludes to the two
  harvests, the Barley Harvest at the
  time of Christ's resurrection, and the
  Wheat Harvest or rapture.
20 Hebrews 12:1
21 I Thessalonians 4:17;   I
  Corinthians 15:52

CHAPTER 3
22 Revelation 4:1; 14:14-16
23 Matthew 27:52
24 I Thessalonians 4:17;
  Revelation 11:12
25 Revelation 1:13-15
26 Revelation 14:14
27 Revelation 14:15
28 Daniel 12:2, 13
29 John 11:11
  If Jesus was born in 5BC or 6BC as
  Herod feared (Mt 2:16), then the

Harvest would theoretically occur
in 9/2021 or 9/2022. As Matthew
24:36 states, no one knows the day
or the hour, so this recalibration
of the calendar is offered as
a prognostication based on a
millennial theology viewpoint.
30 John 11:25
31 John 15:13
32 Revelation 1:14
33 Genesis 28:12
34 Isaiah 14:13-14; 41:25
35 Rosh means 'Head,' Ha means 'the,'
  and shanah means 'year.' Head-of-
  the year, or new year.
36 Exodus 31:17; Genesis 2:2-3;
  Exodus 20:11
37 II Peter 3:8; Psalm 90:4
38 Revelation 20:4-6
39 Daniel 12:13; Ephesians 4:7-10. The
  end of the age occurred when Daniel,
  along with the Old Testament saints
  were resurrected with Christ and
  were taken up into Heaven. See also,
  Hebrews 9:26 where Christ put away
  sin at the"consumption of the ages."
40 Daniel 12:4; Matthew 24:36;
  Revelation 22:10

CHAPTER 4
41 Revelation 21:19-20; Ezekiel 1:28
42 Joel 2:3
43 Exodus 19:2
44 Ezekiel 28:16, 18
45 Revelation 22:2; Genesis 1:11
46 I Samuel 17:4
47 Matthew 14:15-21
48 John 20:29; Psalm 30:7; Isaiah 54;8;
  57:17-18; Ezekiel 39:23-26
49 Romans 1:17; 3:21-22; 4:1-8
50 I Corinthians 15:39-40
51 Romans 8:19

CHAPTER 5
52 1 Peter 5:5
53 Psalms 68:15-18
54 Revelation 4:6; 15:2
55 Revelation 14:1; Psalm 125:1;
  Hebrews 12:22
56 I Corinthians 15:53-54
57 I Corinthians 15:50

58 Exodus 33; Hebrews 8, 9;
Romans 12:1
59 Exodus 25, 26, 27
60 Hebrews 8:5 and Hebrews 9:23.
61 John 1:29, 36
62 Revelation 22:5; Isaiah 60:19;
Revelation 21:23
63 II Corinthians 12:2-4
64 I John 2:16
65 Revelation 4:1; I Thessalonians 4:16-
17; I Corinthians 15:52; John 5:28

CHAPTER 6
66 Acts 10:9-16; Mark 7:18-19
67 Exodus 19:12
68 Exodus 17:15
69 Revelation 4:6; 7:9; 15:2
70 Ephesians 4:8; I Peter 3:18-20;
Colossians 2:15; Isaiah 61:1
71 Peter 3:19-20; Ephesians 4:8-10;
Romans 10:6-7. Two harvests were
denoted in Scripture: the Barley
Harvest and the Wheat Harvest.
The O.T. saints were taken up in the
Barley Harvest as noted, whereas
the N.T. saints in the Wheat Harvest.
Note Ruth 2:21,23
72 Revelation 4:5; 11:19; 16:18
73 Ezekiel 1:24 says the sound of their
wings is like the sound of tumult,
suggesting they are of great size
74 Ezekiel 10:14, 21
75 Revelation 4:7
76 Ezekiel 1:20; 10:17
77 Ezekiel 1:18; 10:12; Revelation 4:6
78 Ezekiel 10:5
79 Ezekiel 1:13; Hebrews 9:4
80 Ezekiel 1:13; Revelation 4:5; 11:19;
16:18
81 Ezekiel 1:22
82 Ezekiel 28:14, 16; Exodus 25:20
83 Revelation 4:5; 1:4
84 I Corinthians 2:11; Isaiah 11:2
85 Revelation 14:3
86 Exodus 19:9; 24:15-16
87 Daniel 7:9, 13; Exodus 24:9-11
88 Daniel 7:9
89 Ezekiel 1:27
90 Psalms 139:16
91 I Corinthians 2:9
92 Jeremiah 29:11
93 Luke 14:8-11

CHAPTER 7
94 Luke 14:8-11
95 Daniel 10:21
96 II Corinthians 4:17
97 Revelation 1:10; 4:2
98 Revelation 4:8; Isaiah 6:3
99 Revelation 5:9, 12
100 Revelation 4:11
101 Daniel 10:18-19; Luke 22:43
102 Psalm 56:8
103 Genesis 1:3
104 Genesis 1:2
105 Proverbs 8:30
106 Isaiah 11:2; John 1:14
107 Colossians 1:15-17; John 1:1-3
108 Proverbs 8:22-31
109 John 1:1-3; Colossians 1:16
110 Genesis 1:2
111 Ezekiel 43:2; Revelation 1:15; 19:6
112 David Crowder
113 Psalms 19:1-2
114 I Corinthians 15:28
115 Job 41:1-34
116 Job 41:33-34
117 I Corinthians 2:9

CHAPTER 8
118 Leviticus 23:32
119 Romans 8:26
120 Isaiah 35:3-4
121 Revelation 15:2
122 Exodus 30:10
123 Leviticus 23:29
124 Daniel 7:9
125 Isaiah 2:9-12
126 Daniel 12:10
127 Psalm 141:2; Revelation 5:8; 8:3-4
128 Revelation 5:1
129 Revelation 5:2
130 Ephesians 2:8-9
131 Revelation 4:5
132 I Corinthians 2:10; Psalm 139:1, 23;
Jeremiah 17:10
133 Acts 2:3
134 Romans 2:1
135 Acts 17:27
136 I John 4:19; John 15:9-10
137 Revelation 5:3; Romans 3:23
138 Zechariah 12:10; Revelation 5:4
139 Revelation 5:5

CHAPTER 9
140 Revelation 5:6
141 Matthew 20:30-31
142 Matthew 20:32-33
143 Zechariah 9:9
144 Matthew 21:9
145 Zechariah 11:12-13; Matthew 27:3
146 Matthew 26:29
147 Isaiah 53:3-4
148 John 19:5
149 Matthew 27:54
150 Revelation 5:13
151 Philippians 2:10-11; Isaiah 45:23;
Romans 14:11
152 Darlene Zschech, Hill Songs,
Shout to the Lord

CHAPTER 10
153 Psalm 29:3
154 Psalm 29:11
155 Psalm 29:9
156 Psalm 24:7
157 Isaiah 42:1-4; Matthew 12:18-21
158 Psalm 91:14
159 Daniel 7:14
160 Revelation 1:12-16
161 Isaiah 61:1-2; Luke 4:18
162 Revelation 5:8, 8:3-4
163 Revelation 5:9-10

CHAPTER 11
164 Revelation 6:2
165 Revelation 6:4
166 Revelation 6:4
167 Revelation 6:6
168 Revelation 6:8
169 Revelation 14:20
170 Revelation 6:7-8
171 Revelation 5:12-13
172 Revelation 5:14
173 Psalm 110:1

CHAPTER 12
174 Matthew 19:28; Revelation 4:4
175 1 Corinthians 15:9
176 John 6:8
177 Hebrews 13:5
178 Matthew 10:16-27
179 Luke 22:32

CHAPTER 13
180 II Chronicles 6:1

181 Revelation 10:1; 19:17
182 Isaiah 2:12; 5:15
183 Leviticus 23:23-44
184 Leviticus 23:26-32; John 14:31
185 Revelation 2:11; 20:6,14; 21:8
186 Matthew 10:28; Luke 12:4-5; Hell
or Gehenna - def. place of fire, or
Lake of Fire. O.T. cites children were
sacrificed by fire to false gods
187 Genesis 4:2-15
188 Genesis 4:14
189 Ecclesiastes 1:14
190 Revelation 21:4
191 Hosea 6:7; I Corinthians 15:21,22;
Romans 5:14; Joshua 3:16 (allegorical
reference)

CHAPTER 14
192 Matthew 27:46; Hebrews 2:18; 4:15
193 Revelation 3:20
194 Hebrews 13:5
195 Job 1:8; Job 2:3
196 Genesis 10:20-23; both Job and
Abraham were of the line of
Shem through Aram (Uz) and
Arpachshad respectively
197 Job 1:1
198 Job 1:6
199 Ezekiel 28:18
200 Job 1:7
201 Job 1:12
202 Daniel 4:17
203 Job 3:25
204 Job 1:21
205 I Kings 18:28
206 Job 2:6
207 Job 4:13
208 Job 4:15
209 Job 4:17-21
210 Job 4:18-21
211 Job 34:14-15
212 Job 31:35
213 Job 38:1
214 Job 40:4
215 Isaiah 53:7; Matthew 12:39
216 Isaiah 55:1; Revelation 3:18;
Hosea 14:4
217 Romans 3:23

CHAPTER 15
218 Revelation 5:4
219 Matthew 10:8

220 Genesis 15:6; Romans 4:3
221 Genesis 15:5
222 Genesis 17:17; 18:12
223 Genesis 17:17; 21:7
224 Genesis 22:2
225 Romans 4:18
226 Genesis 22:5
227 Genesis 22:8
228 Genesis 22:12
229 Hebrews 11:10
230 I Chronicles 21:16
231 I Chronicles 21:14
232 I Chronicles 21:26
233 II Chronicles 7:1-3
234 John 19:30
235 I Corinthians 6:19
236 Romans 9:7,8
237 Hebrews 4:1

CHAPTER 16
238 Matthew 14:30
239 Matthew 8:29
240 John 14:6
241 I John 4:8,16

CHAPTER 17
242 II Corinthians 3:7; Exodus 34:29-30
243 Numbers 12:3
244 Revelation 5:9
245 Genesis 15:13
246 Exodus 3:2
247 Ecclesiastes 2:17
248 Psalm 42:7
249 Exodus 14:29
250 I Corinthians 2:9
251 Joshua 5:3; Jeremiah 4:4;
    Deuteronomy 30:6
252 I John 4:18

CHAPTER 18
253 Daniel 4:17; Job 1:12; 2:6
254 Revelation 3:19; Hebrews 12:7-11
255 II Corinthians 4:17
256 Luke 19:48
257 Romans 1:20
258 Romans 8:32; I Corinthians 2:12;
    Matthew 10:8
259 James 2:8
260 I Corinthians 13:7
261 I Peter 4:8
262 Leviticus 18:6-19
263 Matthew 5:25

264 Matthew 5:26
265 Isaiah 42:20
266 II Kings 6:17
267 Luke 4:18
268 Genesis 44:1
269 Exodus 16:18, 21
270 Judges 7:13
271 I Samuel 21:6
272 I Kings 17:6
273 John 6:41
274 Luke 16:31
275 Greek word "ptoochos" (NT:4434
    which is translated "beggar" or
    "poor man" in Luke 16:20 & 22 in
    this story of Lazarus and the rich
    man) is the identical word that Jesus
    used in the Beatitudes in Matthew
    5:3 where he said, "Blessed are the
    poor in spirit."
276 Luke 16:19-31
277 John 12:9-11
278 Hebrews 6:19
279 John 11:35
280 John 11:6
281 John 11:35-36; Job 30:25;
    Luke 19:41-42
282 Luke 18:17
283 Matthew 10:39
284 Matthew 16:26
285 Matthew 13:45-46
286 Matthew 13:44

CHAPTER 19
287 Matthew 13:24-30; 37-43
288 Matthew 13:41
289 Leviticus 23:36
290 Matthew 13:48
291 Matthew 13:47-50
292 Revelation 5:9
293 Matthew 13:49
294 Matthew 22:9-14
295 Matthew 22:10
296 Matthew 22:12
297 Matthew 22:13
298 Matthew 25:31-33
299 Matthew 25:34
300 Matthew 5:26; Luke 12:59
301 Revelation 20:11-15
302 John 3:16; II Corinthians 4:3;   II
    Peter 3:9
303 Revelation 20:14
304 John 1:29; Romans 11:32. Please

note that some people will be
removed on Day 10, the Day of
Atonement, who are unwilling to
humble themselves per Lev 23:29.
305 Romans 3:19-20
306 Acts 8:23
307 Hebrews 4:15
308 Romans 8:26-27
309 Joshua 24:15
310 Luke 4:18
311 Matthew 6:15
312 John 14:27
313 John 15:11
314 Exodus 12:7,13
315 Acts 10:2,34-35
316 Matthew 24:48-51, Luke 12:42-48
317 Daniel 12:10
318 Leviticus 23:22, 19:9-10
319 Matthew 5:23-24
320 Romans 12:18
321 Matthew 5:25-26; 18:34
322 Matthew 6:9-13

CHAPTER 20
323 Leviticus 23:37; Acts 7:23; I
Corinthians 2:16; Hebrews 10:16
324 Leviticus 23:36; Luke 17:4;
Mark 11:25
325 Luke 20:34-36
326 Ephesians 5:32
327 Luke 6:39
328 Matthew 7:3-5; Luke 6:41-42

CHAPTER 21
329 Leviticus 23:40
330 Matthew 10:34-37
331 I John 4:19
332 Matthew 10:40
333 Matthew 19:26

CHAPTER 22
334 Romans 8:31,33
335 Numbers 16:2
336 Exodus 19:12
337 Ephesians 4:8
338 Exodus 17:3
339 Isaiah 6:1
340 Revelation 3:15-18; Isaiah 55:1
341 Ezekiel 28:14, 16
342 Jeremiah 4:4; Deuteronomy 10:16;
30:6; Romans 2:28-29
343 Psalms 66:10,12

344 Mark 9:47-49; Isaiah 43:2; Numbers
31:23
345 Luke 3:16; Matthew 3:11
346 Daniel 3:19-27
347 I Corinthians 3:12-15
348 I Corinthians 15:50
349 Ezekiel 28:12
350 Ezekiel 28:13
351 Ezekiel 28:13
352 Ezekiel 28:13-14
353 Isaiah 14:12
354 Matthew 22:30
355 Ezekiel 28:16
356 Ezekiel 28:17
357 Ezekiel 28:15; Judges 16:20;
Isaiah 42:25
358 Ezekiel 28:13; John 8:44;
Genesis 3:1-4
359 Hebrews 1:14
360 John 8:44
361 Ezekiel 28:16
362 Ezekiel 28:18; Job 30:19; Malachi 4:3
363 Genesis 2:17
364 Revelation 20:3; 9:2
365 Isaiah 35:8-10
366 Luke 24:32

CHAPTER 23
367 Romans 10:2
368 John 2:24-25; 6:15; Matthew 22:18
369 Matthew 20:1-16
370 Matthew 19:29
371 Matthew 10:42
372 I Corinthians 10:13
373 Joel 2:32; Obadiah 17; Zechariah 2:7;
II Timothy 2:26; Jonah 4:2
374 Romans 2:3; II Corinthians 5:20;
Ephesians 6:20
375 Acts 5:4
376 Matthew 13:30,38-40
377 Matthew 13:48-49
378 Matthew 22:11-12
379 Matthew 25:31-33
380 I Corinthians 9:22
381 John 5:25
382 I Peter 3:19
383 I Peter 4:6
384 John 1:29
385 Acts 17:30; Acts 3:17; Hebrews 9:7
386 I Corinthians 2:7; Ephesians 3:9;
Colossians 1:26
387 I Corinthians 10:13

388 Deuteronomy 30:6
389 Matthew 16:17
390 Matthew 18:21-22
391 Luke 13:28; Psalm 112:10; Matthew 8:12; 13:42; 13:50; 22:13; 24:51; 25:30
392 Job 16:9; Psalm 35:16; 37:12; Acts 7:54
393 Isaiah 66:24; Mark 9:48
394 Matthew 25:29; 13:12; Luke 8:18
395 Matthew 5:26
396 I Samuel 2:6-9; Psalm 107: 10-16
397 Mark 2:17
398 Zephaniah 1:17; Lamentations 3:2,6; Exodus 10:21-22
399 Joel 2:3; otherwise it's a thick darkness - Jude 1:6,13
400 Luke 1:78-79
401 Exodus 10:23; Also, "But the wicked ones are silenced in darkness," I Samuel 2:9
402 John 1:5-9; 3:19-21; 12:35-36
403 Joel 2:2-3; Psalm 68:6
404 Jeremiah 13:17
405 1 John 2:2
406 Psalm 107:10-16
407 Revelation 20:11
408 Revelation 20:1
409 Revelation 20:13
410 Revelation 20:13
411 Revelation 20:12
412 Matthew 10:8; Hosea 14:4; Romans 8:32; 1 Corinthians 2:12; Ephesians 1:6
413 Revelation 20:14; Exodus 32:33
414 Philippians 2:10; Revelation 5:3,13
415 Revelation 20:15
416 I Peter 3:18-20; Isaiah 24:21-22
417 John 3:16; Romans 6:23
418 Revelation 20:14-15
419 II Peter 2:22
420 Judges 17:6; 21:25; Romans 2:14-15
421 Luke 6:38
422 Matthew 18:35

CHAPTER 24
423 Matthew 25:29
424 Matthew 8:29
425 Luke 16:26

CHAPTER 25
426 Isaiah 6:3
427 Isaiah 6:5
428 Isaiah 6:6

429 Isaiah 6:6-7
430 Isaiah 6:8
431 Luke 12:11-12
432 Joel 3:9-17
433 Luke 12:2,3
434 Joel 2:1-2
435 Joel 1:10-15
436 Joel 2:12-13
437 Joel 2:4-9
438 Joel 2:17
439 Acts 2:2
440 Esther 1:8

CHAPTER 26
441 Revelation 15:8
442 I John 4:16
443 II Peter 3:5; Jude 1:18
444 Isaiah 55:12

CHAPTER 27
445 Genesis 50:20
446 Romans 8:28
447 Reginald Heber; John B. Dykes
448 II Corinthians 4:6
449 Acts 2:17-21; I Corinthians 2:12
450 Acts 2:2
451 Philippians 2:10
452 II Corinthians 3:18; Romans 8:29
453 Acts 2:3
454 Joel 2:28
455 Psalm 59:8; Psalm 37:13
456 Psalm 126:2
457 Psalms 126:1-6
458 Romans 1:20
459 Zephaniah 3:11-15
460 Psalm 7:9
461 Genesis 28:15; Joshua 23:5
462 John 14:2-3
463 Isaiah 33:17, 20, 24
464 I Corinthians 3:12-15
465 II Corinthians 3:18
466 I Corinthians 15:54-55
467 Exodus 32:26; Matthew 25:32-33
468 Matthew 13:41, 49
469 Luke 15:7
470 Matthew 22:12
471 Matthew 13:30
472 Matthew 5:26; 18:32-35; Luke 12:59
473 Matthew 11:28-30; Luke 15:11-32 Prodigal's Son
474 James 2:8
475 Numbers 10:33; Joshua 8:33

[476] Isaiah 35:8
[477] John 15:3
[478] Daniel 3:19; Exodus 14:19,24
[479] Exodus 14:13
[480] Matthew 16:4
[481] John 10:4-5
[482] II Corinthians 3:18
[483] Joshua 3:8,11: As the Ark stood still in the Jordan, so it will stand still in the Stones of Fire
[484] 1 John 4:18

CHAPTER 28
[485] Revelation 21:10
[486] Revelation 21:11
[487] Revelation 21:13
[488] Revelation 21:14
[489] Revelation 21:16
[490] Revelation 21:17
[491] Revelation 21:19-20
[492] I Peter 2:5
[493] Revelation 21:21
[494] Revelation 21:12
[495] Revelation 21:22-23
[496] Zechariah 14:8
[497] Zechariah 14:8; Revelation 22:1
[498] Hebrews 12:22; Psalms 125:1; 132:13; 48:1-2; 2:6
[499] Acts 4:32
[500] I Corinthians 2:9
[501] Psalm 139:7-12
[502] Revelation 2:7,11,17, 26; 3:5,12,21; 21:7
[503] Romans 8:17, 30
[504] Song of Solomon 2:4
[505] Numbers 2:12; Tribe of Simeon is located on south-center gate of New Jerusalem; Revelation 21:12
[506] Revelation 22:14
[507] Psalm 122: 1-4
[508] Revelation 3:12
[509] Ezekiel 41:7
[510] Revelation 21:21
[511] Psalm 125:2
[512] I Kings 6:23-28
[513] Exodus 35:35; 36:8
[514] I Kings 7:29
[515] Exodus 35:30-33
[516] I Kings 6:35
[517] John 14:2-3
[518] I Kings 4:29
[519] Psalms 120-134
[520] Breasted, Records, Vol. II, Sec. 288; I

Kings 10:4-9; II Chronicles 9:3-8
[521] I Kings 4:33
[522] Isaiah 65:25; 11:6
[523] Zechariah 6:1; Revelation 20:1-3
[524] Leviticus 25:10-54; Luke 4:19

CHAPTER 29
[525] Isaiah 6:1
[526] Revelation 1:14
[527] Revelation 21:12
[528] Ephesians 4:7, 11
[529] I Corinthians 12:12-27
[530] Ephesians 2:10
[531] Proverbs 22:4; Matthew 5:12
[532] John 15:14-15
[533] Genesis 2:9; 3:22; Proverbs 11:30; Revelation 22:2,14
[534] John 15:16
[535] Revelation 2:7
[536] James 1:12; Revelation 2:10
[537] Revelation 2:11
[538] Revelation 2:17; it is possible Jesus will have us take one of the Stones of Fire that may bear our new name, just as Joshua had the elders take a stone from the Jordan - Joshua 4:3; Isaiah 56:5; 62:6
[539] Revelation 2:17
[540] Daniel 10:21
[541] Revelation 14:1-5; 7:4
[542] Matthew 10:32
[543] Matthew 25:21; Luke 12:44; 22:39-40; Revelation 2:26-27

CHAPTER 30
[544] Matthew 24:7-8
[545] Ezekiel 38, 39
[546] Daniel 9:27
[547] Psalms 133:3 imagined allusions
[548] Revelation 20:12
[549] Numbers 27:21; Exodus 28:30; Deuteronomy 33:8; Ezra 2:63
[550] Exodus 25:10
[551] I Samuel 28:15
[552] Matthew 24:29
[553] Revelation 6:8

PERSONALITY PROFILE TEST

Here is a tremendous resource for helping you to more fully abide in unconditional love. The Personality Profile Test (P.P.T.) is designed to measure the extent to which our personalities rely on conditional love versus unconditional love. All of us attempt to answer the question - "Am I *worth* being loved?" through searching and striving efforts. However, it is only when we relinquish these lesser loves that we can truly come into unconditional love. This instrument will profile your personality in terms of any bonding, performance, control, and behavior issues that you may have. Your profile will include 23 pages of personalized feedback and practical instruction to help you move forward into a fuller expression of unconditional love.

For more on this assessment,
please visit: **DrDaveOnline.com**

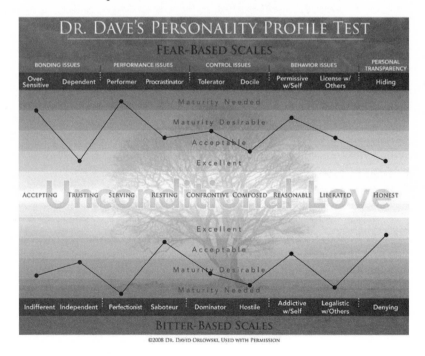

©2008 DR. DAVID ORLOWSKI, USED WITH PERMISSION